A Sheik's Spell

Eboni Snoe

To Jo—
Great meeting you!
Peace & Happiness
Eboni Snoe
12/10/95

Odyssey Books Inc., Silver Spring, MD

Published by
Odyssey Books, Inc.
9501 Monroe Street
Silver Spring, Maryland, 20910

ISBN: 1-878634-06-2

Published in the United States of America
February, 1992

Chapter One

Felicia's scream caught in her throat as tons of rushing water broke through the cracks in the dam. It would only be moments before the massive overflow reached their tiny craft.

"*Allah-u-akbar, Allah-u-akbar*!" the guide yelled as he threw down the oars and dropped to a fetal position in the bottom of the dinghy.

Without thinking, Felicia grabbed the paddles. Frantically, she tried to steer the boat toward the shore.

"Get up! Get up! For God's sake, help me!" she screamed, but by then the wall of water was upon them.

On impact, the dinghy split into shreds of wood, and Felicia felt her entire body being crushed by what had to be tons of water.

Panic set in as she was forced down into water so deep it was darker than any darkness she had ever known. Gallons of water poured into her nose and mouth as she tried to fight her way to the surface.

Is this the way I'm going to die? she mentally cried out to whatever forces might be listening...and she called upon every ounce of strength she had in her attempt to survive.

Thoughts of the research project flashed through her mind...Phillip and the others were waiting for her at Al Uqsur. She could see her mother and her brother, Rodney, as her life began to unfold before her like frames on a movie reel. The dehydration project...her last love–Alvin ... college ... dance class ... her alcoholic father ... women's shelters ... her battered mom.

At last weakness began to set in. Felicia could feel herself fading, yet she continued to struggle as her limbs became heavier. Her hair plastered itself to her face, blinding her, as if it too were trying to drown her. At that moment, she was so aware of how short her twenty-five years had been and her need to live was unfathomable.

As her consciousness slipped away, the last thought that filled Felicia's mind was, *I will not let this be my time to go.*

Chapter Two

Na'im (Ny-eem) lifted his face to the wind and decided to remove the top of his *galabia* to take full advantage of the breeze. Bronzed muscles rippled as he raised his arms over his head, catching his shoulder-length, reddish-brown hair in the neckline of the nightshirt-like garment.

It had been such a long time since he had ridden the slopes of his homeland. Much too long. Now he was back.

He had carried out his father's wishes, spending almost two years in the United States organizing and then trying to close a business deal. Na'im's father had said a son with firsthand knowledge of western business ethics could help modernize his people and bring economic progress to their land. A son who he expected to follow in his footsteps and take over their sheikdom. Na'im was approaching thirty, and his father felt it was time he began to prepare himself.

So Na'im had complied with his father's wishes, knowing that wasn't the only reason his father had sent him to America. He knew they needed the subsidies the Egyptian government offered to businessmen who entered into enterprise with foreigners. Recent years had not been so prosperous for the Rahman clan.

After living among westerners, Na'im Raoul (Ra-ool) Rahman had developed some opinions of his own. He did not feel western ways were the best. He had found corruption in its society that had no face among his people, the rural Egyptians. The business deal he'd worked so hard to obtain had gone sour as a result of the underhanded dealings of westerners. So, Na'im's stay in America had proven to him that his people were civilized in a way that Americans could never be.

The feel of the camel beneath him was familiar, but he needed to once again become accustomed to the continuous up and down movement of the animal's body.

As he looked down the slope through the trees, he could see the River Nile in all its splendor; a sight that he had grown up with and loved. He knew this land like he knew no other, unlike America with its strange ways.

Na'im would have enjoyed traveling nearer to the edge of the river, but he had seen Sirius' position at dawn yesterday, and he did not want to take the chance of being caught in the river's flood. For years it had been rumored among his people that the pressure from the swelling waters of the Nile would soon be too much for the Aswan Dam. Na'im also believed this. That's why it surprised him to see a small boat traveling on the river. He could see its sail from his vantage point, well-hidden within the curtain of trees and brush.

What fool would be traveling the Nile today after the dog star has risen? he pondered. *It must be some greedy merchant who wants to challenge the river and see if he can get his wares to market before it floods.* Na'im scoffed at whomever it was testing the patience of nature.

Resting his spine against the large bundle that was tied to the camel's back, he began to think of his family and the gifts he'd brought back from America. Na'im knew his cousin Fatimah's (Fa-tee-muh) large brown eyes would grow as big as lotus blossoms, as she tried on the jewelry and hair ornaments he'd bought especially for her.

Thinking of this brought a smile to his lips, showing beautiful teeth in a face that could be described as nothing less than classic; not in an elegant way, but in a raw, primitive way.

His hazel-colored eyes, flecked with gold, gave him an animal-like magnetism; the kind of animal that could never be tamed. Thick fan-like eyelashes cast shadows on wide, high cheekbones, divided by a tall imposing nose. Yet it was his mouth that told the most about his personality. It was generous, but at the same time shaped as if it had been chiseled from stone. There was a certain perfection to his lips, that could smile as quickly as turn a deadly frown. Na'im was known to be a man whose heart was hard to reach, but once done, there was nothing he would not do for those he loved.

He decided to dismount and take advantage of a clearing he'd come to high above the Nile. The spot had several acacia trees, crowned with limbs that spread outward like umbrella tops, providing plenty of shade and an intoxicating breeze. He knew it would be a while before he would come to another resting spot as welcoming as this. So he let his camels graze on the plants and grass that were plentiful there.

Na'im stretched his tall, sinewy body out on the soft blanket of grass and thought about all the work he had cut out for him once he reached home. Intermittently, he would close his eyes, drifting off into a languid sleep.

Abruptly, he was awakened by an explosive sound. There was something familiar about it. It was the sound of rushing water. More than once while traveling with the men he had heard it as the Nile's bank began to overflow.

Na'im thought of the small craft he'd seen earlier on the river and leapt to his feet, straining to see if the boat was still in sight. Just as he caught a glimpse of it, it was overtaken by a wall of water and disappeared beneath its masses. Seconds passed as Na'im waited to see if the small craft would resurface, but he knew within his heart that it could not have stood up to the water's weight.

It didn't take long before the swollen river reached the coast beneath him, and it began to climb the riverbank. He could feel the power of the Nile as he watched it overtake small trees and brush in its way.

Almost instantaneously, the force of the river pushed a body to its surface. The foam from the tumultuous water constantly covered and uncovered a black head that rested on a broken board, a remnant of the tiny boat.

Without hesitation, Na'im started making his way northward down toward the riverbank. The currents of the river were so high that he dared not go too far for fear of being swept away in its path. Upon reaching a large tree whose roots had been uncovered from years of erosion, he latched onto it with his left hand and waited for the growing river to bring the body into his reach.

Na'im could barely see now because of the river's spray. Blindly, he reached and groped in the raging torrents, praying that the tree's roots would hold him. Within moments, his right hand seized a piece of cloth, but the force of the water was so strong it tore out of his grip. With quick reflexes, Na'im extended his arm to its full length, making one last effort to grab hold of the body.

Chapter Three

It took all the strength Na'im had to pull the small body up, and out of the water. Had it been a larger person, it would have been impossible. He could feel the tree's roots tearing out of the ground as they bore the additional weight. Finally, he was able to grab the young woman by her waist. Holding her close, Na'im climbed back to the top of the slope.

At first he could do no more than lay flat on his back with her encircled in his arms, as he panted heavily, attempting to catch his breath. Moments later the young woman began to emit a choking sound as her body tried to rid itself of the unwelcome water. Exhausted himself, Na'im managed to roll her over onto her stomach and began to pump with his palms in the middle of her back. He could hear her cough and sputter as she desperately tried to breathe.

The coughing stopped and Na'im carried her limp body under a nearby acacia tree. She laid there as still as death. But he knew from her faint breathing she was alive.

Na'im stared into the smoldering flames of the small fire he'd built outside the bedouin tent. Not once had the young woman awakened since he'd pulled her out of the overflowing river. She had responded strangely, taking quick breaths as he removed the wet clothes from her body in order to dress her in a dry *galabia*..

Na'im couldn't help but stare as he undressed Felicia's unconscious form. Nearly uncontrollable urges began to stir as he looked at her perfectly-formed body.

Her chocolate brown skin was even-toned from her face to her feet, with hints of honey brown between her breasts and inner thighs. Large tips highlighted full breasts that Na'im knew would sit high and proud without support or pretense.

Accidentally, his hands brushed against silky smooth skin as he pulled the top down past Felicia's well-rounded hips and thighs. Na'im's breaths became labored as his eyes involuntarily focused on the triangle of thick, curly black hair that lost itself in the honey brown valley below.

Reluctantly, he completed his task and picked up Felicia's wet clothes. As he carried them outside to dry on a tree limb, a matted book of United States stamps fell from the pocket of her shirt. Na'im wondered what had brought this woman alone to Egypt.

Streams of steam rose from the pot of broth that Na'im managed to make from a leftover meal. He made it with the young woman in mind. It aggravated him to think that already he had another human being's welfare to be concerned about. He had been ready to take on such responsibility once he reached Karib, but that was days in the future. This woman was a foreigner, one he knew nothing about. She was an American, and he felt she could not be trusted.

Na'im determined that as soon as the woman was able, he would take her to the nearest oasis where she could care for herself, and he would no longer feel as if she was his responsibility.

As he covered the makeshift pot, a chilling scream broke the night's silence. Quickly, he opened the tent's flap and stepped inside.

It didn't take long before his eyes adjusted to the dim light filtering in from the dying campfire, and he saw the young woman thrashing about on the pallet he'd made. Gently, Na'im attempted to hold Felicia still so she would not injure herself.

"Come now, *aros al bher,* you are safe now. You no longer have to fight the River Nile. Na'im has fished you out of the water. It is by the grace of God that you are alive at this moment. You should rest now and gather your strength."

The soothing sound of Na'im's voice seemed to reach Felicia through her delirium. She began to clutch at his arms and chest, unconsciously seeking to get closer to the warmth of his body.

Na'im laid back and allowed Felicia to make a pillow in the crook of his arm. He began to stroke the tiny braids of black hair away from her face, that was wet with tears and sweat. Na'im felt a mixture of emotions as he looked down into her troubled face, and he knew if he were not careful he could be in for more than he'd bargained.

▲

Felicia's head ached so badly that at first she dared not open her eyes. She felt comforted by the warm arm that held her and the steady movement of the muscular chest upon which her face rested. She was also thankful for the cover that blocked out the bright sunshine coming through a slit in the material cocoon. She did not know where she was, but for some reason that didn't seem to matter very much.

Na'im, too, had awakened, and looked down to see confused dark eyes staring back at him. "Well, how do you feel, *aros al bher*?"

The sound of Na'im's voice vibrated against Felicia's ear and it sounded as if it were bubbling forth from an underground stream.

"I don't know. I feel a little weak and disoriented." She tried to sit up, but her arms were too weak to hold her.

"Well, you should," he replied, "you are blessed to be alive. You nearly drowned yesterday."

Na'im lowered Felicia's head down upon the pallet as he slid from beneath her. He then reached for a large bundle that was nearby and propped the stunned Felicia up against it. Nervously, she looked down at her hands and at the clothes she was wearing before asking, "Drowned...but where am I?"

"You are in my tent," Na'im said with a mischievous, boyish smile. "The tent of Na'im Raoul Rahman." He could not help but pity this beautiful woman, who at the moment appeared so bewildered and helpless. "And who are you?"

"Felicia Sanders. I...I'm a research scientist." Felicia placed a trembling hand up to her forehead. "My head is pounding so. Everything seems a little fuzzy right now."

She ran both hands over her face and back through her

hair. Her fingers caught in some of the tangles, as she made efforts to smooth it and collect her thoughts.

Suddenly she turned accusing eyes toward Na'im. "Was I with you when I almost drowned?"

"Oh no," he raised one defensive eyebrow. "I am the one who fished you out of the River Nile. That is why I call you *aros al bher*, 'little mermaid'. As a matter of fact you owe me your life."

Na'im was sitting cross-legged, no more than two feet away from Felicia. As a final gesture to his pronouncement, he crossed his muscular arms and waited for Felicia's reaction.

Felicia's mind had blocked out the events surrounding the accident. All she had to go on was this stranger's word.

There was an awkward silence for a few moments. When Felicia finally spoke, Na'im could barely hear her.

"I don't know what to say. The pain in my head is unreal, and I feel so confused. I've got to believe you because my mind seems to have blocked out everything that happened."

Tears began to well up in her eyes, even though Na'im could see that she fought to keep them from flowing.

"I don't know how to thank you enough for helping me, but as soon as I can, I'll pay you back."

Na'im shifted his weight uncomfortably. "I know one reason you are feeling so bad," he said with false gaiety, "you have not eaten since I rescued you, which was early yesterday afternoon. I probably would not feel so good either if I had not eaten since then."

Felicia looked at Na'im with dark eyes surrounded by lashes glistening with tears and rewarded him with what he sought--a smile, albeit a weak one.

"I will just reheat some of that broth I made for you last

night. I am sure you will feel much better after you have had some."

She watched him rise to his feet and exit the tent.

Now that Na'im was gone, Felicia took a good look around her. The tent contained the bundle Na'im had placed behind her back, two larger ones, and the blanket he'd placed over them while they slept.

Felicia felt so bad it didn't really matter to her that she'd slept with Na'im. Plus, she instinctively felt sleeping was all they had done. He didn't appear to be the kind of man that would take advantage of a half-drowned woman.

Felicia wrapped her arms around her knees, hugging herself in a natural gesture of comfort. In doing so, the large shirt she wore slithered upward against her skin. For the first time she realized she was completely naked beneath the airy material.

Her eyes focused on the outline of Na'im's large frame outside the tent. An involuntary tremor ran through her as she pictured him dressing her.

It didn't take long before Na'im had built a new fire; dry twigs and sticks were plentiful. As he sat stoking it and waiting for the contents of the pot to simmer, his thoughts naturally evolved around Felicia. Evidently she'd injured her head and was probably suffering from some kind of concussion. But that wasn't what bothered him most of all. It was how *he* was so anxious to please her. It was contradictory to his very nature to be taken in by a pretty face. Beautiful women had never been a problem for him in Egypt, America or anywhere else. As a matter of fact, they had all proven to be quite dispensable.

Na'im knew his father had plans to put an end to what he called his son's 'unstable ways'. Sheik Rahman did not feel it was wrong for a man to take his pleasure wherever he could find it. He simply felt it was in bad taste not to have a wife, at least giving the impression of stability. Na'im also knew his father was plotting to marry him off to some Egyptian miss whom he felt would yield strong sons for the perpetuation of the Rahman clan. It would be a plus if her family had money and influence.

But Na'im had plans of his own. He would not marry anyone except a woman of his choosing. This much the West had taught him. Women were definitely different. Some could be as warm and satisfying as a campfire on a cold desert night, while others were as undesirable as the cold itself. From the treasures Felicia Sanders possessed, he would guess she would be the former. Yes, he would have to be careful around this one with her velvety eyes and upright manner.

Na'im handed the lukewarm liquid to Felicia. "It is not much, but I think it is all you should have at this time, along with some bread."

He maneuvered his body and pulled the larger bundle closer within his reach. Digging inside, he untied a dark brown cloth which housed some pita bread. He tore off a large portion of it. Then he pulled off a smaller piece of that and gave it to Felicia. As Na'im replaced the covered bread into the bundle, he retrieved a more colorful package. From its contents, he produced a comb and brush and placed them by her side.

"Here. I think you can make use of these. The clothes

that you were wearing when I found you should be dry, so once you finish eating I will bring them in to you."

Felicia didn't quite understand why, but she was sure Na'im was being a bit more brusque with her than he had been earlier. Not once while speaking did he look at her directly. His tone no longer contained the comforting, reassuring lilt it had possessed during their earlier exchange.

"These must be for someone special," she commented and motioned toward the comb and brush that lay by her thigh.

Na'im simply nodded his head affirmatively and went back outside of the tent.

Felicia admonished herself for looking for comfort from this man whom she knew little about. She was not his responsibility. She should be grateful for everything he had done for her and not expect any special treatment in the future.

Felicia found the broth and bread to be satisfying and after she'd eaten it, she began to untangle her hair. It took quite a while to comb out the loose ends of her micro-braids that had dried into stubborn clumps of hair.

Once done, she found even that task seemed to zap all of her strength, and before she knew it she had fallen asleep with the comb still in her hand.

The tent was engulfed in darkness when Felicia awoke again, except for the sliver of pale light that shone through an opening in its flap. But this time she did not awake to the steady, rhythmic breathing of Na'im's chest beneath her head. She could see his sleeping form lying several feet away.

As Felicia fell back into the sleep of one whose body and mind have been taxed to their limit, she fought unwanted feelings of wishing she were in the comforting arms of the Egyptian.

Chapter Four

Harsh sunshine and a persistent scraping noise awoke Felicia the next morning. Her hands flew to her eyes to shield them from the intrusive light. It only took a few moments for Felicia to realize this was Na'im's abrupt way of awakening her.

"We will leave the camp this morning," he said without glancing her way. "Your clothes are beside you. There is some fish, bread and tea for breakfast. I would eat all I could if I were you. We have a long ride ahead of us."

Before Felicia could open her mouth to reply, Na'im was on his way out again, dragging another bundle and closing the tent's flap behind him.

A long ride where? What is he talking about, she thought in a sleepy haze. Felicia had never been known to be the most congenial person right after waking up. Especially after such a rude awakening.

She was glad her head only pounded slightly as she sat up to dress herself. Buttoning her blouse with near-steady hands, she thought of Phillip and the other research team members waiting for her at Al Uqsur. *I'll just have to tell him to drop me off there. That's all. We can't be that far away. It would have taken a few hours by boat, so it can't take much longer riding a camel.*

Satisfied with her plan, she braided her unruly locks in a thick plait at the base of her neck and stepped outside the tent. No sooner had she done so than Na'im whisked by her to retrieve the last bundle.

"Good morning," she said, following him back inside. "This is rather awkward. I was so messed up yesterday, I don't remember what you said your name was."

Passing her on his way out without breaking his stride, he replied, "Na'im Raoul Rahman."

"Well, I guess I can call you Na'im, if it's alright with you?" Felicia waited for a response that never came. A perturbed twist set upon her lips as she crossed the campsite and stood behind Na'im while he fastened the bundle to the camel's back.

"Look, I don't know what you're thinking. I'm sure you've got things you need to do and I really do appreciate what you've done for me so far."

Na'im ducked beneath the camel's neck to fasten down the other side of the bundle, completely blocking Felicia's view of his face. Riled by his insolence, Felicia tried to calm herself. *Remember, you need this guy who is beginning to act like a total jerk.*

Imitating Na'im's body movement, Felicia thumped her head against the animal's hairy neck as she straightened up precisely at the moment when the camel decided to move its head. "Dog-gone it!" Holding her head that throbbed more from the previous injury than the one she had just received, she spoke through her irritation. "All I want you to do is drop me off at Al Uqsur."

Na'im turned and pinned her with steady, golden eyes. "I am not going to Al Uqsur. I will take you to Al Kharijah.

From there you should be able to get transportation to any place you want.''

''But I don't have time to go anyplace else. I've already lost a couple of days because of this accident. I'm working on a very important dehydration project and...''

''Your work is not my concern.'' Turning on his heels, Na'im headed for the campfire with Felicia behind him.

Felicia held out her hands in frustration. ''I don't believe this,'' she said as Na'im passed her a brass plate with a piece of fish and pita bread on it.

They sat and ate in silence.

How could one man be so contrary. *He says he saved my life, but he's so arrogant he won't even listen to what I've got to say.*

Pushing a lump of bread into her cheek, Felicia offered Na'im an alternative. ''Okay. So you don't have time to take me there. Just give me one of your camels and a little bit of food. I know if I follow the river, going north, it will take me straight to it.''

Na'im's response was not what Felicia expected.

''Rumor has it, a group of men are pillaging the smaller villages and kidnapping some of the women. You would not stand a chance riding alone.''

''Men kidnapping women? Aah, come on.'' *This guy must think I lost my mind when I hurt my head.* ''Look, if you don't trust me with your camels just say so; I can understand that. But I can promise you, I'll take care of the animal, and you'll be well paid once I can get to where I'm going. Just give me your address or something. I'll take care of it,'' Felicia said in her most business-like tone.

Na'im stood drinking the remainder of his tea. ''I do not need your money, Ms. Sanders. As I said before, we are going to Al Kharijah.''

Felicia fumed as she ate the rest of her breakfast and watched Na'im gather the last remnants of the campsite together. When she finished, she did as he instructed her to do, cleaning her plate with mounds of sand.

Felicia's patience had run out when it came to this high-falutin' Egyptian. *I'm just going to have to take matters into my own hands.*

She waited until Na'im was well-engrossed in dismantling the tent before she made her move. Grabbing one of the water containers and the remainder of the pita bread, Felicia rushed toward the second camel. Running gave her the momentum she needed to clamber upon the surprised animal's back. Even if she didn't manage to get far, he'd see how determined she was, and hopefully be more open to seeing things her way.

The camel let go a noise similar to a small roar. Na'im, startled by the animal's protest, applied too much pressure on the remaining side of the tent, causing it to come down in a cloud around him. Clawing to remove the billowing material from his head, he managed to do so just as the animal bolted forward with an ill-prepared Felicia on its back.

Chapter Five

“Ei-ei-ei-i,” Felicia screeched as the animal took off, loping with gigantic strides. Within moments she found herself on the ground, landing with a thud, causing her head and her backside to ache. Throwing her head back in anguish, she could see Na'im removing the remainder of the fallen tent from about him. The arrogant son of a biscuit acted as if he didn't know or even care about what she'd done.

He methodically finished taking down the tent. Then he went after the camel that had stopped about a half mile away. The pain in Felicia's head and her rump, plus Na‘im's attitude, had made up her mind. She'd simply get transportation from Al Kharijah to Al Uqsur.

Felicia had no idea how long they'd been traveling in the merciless sun, but she knew her backside cried for something softer than the hard flesh of Na'im's camel's back. At first she'd tried not to lean against him, but as time passed and she began to feel weak from the heat, physical need overtook her pride.

At the beginning of their journey, he'd acknowledged her presence by passing her a *galabia* top and head wrap saying it would protect her from the sun. Other than that, no other words had passed between them.

Most of the landscape looked the same to Felicia once they had traveled several miles inland, away from the Nile. They traveled all day across coarse gravel and rock outcroppings, stopping only to eat a small midday meal.

The sun had begun to sink behind a group of sandy hills in the distance when Na'im finally decided on a place to bed down for the night. As Felicia dismounted the camel's back, Na'im noticed she winced with pain as he held her arm to aid her descent.

Felicia felt as if she'd been flogged with a cat-o-nine-tails. Her flesh burned from the sun's pitiless rays, in spite of the layers of clothing she wore, and her bones ached from the relentless movement of the camel's body.

Na'im removed all of their gear from the beast of burden so he, too, could rest. Looking about, he decided to pitch the tent in an area that was almost entirely surrounded by gigantic stones. Felicia could tell that over the years many nomads had used this same spot with the same purpose in mind. While Na'im worked, Felicia sat motionless on a flat stone nearby, not caring that she did not offer to help.

"If you go through the opening in the rocks, you will find a small water hole. It should help soothe some of the pain that you helped to bring upon yourself."

Felicia was in no mood or shape to play verbal volleyball with this man, so she followed his suggestion without protest.

The new moon was high in the sky by the time Felicia reached the water hole. She mechanically began to undress in the privacy of an alcove of stones and rocks. The need to shield herself was done more by instinct than thought, and she stepped out from her self-made dressing room with little care of being seen by Na'im, or anything or anyone else.

The water hole had many boulders surrounding it, with scarce vegetation growing where it could between the rocks near the water's edge.

Once Felicia entered the water, she found a place where she could sit and be completely covered, except for her head and neck. She took solace in the prickly pain created by the coarse gravel that blanketed the bottom of the pond. At least it took her mind off her sunburnt skin and the other aches and pains bombarding her. But there was one pain it couldn't take away.

Despite the strong exterior she'd shown to Na'im during their journey, the hurt of loneliness and alienation was heavy. It wasn't the first time in her life she'd experienced this. As a matter of fact, to cope with the problems that had inundated her childhood she'd become an expert at dealing with denying her true feelings.

That's why it took her by surprise when she felt moisture upon her cheeks. *Tears?!* She couldn't remember the last time she had actually cried. Was it when her mother lay balled up on the kitchen floor holding her arm that hung strangely from her shoulder? Or when her brother, Rodney, was accidentally shot by drug dealers wanting to even the score with one of their neighbors? These were the highlights of scarring incidents that had dotted her life.

The pond's water on her fingertips mixed with the tears on her face as they began to flow in earnest. Maybe it was the near-death experience that fueled this outpour of emotion and allowed Felicia to give in to her pain. She cried because of the physical, mental and spiritual desolation she felt. As an adult, she cried the tears that as a child she could find no more of. Now, once again life had thrown her a curve. She had vowed at thirteen, when her father deserted them, never again to be at the mercy of anyone. She told herself she would not be at the mercy of Na'im Raoul Rahman. She knew it would be so easy to take comfort from a few kind words, from his touch. There was something about him that stirred all of her senses to their peak. The smell of his hair as she sat behind him, the feel of his broad back against her cheek, and the way her thighs had molded against his as they rode in the desert.

"I'm not going to let him get the best of me," she whispered aloud into the cool night air. "No way."

Chapter Six

As Felicia approached the campsite, she was surprised to see Na'im quietly conversing with another man. Both men looked up as she entered the circle of light created by the glowing fire.

Felicia made quite a captivating picture with her wet tendrils and Na'im's *galabia* clinging to her body in places where her skin was still damp.

The water had worked in soothing her body and lifting her spirits. As she had slipped the soft material of the *galabia* over her naked flesh, she thought of Na'im. He had seen her like this before. He had even dressed her. Just the thought of Na'im's muscular body being so close to her's under those circumstances sent exciting messages to the core of her femininity.

Felicia knew she could have used more discretion in dressing, but that wasn't what she wanted to do. *Maybe now I'll get his attention, since he wants to be so aloof and nonchalant. I'll just have to see how much he can take,* she thought.

But Na'im's handsome face remained as impassive as stone as he gazed upon her beyond the campfire. It was his companion who showed surprise and pleasure as he took in her womanly curves, clearly outlined by the fire's glare.

Felicia's feet felt as if they were rooted to the ground. She was paralyzed by the thought of what she must look like to this total stranger. It didn't take long before the man made it known just what he thought of her.

Felicia's almond eyes widened in total disbelief and outrage as she watched him pull a pouch out of the folds of his garment. She could hear the coins jingle as he threw it up enticingly in front of Na'im.

Felicia didn't know much Arabic, but there was little doubt in her mind as to what the man was saying to Na'im, sounding as if he were bargaining for wares at one of the village bazaars.

It infuriated her to think that this person felt he had the right to try and buy her. If he or Na'im thought for just one moment she was going to go along with this, they had another thought coming.

It was Na'im's voice that brought her out of her state of disbelief. He calmly, but with authority, told her to go inside the tent. For a moment Felicia thought of resisting him; then she looked at the stranger and changed her mind.

It wasn't long before Na'im followed her. "Why did you just stand there, showing yourself in front of us?" he asked heatedly.

Felicia felt her face become warm with embarrassment and anger. "Well, how was I to know there was someone else in the camp? You could have come and told me!"

"Keep your voice down, you have already caused me enough shame."

"Shame? How have I shamed you? I am the one who should feel ashamed," she threw back at him, but in a more hushed tone.

"I told him that you are one of several wives, and a favorite at that...so now you will act accordingly."

"You told him what?!"

"You heard what I said. What else was there to say with you standing there where we could see straight through your clothes. Even if you did not know he was here, you could have had more respect for yourself and dressed like a decent woman around a man you hardly know! And I am referring to me. Is that so much to expect from you?"

"Well aren't you something. Here's a man who says he saved my life, but who acts as if I have some kind of plague. And now he's trying to tell me how to act," Felicia retorted on a shrill note.

"Well, you won't have to worry about that tonight. We'll be sharing the same pallet. Shabazz seems to have accepted my explanation, but I'm sure he will be looking for signs to prove that I was not telling the truth. Ravaging a woman who he feels blatantly asked for it would not bother a man like him a bit."

"I'm not sharing anything with you," Felicia managed to get out with obvious indignation. "What have I done to you, anyway? Why do you dislike me? I would think we could be friends under the circumstances. Maybe you're one of those men who finds solace in solitude or something like that. But I must honestly say I'm not that kind of person, and at this particular point in my life, with all that has happened to me, I could use a friend."

"You surely were looking for more than friendship to come back here dressed like that!" Na'im's golden eyes blazed down on her. "You forget I've already seen all that you have to offer and I am not having any part of this cat and mouse game you Western women tend to play. With women from my country, a man knows where he stands. With you all, there is nothing but games and more games.''

Na'im didn't know it, but he'd struck the right cord and that incensed Felicia even further.

''How do you know so much about me? You haven't shown the slightest interest in what I'm thinking or feeling. So I'll thank you to keep your stereotyped opinions to yourself.''

Felicia then turned to sit in the furthest corner of the tent that she could find. Refusing to look in Na'im's direction, she concentrated on plaiting the ends of her hair.

''You are not going to make a liar of me. If it was not for you, none of this would have happened in the first place. There will be one pallet in this tent tonight, if you choose to sleep on it or not. The earth becomes very cold and hard at night in the desert, and your journey tomorrow on the camel's back will be even more painful if you decide to make the bare ground your bed.''

With that, Na'im took out several woven blankets. He padded the ground with some and the others he said would be used as cover during the night. Then he left the tent.

Felicia began to feel the chill of the desert night air shortly after Na'im had gone. Her hair was still damp and the *galabia* did not provide much protection from the elements.

''I'm one of several wives, am I?'' she mumbled out loud. ''If he had to say anything of the kind, why couldn't I just have been his wife?'' It all sounded so demeaning. What if he did have several wives? Felicia hated to admit that was the thought that brought her the most frustration.

She assessed the amount of blankets Na'im left on top of the pallet, and she concluded there were enough blankets for two pallets. So she took two of them, leaving one for Na'im.

Just as Felicia was wrapping the blankets around her, Na'im reentered the tent. It took a few moments for his eyes to adjust to the darkness, but when he saw what Felicia had done, he made no comment.

Na'im began to slowly remove the *galabia* top he was wearing. After he'd taken it off, he flung it on top of a nearby bundle of gear. Felicia tried to act as if she wasn't paying him any attention, but it was very hard to do. Na'im's size took up so much space in the small tent. And Felicia was hard put to draw her eyes away from his wide, muscular shoulders and chest, that tapered to a flat torso and trim waistline. Na'im threw back his head, yawned and began to stretch, showing even more of his well-defined frame.

Felicia lowered her eyes, closed them and inhaled deeply. As she released her breath she trembled. Upon opening her eyes she was startled to see Na'im standing right in front of her. Placing both hands on her upper arms, he raised her to her feet. She could barely see his eyes in the dark as he looked directly into hers.

Slowly and purposefully his mouth descended on hers. The contact was so light as he rubbed his closed, but firm lips back and forth against her mouth. Felicia's eyes were held captive by the golden ones that seemed to probe into her. The feeling of moisture heightened her senses as the tip of Na'im's tongue outlined her full lips, leaving a tingling path wherever it touched. So vulnerable was she to Na'im's unprecedented show of affection, Felicia's lips parted in surrender, allowing him access to the wetness inside. Of this Na'im took full advantage, his tongue tasting her welcome. With skill Felicia had not known before, it lashed out incessantly until she joined him like two serpents in a mating dance. Felicia could think of nothing else as she cradled Na'im's face in her hands. Her entire being screamed for more.

"You're not the only one who knows how to tease, *aros al bher*," he spoke against her lips as he encircled her in his arms.

Closing her eyes, Felicia didn't care what happened next. All she knew was she wanted to be close to him, and she swayed with anticipation.

Na'im had also been waiting for just the right moment. As he felt Felicia's body begin to give in to his, he yanked the two blankets from around her, sending her into a half spin. She would have landed on the ground, if he had not caught her.

"Like I said, there will be only one pallet in this tent tonight." Na'im turned his back and started toward the pallet he'd prepared.

"Why you dirty, conniving..." All of Felicia's frustrations surfaced, as she launched an animal-like attack on Na'im's expansive back. She took out on him all the anger, hurt and fear that had been mounting inside. She kicked him and gouged her fingernails into his skin, drawing blood in her rage. "You think I'm going to let you get away with this?" she said between tears and clenched teeth.

Na'im had no idea how Felicia would react to his ploy, but he certainly hadn't expected such fury from one so small. There was simply no way of controlling her until he pinned her on her back, arms and legs outstretched.

"*Azizi. Aros al bher*, what would you have me do? Take advantage of you at a time when you are the most vulnerable?"

Na'im tried to penetrate her fury that he felt welled forth from wounds much deeper than the one he had inflicted. "I don't want to do that. I have used all the restraint that I know of in respect of your situation, and you come back here tonight ready to taunt me."

Felicia looked up into Na'im's tortured eyes as he reasoned with her beneath him.

"Do you want me to say I want you? That I'd love to be where I'd hate to think any other man has been?"

The emotion and sincerity in Na'im's reluctant confession vanquished the fight within her. Felicia knew she wanted Na'im, but life had taught her to hold back her heart even if her body longed to be taken.

"Don't you understand? I need you to make love to me. We've been through a lot together during the past two days, and more than you can imagine, I've wanted you to hold me. I need the comfort of your touch. Ever since this trip started, the reality of my life has been bubbling up within me, not allowing me to forget the past. I want to forget, Na'im. You can make me forget."

"*Habibi. Azizi.*" Na'im leaned forward blazing a trail of kisses across Felicia's face.

All kinds of questions flashed through his mind. How could there be so much torture and pain behind eyes so beautiful? The reasoning side of him yearned to know, but his physical need for her was unbearable.

Na'im did not stop kissing Felicia's face until he reached her mouth, which was waiting for his. This time there was no hesitancy in Felicia's response as she gave into the sensations he invoked in her. They kissed with fervor and longing, as if through it they could touch the depths of each other's souls and all questions would be answered.

It was Na'im who reluctantly drew back from Felicia's clinging lips. "Tonight, *aros al bher*, everything would feel right to us. We would justify our physical urges and quench them with little thought. But I fear tomorrow you, more than I, would regret our actions. I cannot afford to think at any time you may look at me with disgust for taking advantage of you.''

Felicia began to shake her head, denying the words that he was saying.

``No, you must listen. Your need for me now is the result of the horrible experience you've just been through. I am not saying it is the only reason, but you said it yourself, what you truly need is a friend. I will be that for you now, Felicia. If the rest is in our future, it will happen.''

Silently he rose, offering Felicia his hand. Upon her acceptance, he led her back to the pallet he'd made, adding one of the blankets Felicia had coveted for herself.

As they lay together with Felicia's body tucked snugly against Na'im's back, Felicia was the first to give in to sleep, thereby assuring Na'im he had done the right thing.

It was not easy for him to do the same. His body was still tense with desire. But sleep finally came, his mind, at peace, clearing the way.

Chapter Seven

When Na'im, Felicia and Yusef (Yoo-sef) Shabazz first entered the oasis, they had to cross stretches of irrigated fields where dates and citrus trees were being grown. The contrast between the desert's dryness and the greenery of the oasis was amazing.

Felicia discovered Na'im had not exaggerated a bit when he said Al Kharijah was no small settlement. It was quite vast and the closer they got to the inner village, the more colorful it became.

There were carts filled with all kinds of goods, and salesmen peddling their wares, drawing attention to themselves by calling out to passersby or by waving samples in the air.

There were musicians playing flutes in brightly-colored *galabias* and vendors selling street snacks throughout the crowd. All of the people, sounds and smells instinctively made Felicia know how different Egypt would be from America.

Felicia released a sigh of relief as they left the camels drinking at a water hole and proceeded down one of the main thoroughfares, where a street sign that read "American Consulate" hung from one of the buildings. It was at this point that Yusef Shabazz bid them "*As-Salam-Alaikoom.*"

Felicia was glad. Over the past day and a half, as he rode with them, she had never felt comfortable around him. Na'im never said it, but she knew he felt the same.

The American Consulate building was not that impressive from the outside, but it was comfortable enough once they entered its quiet surroundings. The room was bright with sunlight. It was also quite clean and had several posters of cities of the United States adorning its walls. Felicia found herself wandering from poster to poster. There was a nervous feeling inside of her; something she couldn't explain, but she knew it had to do with Na'im.

They were greeted by a small Arab who said he was the receptionist. "Mr. Johnston, the representative, is not here right now. I do expect him back at any time. Please feel free to wait for him if you like," he said, pointing to the wooden chairs that lined one of the walls.

"Thank you," Felicia smiled in acknowledgement, as Na'im motioned for her to follow him back outside.

"I have several things I need to look into while I'm here. I don't know how long its going to take, but here are several *piasters* for you to buy something to eat in case you get hungry."

Felicia looked at the coins Na'im held in his outstretched hand. She was reluctant to take them, and it wasn't just because she didn't want to take money from him. Common sense told her to take them anyway.

Anxious feelings arose in her as she watched him disappear in a sea of *galabias*, western-styled clothes and *melayas*. She decided to get something to eat before she returned to the building.

During their last two days together, Felicia and Na'im had shared his pallet, but that was all. With Yusef Shabazz accompanying them all the way to Al Kharijah, they had kept up the pretense of man and wife for Felicia's sake.

Na'im was different after their night of confrontation. He treated her kindly, but he kept her at arms length. Felicia felt her open invitation for him to make love to her was the reason why. Na'im now saw her as a loose woman, unworthy of his affection. Today, there was no doubt in her mind that he had made the right decision in not accepting her offer. She was thankful that he had.

Na'im had made it clear on the second day of their journey that Felicia would have to take on the duties of a nomad's wife, preparing the food and fetching kindle for the campfires. She had fulfilled her end of the bargain without protest.

It had taken them exactly two days to reach the outskirts of Al Kharijah, where they camped until sunrise the following day.

Felicia couldn't fathom how long she had been sitting in the small office waiting for the representative to return. Her head began to ache in a fashion to which she'd become accustomed since the accident.

She threw away the empty sack that had held the street snacks she'd bought not far from the building, while the receptionist offered another apology for the delay. Her nerves were on edge as she studied the yellowing posters of cities in different countries, including the United States.

Constantly, Felicia's eyes strayed to the bare window that looked out onto the street. Her thoughts were not on the representative, but on Na'im.

▲

The mail clerk was surprised and pleased to see Na'im as he entered the sunbaked building. Through the years Na'im's face had become quite familiar, and of course he had known of Na'im's visit to the United States through the steady flow of letters written between he and his father.

"*As-Salam-Alaikoom,* Halil (Ha-leel). It is good to see you."

"*Alaikoom Salam,* and you as well, Na'im. You could not have arrived at a better time. I have a letter addressed to you from the sheik that I was about to send out. Evidently your arrival will be a surprise for him."

"Yes, and that is how I have planned it," Na'im replied as he opened the sealed envelope and read:

"*Naim,*

Your mother and I are well. This letter is a request for you to return home as soon as possible. Several changes have taken place in the area and your help would be of great value at this time.

Your father,
Sheik Ahmed Salim Rahman"

It was not like his father to be evasive, so Na'im knew there was some kind of trouble going on. He had to get to Karib without delay.

Na'im thought of Felicia, and he knew she was at the best place for her, the American Consulate. There she could get the help she needed. Once he got things in order in Karib, he would check back with the consulate and find out exactly where she had gone.

With this resolution in mind, he jotted down a message and asked that it be delivered to Felicia at the consulate.

▲

Felicia's heart lurched as the phone rang. She had just finished reading the note she'd received from Na'im. The representative's low-toned, hesitant conversation on the phone gave her the feeling her troubles were just beginning.

"Ms. Sanders, I am so sorry. An emergency has come up. Mr. Johnston has been sent to Cairo and will not be back for a couple of days."

"This is really awful...I don't have anyone I can contact. I know that sounds a little crazy, but you see, everyone I know is at the research site, miles away from here. They can't be reached by phone and I only have a little bit of money. I lost everything I had in an accident. I have some money that was given to me by the gentleman who brought me here, but I'm sure it's not enough to provide for several days' stay," Felicia concluded in utter frustration.

"I'm sorry this has happened. I would help you if I could but it is not my job to communicate with the main office in Cairo, and I simply would not know what to do. I will tell you what I will do. I will send a message to my Majidah (Ma-jee-duh) and see if you can stay with our family for a couple of nights. I am sure she will not mind. We run a small motel here in Al Kharijah. It is not in the inner city, but it is not far. I will check with her; I am sure it will be fine."

Felicia looked at the small man with the large, dark, kind eyes and decided once again there was nothing she could do but accept his help. "If you really think it will be alright...," she replied with her heart pounding, so much aware of her vulnerable situation.

"Sure, it will be alright. My Majidah is a good woman. She will be glad to help a young woman as yourself. By the way, my name is Najid Mu'adin (Na-jeed Moo-ah-deen)."

"I am pleased to meet you, Mr. Mu'adin."

Najid returned to his desk and scribbled a note on a small piece of paper. Stepping outside the building, he walked to one of the nearby peddler's carts where a Berber was selling many beautiful rolls of cloth. Najid spoke to him in rapid Arabic, and the Berber nodded his head in understanding, taking the paper from him.

"Raoul, Raoul, take this note to the house of Najid Mu'adin," the Berber called out to the young boy who appeared.

It looked as if the child wanted to put up a protest, but before he could, the Berber inspired him in a somewhat more ominous tone.

"Now! You lazy child! What else have you to do but ask me for money all day so that you can eat everything that is sold in the marketplace," and he placed his hand menacingly on a braided belt made from camel's hair.

With this, the young fellow took to his heels, followed closely by a scraggly brown and black dog.

Chapter Eight

Her dark, shoulder-length hair swayed like a flag in the wind, as the small, brown-skinned girl jumped up and down, waving her arms in a welcoming gesture as Felicia and Najid approached the inn.

"Mama, they are here. They are here, Mama," she cried as she ran toward them leaping into Najid's outstretched arms.

"This is my littlest one, Sana. As you can see, she is our welcoming committee. She always has her nose in the windows looking for anyone who may be coming."

Sana smiled boldly at Felicia, wriggling her small frame until her father was forced to put her back down on the ground. Skipping back to the building alongside them, she began to hum a traditional tune.

Felicia felt relieved to see Najid's daughter and the smoke coming from the chimney of the inn, which also served as the Mu'adin family home. The entire scene seemed to take away most of the apprehension she had been feeling as she walked with Najid, whom she barely knew, to a place she knew nothing about.

As they approached the doorway of the mud and rock structure, Majidah appeared, giving her husband a hug and voicing a soft but sincere welcome to Felicia as she beckoned for the two of them to follow her through a low, dark hallway. As the group emerged on the opposite end, they were greeted by a room embossed in a soft, shimmery light produced by several oil lamps.

A young woman was placing bowls and eating utensils on the table as they entered, but she halted her task long enough to give her father a peck on the cheek and greet and welcome Felicia.

"This is my daughter, Jamillah (Jah-mee-luh). She is the middle child, and there is my son, Ali, the eldest."

A handsome, honey brown-skinned man began to cross the room toward them as Najid spoke his name. Ali, too, gave his father a hug and turned to greet her.

Felicia felt somewhat overwhelmed by the family love that was obviously shared between the Mu'adins. She was engulfed by a sense of profound loss as she reflected on her childhood and her current plight. But that moment wasn't allowed to last for very long as Najid guided her toward the wooden table that dominated what was the family's dining area.

Majidah entered with a hot, steaming cup of cinnamon tea, offering it to Felicia. She accepted it graciously.

"It is old Egyptian custom, offer guest hot drink when enter our home. We are so glad you accept our welcome," Majidah crooned with a serene smile.

"My Majidah's English is not the best, but we have all attempted to teach her what we know. The children have studied your language in their schools, and I must speak it on my job, so we share with her whatever little knowledge we have, whenever we can," Najid added.

Felicia was told to make herself comfortable; then they all went their separate ways, becoming involved in their own duties. All except for Sana, who sat on a little mat in the corner playing with a handmade doll. Every once in a while, she would look up at Felicia with an impish grin as she continued to play with her toy.

Felicia was glad to have a moment of semi-solitude as she sipped on the aromatic cup of tea. Her feet were tired from the walk to Najid's home that had taken them nearly an hour, but she was glad she had come.

It was late in the afternoon when Felicia arose from the small bed in the room given to her by Majidah. Bright sunlight was shining through the tiny, high-set window, and Felicia could hear movement in other parts of the inn.

Swinging her feet off the bed onto the floor, she noticed her jeans and shirt had been removed from the back of the wooden chair on which she had placed them the night before. In their place was a colorful, floor-length dress and a pair of heelless, leather shoes.

The material from which the dress was made was truly beautiful, and Felicia found herself stroking its fine fabric between her thumb and index finger. As she marvelled at the texture, there was a tap on the door.

"Yes?"

"It is Jamillah. May I come in, please?"

"Of course, Jamillah."

"We hope you like the dress. Mama thought it would be just perfect for you. It used to be Mama's until she gained a few pounds. She thought you might wear it today while your clothes are being washed."

"I simply don't know what to say, or how to thank you all. I explained to your father that I do not have much money, but I'm sure I'll be able to pay you when..."

"Oh, no, no, no, it is not for pay that we do this, Ms. Felicia. My father has told us of your troubles and it is because of Allah's grace that you have been sent to us. We are only to do his will."

Felicia could do no more than look down at the dress she held in her hands. She wished the large lump forming in her throat would disappear, along with the tears that were welling up in her eyes.

"Breakfast is already over with, but once you are dressed you are welcome to any of the dishes Mama has prepared for lunch."

With these last words of encouragement, Felicia reached out and touched Jamillah's hand. "You are so kind. I'll get dressed and come down and join you right away."

Felicia put the finishing touches to her hair. It fell in a series of dark waves and curls across her brow and down the side of her face, onto her shoulders and upper back. She firmly pushed the remaining side behind her ear as she assessed herself in the broken mirror that hung over an old wash bowl.

The image that looked back at her was quite a pleasant one, but there was a lifelessness about the eyes that Felicia knew reflected the turmoil she continued to feel inside.

Strife was not a stranger to her. As a matter of fact, she considered herself to be a master at controlling it. She knew if you pretended long enough that everything was fine, after a while you'd even be able to convince yourself.

She made herself focus on the reason she was in Egypt. *I'm a research scientist. One who is on a very important project that could end up helping thousands of people in the long run. I'm finally doing something I've always dreamed of doing. I'm in control,* she proclaimed in an effort to combat her thoughts of Na'im, without much success. *I'm not some helpless female like my mother who had to take anything from a man just to survive.* Felicia regretted the negative thoughts about her mother as soon as they entered her mind. She loved her mother, but she resented her for not being able to protect her as a child.

She couldn't help but wonder if she'd ever see Na'im again. She chastised herself for feeling deserted. Life had already taught her that all a man wanted was to possess and dominate you, and then leave as Na'im had left without a second glance.

He had saved her life and they had spent four days of their lives together. Did they not share a common bond because of this? How could he simply put her out of his mind, like some stranger you'd pass on the street? His note to her had been short and simple: *"Must go on to Karib; will contact you at the consulate as soon as possible. - Na'im."*

Felicia looked down as a slow, steady sigh passed through her lips. At that moment, she determined that with so many other problems to solve, Na'im Raoul Rahman was the least important to be concerned with.

Chapter Nine

There was much dancing and celebrating in the sheik-dom on the outskirts of Mut. Na'im's father spared nothing in welcoming his son back home.

The melodic beat of ethnic drums vibrated through the night, accompanied by flutes and clappers, while Na'im and his father sat in the seats of honor before a majestic feast.

There were kebobs of all kinds, *mahshi*, and *baklava*, a crisp, flaky pastry with many layers, oozing with syrup and ground nuts. Turkish coffee and the aroma of Arab breads filled the air, along with the fragrance of fresh mangoes, oranges and figs.

The spirits of everyone in the small settlement seemed to be high, some boosted by homemade wines fermented from grapes and dates. Na'im had to admit he was glad to be among his people.

Na'im's father talked of nothing else but Na'im's travels and the education Na'im now possessed that would allow him to lead his people further into economic progress. Na'im sat beside him, content to let him rave on.

Soon a group of women began a ritualistic number to

the captivating sound of a solo flute. Fatimah (Fah-tee-muh), his cousin, twirled amongst the fluid dancers, giving Na'im an obvious wink as she went by.

My, she has grown into such a lovely woman. Na'im always knew she would be one of the prettiest girls in the village, but he had not expected such grace and elegance from his cousin, whom he remembered as no less than awkward–always stumbling about and knocking over anything within her reach.

Na'im smiled generously at Fatimah as the dancers formed a swaying, tightening circle. The dance ended abruptly in a final crescendo of drums and tambourines.

Slowly and almost imperceptibly, the lone sound of a haunting oboe began to fill the air, and the dancers' circle parted to reveal a crouching figure in its center.

The solo dancer's movements were so much one with the instrument that her undulating body appeared to move without conscious effort. As the drums joined in and the melody began to pick up its pace, so did the gyrations of the woman's body until she became a fiery energy ball, captivating and spellbinding all who gazed upon her. This included Na'im, toward whom her rhythmic steps were advancing.

Na'im's nostrils tingled from the smell of sweat rising from the dancer's caramel-colored frame as she came down on her knees no more than a foot in front of him. Her entire body shook with tremors, making the flesh at the top of her glistening breasts tremble. Her limber back bent backwards until the top of her dark brown head lay in the dust and her long, slender arms extended outward as if beckoning for Na'im to take her.

"Your father can see that this one rouses your interest."

"My interest is not the only thing that has been roused, my father," Na'im replied, as the woman bowed to him, never breaking contact with his eyes.

"Aha!" Na'im's father chuckled, "I have not forgotten my promise to you that I would find you a suitable woman to wed. I have searched many territories and this one, Waheedah Faruuk (Wah-hee-duh Far-ook) of Khartoum has been so honored as my choice."

"My father shows good taste in women, at least when it comes to their physical attributes."

"And their mental abilities as well. If not, I would never have married your mother."

"What do you know of this one's mind, Father?"

"No more than what her father has told me, which I confess has not been much. But she comes from a good Egyptian background. One that would be politically and economically helpful to Karib. And from what I can see, she should be able to keep you happy. Even though your mother does not agree with me when it comes to her."

"Oh, my mother does not? What does she have to say about this?"

"You know your mother. She is always consulting her 'guides', who she says do not bring forth good feelings toward the girl. The older she becomes, the more she talks of them. She says it is because she is growing wiser and journeying closer to 'The One'. I am careful when it comes to teasing her about it, for as you know she has proven to be right on more than one occasion. It has not been easy for her, choosing to hold onto the beliefs of her forebears. It is because of my power and influence that she has been left to believe what she wishes. She says it is because she is protected by 'The One' who exists inside of us and throughout the universe."

"Where is my mother? Why is she not beside us here enjoying the celebration?"

"One of the women is in labor tonight. Yasmin (Yazmeen) wanted to see if there was anything she could do to comfort her."

"My mother has taught me many things through the years and I find it has helped me to keep an open mind. I have learned it is good to keep an open mind when it comes to the spiritual world."

"I understand, Na'im, but it is not always safe to voice your views to others who may not agree with you."

"Are you attempting to make Na'im as overprotective of me as you are, Ahmed ?"

Na'im looked up at his mother's face as she knelt behind his father, placing both hands gently on his shoulders. She had not aged much during the past two years, and the small lines that had begun to appear simply added character to her strong features.

"No, Yasmin, this is not true. I simply wish that you would be a little less outspoken when it comes to some things."

"But my husband, this is not the time to be silent. Have you not told Na'im of the problems we face because of Sharif Hassan (Shah-reef Hah-sahn)? Many of the younger women and older girls are being stolen from their villages, Na'im. And it is believed that Hassan is behind this."

"Right after you left for America, his village suffered a great tragedy. Somehow their wells became tainted. In the beginning, they could not tell that there was anything wrong because the water tasted and smelled the same. So before they realized this, all of their village drank of it for a few days. Then some of the people began to get sick; the old ones and the women and children. When it was all over, all of the old ones had died and only a handful of the women and children were left. The majority of the villagers are now males. Hassan's wife was among the dead.

"The villages that have been hit by Hassan are the small ones that do not have enough men to protect them against him. We do not think he will take on a village of our size, for these abductions have taken place in broad daylight, with brutal force. Still, we felt concerned because our cotton crop did not produce nearly as much this year. It would be devastating for this problem to be coupled by an assault from Hassan. Yasmin and I both felt that maybe you could think of a way to convince Hassan that this is not the way. Do you not know his son, Abdul (Ab-dool)?"

"Yes, I do. But by what I know of him, it would not do us any good to approach him. He is easy to provoke, no matter what the situation."

"Let's end this kind of talk; you are home now after being gone for so long. Let this be a night of happiness and celebration, not of things that I dare say are not nearly as pleasant."

Na'im nodded his agreement as Sheik Rahman motioned for the acrobatics to begin.

Na'im sat through the first half of the performance, but then begged his father and mother's forgiveness for wanting to retire so early. He was sincerely tired from the last few days of travel, but he also wanted some moments alone.

After reaching his tent and settling himself down on his pallet, Na'im reached for the wine that had been left for him to drink. As he looked down into the copper goblet that held the rich dark liquid, sad dark velvety eyes stared back at him. He downed the blackish brew quickly and rubbed his hands over his eyes, shaking his head in an attempt to clear his mind of Felicia.

After the night Shabazz had appeared in their camp, he knew how much he cared for her. He could not risk taking their relationship any further without knowing more about her. No, she had not worn a wedding ring or a locket showing that she had committed herself to someone else. But it was strange to hear a woman invite a man to make love to her with no strings attached. He'd known plenty of American women who'd say anything to get what they wanted. But what would she have accomplished? She didn't know he was the son of a sheik. No, it was best that he had said and done what he had.

Laying back with sleep rapidly overtaking him, Na'im's dreams were filled with many images. He found himself drowning in the River Nile and being saved by a female whose features he could not make out.

Then he was back at his father's feast with Waheedah dancing only a few inches in front of him, her tanned body twisting and churning, becoming darker in color until it was a luscious chocolate. Her head was bent backwards to the ground, her arms outstretched to embrace him. He wrapped his cord-like arms around her bare waist, burying his face in her abdomen, his tongue a fiery thing as it flicked her navel and she cried out her pleasure. Na'im's head was molded into her belly as she ran her fingers through his thick mane. Suddenly she jerked his head back as she lifted her head upward, no longer Waheedah but Felicia.

Chapter Ten

"Na'im! Na'im! Come quickly! Several women have been taken from the camp, including Fatimah and Waheedah of Khartoum."

There was rising commotion throughout the camp as Na'im headed for his father's tent. Before he could reach it, he could see the sheik standing outside surrounded by a crowd of people. Several men were shouting and an elderly woman was crying. Sheik Rahman attempted to quiet them, but to no avail.

"Quiet. Do you not hear my father speaking? I know you are upset, but fighting amongst ourselves will get us nowhere," Na'im shouted above the crowd.

"Well, what are we going to do about this?" the father of one of the younger girls asked.

Na'im looked questioningly at his father. Sheik Rahman nodded for him to go ahead.

"We will form a search party and go after them. I will need at least twelve men. But the rest of you are to remain here, making sure the women are settled back safely in their homes."

"I want to go, Na'im. Fatimah is my concern."

"And also mine, Ilyas (Eel-e-yas)," Na'im replied as he looked down at the young man who had voiced his intentions toward his cousin a year ago.

The father of one of the missing girls, and several others who had personal concerns about the women who had been abducted, stepped forward. Soon Na'im had his twelve men.

He entered his father and mother's tent, surprised to find Yasmin ministering to his father, and he allowing her to do it.

"My father has become very spoiled with the years," Na'im commented jokingly.

"No, Na'im. Your father is not well. This is another reason why your mother and I wanted you to return to our home. As you could see outside, I no longer carry the force needed to command obedience from our people. I am not saying they do not respect me. But they have known of my recent bouts with sickness and this has filled them with fear. The fear that they will be left without a leader. Now that you are here, they see youth and strength and their fears will be calmed. You can see, my son, these are not the easiest times."

"I agree, and I will lead the search for our women, but our people will always need your wisdom."

"My husband has tried to do too much, Na'im. I warned him that he should rest. He says rest is for those who lie in the ground. But now that you are here, we shall see that he does rest. Won't we?"

Na'im could see the love and concern in his mother's eyes for his father.

"Of course we will. Starting today."

Chapter Eleven

Jamillah knocked on the worn, wooden door and opened it slightly as she called out her aunt's name. Every week it was her duty to bring her aunt fresh bread, and today Felicia accompanied her.

The walk had taken them nearly two hours, but it was pleasant enough with Jamillah to talk to. Though only sixteen, she was very knowledgeable about many things, and the time had passed quickly.

"Aunt Esme (Ez-may)," Jamillah called once more, poking her head inside the small house but still getting no answer.

"She is not here." Jamillah looked further down the road at the small houses that lined the way. "She can't be far."

Felicia had to agree with her. The village was so small, there were not very many places she could go.

An elderly man emerged from the house next door and began sweeping off the stoop in front of it with a home-made broom. He peered at Felicia and Jamillah.

"If you are looking for Esme, she is at the healer's," he said, pointing toward a house sitting further back from the road than the others.

Jamillah and Felicia thanked him as they headed toward the house.

As they stood waiting at the door, Felicia found herself staring at vast amounts of quartz crystals lining the inside ledges of the house's window sills. Each one seemed to catch the sun's light, turning them into small rainbows of color. Felicia felt awed by the sight and wondered what manner of person would surround themselves with such an array of nature's beauty. She didn't have to wonder long, for just as she stepped over to one of the windows for a closer look, the door opened and the two young women stepped inside.

The room into which they entered was alive with scents, all mingling together in a fashion that assaulted their senses. There were countless shelves lining the walls, most of them possessing rows and rows of canisters and containers. Some seemed to be made from precious metals such as silver and gold.

The perfectly-preserved buds of dried flowers lay interspersed between these objects, adding to their wonderment.

One corner of the room displayed various stones of all colors and sizes ranging from a large pale pink rose quartz to a minute, shiny pitch black obsidian. It was as if Felicia had stepped into a time and place that captured the essence of nature's gifts, and the petite elderly woman who welcomed them inside was the most alluring of them all.

The top of her silver gray head came no higher than Felicia's shoulder, and she wore her floor-length hair in one silken braid that hung like lightweight hemp down her back. It too was adorned with hair ornaments made from the stones that surrounded her. Her delicate oval face had not been spared the lines of time, but it was her large slate gray eyes that dominated her facial features. The woman's small body was covered in a long violet robe made from the lightest of materials, while handmade embroidered shoes graced her tiny feet.

"I bid you welcome to the house of Aisha (I-ee-sha)."

Felicia was so taken aback that she stood motionless, unable to speak, as she took in Aisha's tiny presence. She didn't know what she'd expected to see when she entered "the healer's" abode, but it surely wasn't this angel-like creature who addressed them now.

Jamillah, on the other hand, was locked in a bow pose extending from her waist.

"There now girl, there is no need to act as if you were greeting 'Ra' himself," Aisha remarked, her voice sounding like the wind whistling through trees.

Jamillah stood upright. Her face was extremely flushed as she looked at Aisha, and then at her aunt who was seated in a padded chair not far away.

"Jamillah, I am glad you have come. Your counsin Akeel (Ah-keel) is here today also, visiting from Va. I told Aisha that I was expecting you. We knew that you would not have a problem finding out where I had gone. Who is this young lady with you?" she nodded in Felicia's direction.

"This is a guest of our house, Aunt Esme. Her name is Felicia Sanders. She is an American."

"Oh, a foreigner! You certainly could not tell that by her looks or dress!"

"No, the dress is Mama's, and I agree with you, she looks very much like one of us."

Felicia was becoming accustomed to being the center of conversation, but not being able to completely understand what was being said. She waited for Jamillah to explain.

"She is staying with us until the representative at the American Consulate comes back from Cairo. Hopefully, once he returns he will be able to help her."

"What pains you, my child?" Aisha asked, as she watched Felicia close her eyes and wrinkle her brow.

"I had an accident a few days ago; ever since then, from time to time, pains shoot through my head and I have trouble focusing and remembering things. But during the pain I seem to have flashbacks of the very things that I would forget if I could," Felicia replied, rubbing her hand across her brow. "It only lasts a few seconds, and then it's gone."

"Your pain stems from more than a physical injury."

Felicia's eyes opened wide with surprise from the woman's unexpected remark.

"It is time for you to confront your own fears," she said quietly and crossed the room to Aunt Esme's side.

"What does she mean by that?" Felicia asked Jamillah in a hushed tone.

"I do not know. But I do know she is a very powerful healer. Her power is known through many towns and oases. It is said she has the gift of resurrecting."

Suddenly, with a nymph-like hand, Aisha motioned for the young women to be quiet and pointed to some chairs surrounding a table in the center of the room.

Without another word, Aisha stood behind Aunt Esme with her eyes closed. Her hands were spread apart and held no more than six inches above Aunt Esme's head. She stood there so still, and for just a moment she reminded Felicia of the stone carvings she had seen in Al Kharijah. Then slowly Aisha's hands began to descend the sides of Aunt Esme's head, stopping intermittently as if feeling for something unseen. As she reached her neck and was about to continue down the sides of her shoulders, she halted abruptly. Felicia noticed a change in the expression on her face, which had been blank up until that moment. Now it appeared as if Aisha was feeling pain or discomfort. Her thin eyebrows came together in a slight frown.

"It is here, Esme, that I feel the imbalance. The energy does not flow here as it should."

At that time, Aisha placed both of her hands on the base of Esme's neck at the point where it entered her shoulders. Now it was Aunt Esme who reacted as if she had been hit with a small bolt of lightning, but the expression on her face was not one of pain, but one of relief.

Aisha kept her hands on Aunt Esme's shoulders for only a short time. She opened her eyes as she removed them and advised Aunt Esme to do the same.

"Now I will have you smell of this," and she turned to remove a container from the shelf behind her.

"This holds the essence of a very special plant. It will help you to relax and harmonize the imbalance in your upper body. I will give you a measured amount, but you are not to use it except at bedtime."

Aunt Esme closed her eyes once more, inhaling the fumes from the container that Aisha held. Felicia observed the entire scene in complete bewilderment. Jamillah too was awed by what she was seeing. The kindly woman bestowed a moderate smile in the young women's direction.

"It is not as magical as you two may think. For many centuries in Egypt, high priests and those with the knowledge of healing used this method to bring comfort to the sick. Because I, and those who come to me, are still of the old beliefs, the aromatics are still able to manifest their powers to cure."

"Now, Esme, you should go rest. Have your niece, Jamillah, take you home and visit with you for awhile. This will give me an opportunity to talk with the girl."

Aunt Esme motioned her agreement and began searching in the folds of her *melaya* for her coin pouch.

"You know I do not want your money, but a portion of the fresh bread Jamillah has brought you would be most welcome."

Aunt Esme nodded her compliance.

Felicia's eyes wandered back and forth beneath their closed lids as she took in each breath. Aisha had told her to just relax and breathe naturally; to concentrate on each breath, and it would be through the power of her own breath that the rebirthing would work for her.

Felicia found herself wondering why she was cooperating with Aisha's instructions. She no longer believed in anything other than what logic and science could prove to her. She'd decided life was best seen in black and white. The hardcore truth is what a person needed to survive in this day and time. Belief in anything other than that would only bring you pain.

She was feeling more relaxed and just a little sleepy now, even though her breathing had picked up its pace on its own accord. A white light began to fill her mind as her breaths became a pant, and it appeared to encase her entire being in its energy like a sea of peace and love. She could see herself being guided upward by a tiny translucent winged being until she was no longer herself but a child. They had reached a cleft high in a mountain ridge where the being left her, but at her feet was a leather-bound burgundy book with pages trimmed in gold. As she turned the pages, she saw they contained the story of her life.

A primordial scream brought Felicia out of her altered state. It was her own scream that she heard. The scream of someone on the brink of death. The scream she would have emitted if her mouth had not been filled with water from the Nile.

"You are fine, Felicia. Don't worry, I am here. And now you are here; all of you. There will be no more physical pain or pain of the mind from things you wish you could forget. Now you will be able to accept the hand fate has dealt you and begin to live your life without reservation."

A shaken Felicia looked at the tiny woman who sat in front of her.

"It is through the breath of life that 'The One' constantly reminds us that we are one with Him. I did nothing but allow you to really open up to yourself. For a long time now, you have fought to forget Him. But there are many rainbows in store for you, Felicia Sanders. This you can be sure of."

Felicia touched her own face. For some reason she felt that there would be something different about it. For the first time in years, she felt an acceptance of herself and where she had come from. Somehow deep inside, she knew this event was a turning point in her life.

Aisha busied herself, allowing Felicia a few moments to collect her thoughts.

"Aisha, did I hear Aunt Esme mention a village called Va?"

"Yes, you did. Her son, Akeel, lives there. He decided to visit her today."

"If I'm not mistaken, Va is the village that we were going to get some of our supplies from for the research project. I don't know why I didn't think of that before now. Maybe Akeel will allow me to go back with him. I'm sure I'll be able to contact Phillip and the others from there. I've got to let them know that I'm okay."

"Do whatever your heart speaks to you of doing, my child. It is only from inside of yourself that the true answers will come. And never forget your will is not separate from the will of 'The One'. It is because of that, you can accomplish anything."

Chapter Twelve

Jamillah had been reluctant when Felicia told her of her intentions of going back to Va with Akeel.

"Why not wait for Papa to come home tonight? He will be happy to take you into town with him tomorrow, and from there you can travel to Va. That would be the best thing to do."

"But I'll need a guide and everything then Jamillah, don't you see? I'll practically be in the same position I was in when I first came to Al Kharijah. I just don't feel I can put it off any longer, now that I know how I can contact my research team. See you really don't understand. I have a group of people here in Egypt who are waiting for me. It's been almost a week since I have been missing. I've got to get to Va as soon as I can, to let them know I'm alright."

"I do understand now. I will ask Akeel to take you."

Jamillah and Aunt Esme gave Felicia and Akeel some dried meat and bread and a container of fresh water, to make their journey easier. Aunt Esme wrapped the food, along with a knife, in a piece of cloth.

It was late afternoon when they passed several people on the road; most of them walking, others pitched high on the backs of camels.

Akeel said it would take them about three more hours before they reached the town. Maybe even sooner, since they were making such good time.

Felicia knew that she was in good shape physically. She was quite an exercise and dance buff back in the States; aerobics, walking, and she still frequented the modern dance studio whenever the urge hit her, and that was once or twice a week.

Felicia's face clouded over as she remembered when she had little time for the things she enjoyed outside of work. Alvin Bailey was the reason why. Alvin, with his suave ways and business suits. His condominium and consultant firm. His promises to marry her. His lies. His family in Toledo, Ohio.

It was after Alvin Bailey that Felicia had decided to take this assignment in Egypt. He'd sent dozens of yellow roses, asking for her forgiveness. But two years of being deceived could never be wiped out by flowers.

It had taken an additional six months for the base work to be completed on the project in a lab at William Bowles Hospital in Memphis, Tennessee. But they finally did it.

Phillip and the other research team members had set out a week before she had. She had wanted to spend some additional time with her family in Clarksville. Rodney, her seventeen year-old brother, had been beside himself when she asked if he wanted to keep her Mazda RX-7 while she was overseas. Even though they were eight years apart, they were extremely close.

Akeel and Felicia reached a fork in the road. He said both of them led to Va, but one of them, the more public road, took much longer than the other. Akeel said he was familiar with both and decided they would take the shortest route.

Felicia thought of Phillip and how, by now, he had probably contacted her family. She knew everyone had to be concerned about her, and was pleased with Akeel's decision.

She knew they couldn't be far from the settlement because the trees and brush were becoming plentiful. She didn't want to, but out of necessity, they stopped to rest. They couldn't have chosen a better spot to do it. The place they chose was well off the road, equipped with several boulders on which they sat. Silently, they shared the bread and meat and drank some of the water.

The sun was just beginning to set when they completed their meal, and the sky was filled with the most beautiful hues of magenta and violet. As they began to make their way back to the road, Felicia heard someone weeping. At least she thought she did.

She placed her hand on Akeel's arm, and motioned for him to stop and listen. After a few moments, the faint noise was heard again.

Felicia began to move in the direction of the sound, with a reluctant Akeel in tow. As they got closer, crying wasn't the only thing they heard. Boisterous laughter began to drown it out. Male laughter.

Through the trees Felicia could see three men sitting in a small clearing in the brush. It was the woman with them who interested Felicia the most. The men patted and pinched on her as she passed by, serving them food. It was this woman that Felicia had heard crying.

The men seemed to be having a great time. They knew of the woman's discomfort, but it was obvious they didn't care.

One of the men motioned toward a set of trees behind them. The woman gathered some of the food together and proceeded in the direction of the trees, directly opposite from where Felicia and Akeel were hiding.

As she looked more closely Felicia was shocked to see four bound women.. Ropes encircled their waists, as they sat with the tree trunks supporting their backs and their feet extended outward.

Three of the women snatched the food hungrily, but one refused to take it and her food was left sitting in her lap. It was obvious these women were here against their will. But why? Could these be the kidnappers Na'im had warned her of, and she had brushed him off?

Akeel leaned close to Felicia's ear, his fear apparent in his voice.

"This is dangerous. There is nothing we can do. We must get the authorities."

Felicia's mind flooded with images of police coming to her house after her father had kicked in doors and battered her mother. She felt it would be too late by the time they contacted the authorities.

"It won't do any good then, Akeel. We've got to do something now. I think we'll have a better chance once it is dark."

It didn't take long before the group had a small but adequate campfire going. The men had placed their guns, along with other gear, in two small tents they'd hoisted. Probably, if Felicia and Akeel had not spotted the campsite during the daylight, it wouldn't have been easy to find after dark.

For some reason, against the campfire's glare, one of the men seemed vaguely familiar. Felicia dismissed the thought as she began a wide circle around the clearing.

The woman who refused to eat was the first one that Felicia approached from behind. ''Sh-sh,'' she warned, as she quietly cut her ropes.

The startled woman remained seated as she waited for Felicia to free the others.

Felicia had cut the ropes of a second young girl, when she was grabbed from behind and dragged forward to the middle of the camp.

Chapter Thirteen

Felicia couldn't understand a word that was being said, the man was speaking so rapidly. But when he dumped her at the feet of Yusef Shabazz, she was terrified. She only hoped that Akeel would not try to play the hero like she had, and had gone to get some help.

At first Shabazz spoke to her in Arabic, assuming she understood him. Felicia didn't say a word, because then he would know she and Na'im had deceived him in more ways than one. Her silence did nothing but provoke Shabazz.

She could tell he was explaining to his men where he had seen her before, and he pranced around the fire showing just how he had seen her. At this, they all roared with laughter.

Shabazz laughed louder than any of the others; but once his laughter subsided, another expression appeared on his face–the same one Felicia had seen that night when he and Na'im had sat before the campfire. One of pure lust.

Shabazz toyed with a long stick he'd picked up in the clearing, before he began to poke Felicia with it. She covered her breasts with her arms as he used the branch to circle them. Leisurely, he raised her dress as she clasped her arms tightly to her sides.

"That's enough, Shabazz," a male voice called out from the edge of the clearing.

Felicia could not believe her eyes or her ears as she turned and saw Na'im.

"So you speak to me in English this time, huh?"

"Yes, because I want the young lady to understand everything we're saying. Don't try to go for your guns because I am not alone."

More than ten men, along with Akeel, stepped out of the shadows to show that Na'im was telling the truth.

Fatimah wasted no time shaking off the cut ropes. Relieved, she ran across the clearing to stand between her cousin and Ilyas. The second woman who Felicia had managed to set free followed suit, to another young man in the group.

"How did you get loose?" Na'im asked.

Fatimah pointed to Felicia. "This woman freed us. It was while she was trying to free the others that Shabazz's lookout caught her."

"Where is Waheedah?"

"They split us up once we neared the borders of Al Kharijah. Two of Shabazz's men took her and Khalilah (Kah-lee-luh) with them. I do not know where they have gone."

"Where are they, Shabazz?" Na'im demanded.

"They are being taken to Hassan, but don't worry, nothing will happen to them. At least nothing that you'll be able to look at them and tell. I understand you have a special interest in..."

"You only need answer the questions that I ask you, Shabazz, and nothing else."

Na'im crossed over to Felicia and lifted her up from the ground.

"I must say, Na'im, you seem to have impeccable timing."

"Only where you are concerned, *aros al bher.* As my mother would say, our karmas are intertwined."

Feeling a flow of heated relief rush through her, Felicia responded, "Whatever the reason, I'm thankful for it."

Na'im decided to remain at the campsite the rest of the night. After all, the women had had enough excitement for one day.

Felicia was put into the tent with all of the single women. The other tents contained the men and one married couple. Shabazz and his men looked on from their vantage point, tied to the same trees that had earlier held the women captive.

Na'im had been busy with the men, getting the camp ready for the night, securing the tents and taking care of the camels. The women took on other chores. Once Na'im was done, he asked Felicia if she'd like to walk with him.

All eyes were upon them as they left the campsite. Felicia had noticed how everyone looked to Na'im for instructions and how he naturally commanded and got their respect.

"So who is this Na'im Raoul Rahman that can order a small army of men about without the slightest show of disobedience? Don't tell me I've been in the company of a king or prince and I didn't know it."

"No, sorry to tell you, I'm neither of those. The men are all members of our village. Every one of them had been personally affected by the abductions and wanted to do something about it," Na'im explained with a casual air.

"But I didn't ask you to walk with me so I could talk about myself. I want to know more about Felicia Sanders."

So Felicia began to talk. She was careful not to tell him much about her childhood because, in some ways, she felt life had truly begun for her once she left home and went off to college.

It didn't take long before her talk had brought her to Egypt. She told him of Aisha and the rebirthing. Of how fate had placed Akeel in her path, providing a way for her to contact her research team members. Lastly, she told him of how they had come upon Shabazz and the women he and his companions were holding captive.

"So despite the danger to yourself, you risked your life to save a group of women you knew nothing about? There is much more to you, Felicia, than one would ever suspect."

"In America, we say you should never judge a book by its cover."

At this, Na'im laughed. " That is very true."

The night was alive with nighttime sounds, as they entered a circle of trees. Na'im sat down on the spongy grass and Felicia did the same, a few feet away from him. She stared up at the moon. Lackadaisical clouds drifted high above leafy tree branches, resembling pieces of lace against the dark blue sky.

"Sit closer to me, *aros al bher.* I have been so busy at the camp. Now I'd like you to be near me. Days have passed since we've seen each other. I must admit, I had become accustomed to your company."

"So now I guess your perception of me has changed. Now that I helped your people. Does that make me more worthy of your affection?" she looked at him pointedly. "Let me tell you something, Na'im. I am the same woman now as I was before this happened."

Na'im moved closer to her side. "I know that."

"And in my country, it is common for a woman my age to feel and display the kind of emotions I have shown. And if I was not good enough for you then, I guess I'm still not good enough." She lifted her head defiantly.

"*Aros al bher,* I kept my distance from you because I was not sure if the whole thing between us wasn't just an emotional need, resulting from your near drowning. People do and say strange things after those kinds of experiences. It would not have been an honorable thing to do. Can you honestly say you were thinking clearly that night and knew what you really wanted?"

Felicia laid back on the blanket of grass. "No...I can't. But I know what I felt."

"And I know how I felt then, and still feel."

Na'im leaned down toward Felicia and placed a soft kiss upon her lips. "*Aros al bher*, when I take you for the first time, I want you to know how much I want you. And I want to know that you truly want me. I want every part of you to know how precious it is to me."

Na'im sat back and began to remove his *galabia.* Felicia endeavored to do the same, but Na'im stopped her and motioned for her to lie still. After removing his clothing, Na'im turned to Felicia and eased the dress over her head.

"How could you ever think I did not want you after seeing you like this?"

A small moan escaped Felicia's lips as she saw the urgency in his eyes and heard it in his voice.

Na'im lifted Felicia's palm to his lips and pressed a kiss right in its center. Slowly he moved his mouth upward, nipping at the tender skin that led to her fingertips, leaving none feeling undesirable.

After giving reverence to both hands, Na'im continued his onslaught of Felicia's senses. Burying his face in her breasts, he held her as if she would disappear if he let go.

By now, Felicia's chest was rising and falling rapidly. The tips of the two dark mounds that graced it beckoned for Na'im to caress them, which he did in every way. Hairs so small that Na'im could hardly see them began to stand on end, as he licked skin reminiscent of chocolate.

Na'im's hand stroked Felicia's thigh, moving upward until he reached the oasis of her being, and he found it ready to give of its resources.

Rising above Felicia and looking passionately into her eyes, Na'im asked, "And now, *aros al bher*, if I did not desire you, would I drink from the well from which your femininity flows?"

Felicia could not answer him; nor did he expect her to as his lips sought out the center of her pleasure. She moaned as they played havoc with the very core of her.

He had brought her to near delirium before he entered her–a pulsing, throbbing mass. Once inside, Na'im's pleasure was so intense he lost all sense of place and time, his body performing to a beat older than time itself. Over and over he plunged. His only awareness...Felicia.

Her legs and thighs clung to him, urging him on until she exploded with intense pleasure, his own release following in spurts of passion.

The two of them remained there in each other's arms until the nighttime breeze made them know they were no longer welcome. Only then did they head back to the camp.

Chapter Fourteen

Felicia looked into the anxious faces of the crowds filling the streets of Karib as she rode in front of Na'im on his camel. She could tell the village was not a very large one, but she was surprised to see more than two hundred people cheering them on as they progressed toward the center of the town.

"Rahman, Rahman," they chanted in unison. Felicia was astonished to hear them calling Na'im's name. She dared not look back into his face, for as she attempted to do so, she could feel his arms tighten around her waist, keeping her still.

"Na'im, are you going to tell me what this is all about?" she asked.

"What do you mean? They are glad that we have been able to recapture most of the women."

"Then why are they shouting your name?"

"Mine is the oldest family name in the village; it is rightfully so that they do this."

They entered an area surrounded by a high white wall that resembled a courtyard, and Na'im dismounted. A young boy came forth smiling and greeted Na'im.

"*As-Salam-Alaikoom.*"

"*Alaikoom-Salam,*" Na'im replied, lifting Felicia from the camel and handing the reins over to the boy.

Felicia followed Na'im until they entered a round foyer filled with exotic plants and marvelous Egyptian sculptures and art. It led to what appeared to be five separate areas of the building.

"This isn't where you live, is it?"

"And if it is?"

"Well, my goodness, you're talking to a girl who grew up on the south side of Memphis, Tennessee, you know. I feel like I'm in some kind of palace or something."

"My family's taste has been quite extravagant through the years. So what you're seeing is just an accumulation of contributions by generations of my family...what would you call it? Heirlooms? So now, if you'll just follow me this way, I'll show you where you'll be staying."

Felicia followed Na'im through a long, screened-in, domed sunroom, overflowing with blossoming plants and colorful birds that were allowed to fly about as freely as they pleased.

"This is my mother's favorite room. She and my father are away for awhile, taking care of some personal matters. And this is the sitting room that connects to your bedroom."

Na'im threw open the doors to an expansive, well-lit area, adorned with two overstuffed chairs, a couch and various artifacts. There was a portrait that looked remarkably like Na'im hanging on the east wall.

Na'im crossed the room and opened another door. "This is where you shall sleep."

Felicia had never seen a more beautiful bedroom. Several shades of purple, lilac and magenta had been combined in the most refreshing way–from prints to solids, from curtains to rugs.

Felicia made a graceful, backwards swan dive onto the full-sized bed that dominated the room. "Now I could surely live like this for awhile."

"And so you shall, *aros al bher*, for as long as you like."

Felicia could hear the serious tone creep into Na'im's voice, as he watched her from across the room. She thought of Na'im and everything he had done for her.

"Na'im, I want you to know that I owe you my life and I'll never forget that. I promise you that I'll do anything I can for you."

"Is that a true promise, *azizi*?" Na'im asked in a tone so soft, Felicia could barely hear him.

Sitting up on the bed and caressing him with her eyes, Felicia replied, "Yes."

Felicia and Na'im stared at each other for a long time, the electricity between them a tangible thing; their ethnic backgrounds a major obstacle in both their minds.

Felicia was the first to look away. "Na'im, I've got to contact the other members of my research team."

"It's no problem. I will send Kareem (Kah-reem) to you, and he will deliver your message to the center in Al Kharijah. From there, I'll make sure it reaches any village you want to contact in Egypt."

"Ooh, that sounds powerful," Felicia chided him.

"Not really. It is just true." Na'im pointed to a pair of double doors. "You will find an assortment of clothes in the closet there. Something should fit you. I must go now. I've got a lot of things to do. I'll see you later."

Felicia watched Na'im's retreating form as he closed the door to her room, and she wondered what she was getting herself into.

Chapter Fifteen

"Is all?" Kareem asked, while bowing at the same time.

"Yes, that's gonna do it, Kareem."

He bounded for the door with Felicia's last approval, almost knocking Fatimah over as she stood at the entrance.

Fatimah admonished him in Arabic for his careless actions, causing Kareem to bow several times in succession as he backed out of the door.

"You must forgive Kareem, Felicia, he is not accustomed to working inside of the home. Na'im has kept him around because his mother died while in the Rahman's employ. Rarely has he been allowed to come inside and perform tasks. Na'im is trying to see that he has good training in both areas."

"Believe me, I'm not accustomed to anyone waiting on me in my home at all. So to be honest with you, I was a little impressed with how anxious he was to take care of that for me."

Fatimah smiled and Felicia couldn't help but admire how lovely she was. Her skin was a little lighter than Felicia's, a rich brown with red tones. She wore her waist-length hair in a decorative ball at the top of her head, allowing the back hair to hang free. The festive plum and mustard, floor-length dress she wore accentuated her natural beauty.

"So, are you all settled in now? Na'im told me to check on you. He wants to make sure you are comfortable while you are here. I am happy. This will give me something to do. Give you companionship, and help you understand our ways a little better."

"I definitely appreciate all of this. But you see, I really don't know how long I'll be here. That's why I sent a letter by Kareem to the message center in Al Kharijah. The reason I am in Egypt is because of a research project that I am working on. And, I'm afraid to say, so many things have happened since I got here that I haven't been able to work on the project at all."

"What kind of project is it? I completed secondary school in Cairo so I am somewhat familiar with these kinds of things."

"Well, you probably know that the Sahara Desert is spreading, and much of Mauritania is being overtaken by it. This, of course, is causing a water supply shortage and thousands of people are beginning to move further inland. There's extreme crowding in the places where they are relocating. We are attempting to develop an inoculation that would help humans maintain moisture in their bodies longer than normal. Then the water shortage will not be such a pressing problem, and survival will not be so difficult.

"Yes, I am aware of the problem with the Sahara. So must you go to Mauritania to develop the medicine?"

"No, though I was there about a year ago to do some initial research. Right now, we need a place where we can do some of our tests over again. I lost the Phase I serum during my accident. The camels that we initially performed the testing on have been sent back to the organization that owned them.''

''Na'im has a vast number of camels. His family breeds them to be sold to other sheikdoms such as his own.''

''To other what? Sheikdoms? Like in Rudolph Valentino?''

''I do not know of Sheik Valentino. But my uncle, Sheik Rahman, is the head of our village. It is a position of great honor.''

''I don't believe I'm hearing this.''

''I'm sorry if I have said something to upset you.''

''Believe me, it's not you, Fatimah.''

''Good, then everything is okay now. Dinner is being served in one hour. You will dine with us, won't you?''

''No. I think I'll pass up the royal dinner,'' Felicia mumbled.

''Well, I will have something brought up to your room. If you wish to bathe, you should do so soon. All electrical power is cut off at five o'clock. We do not have enough power to keep it going day and night. That is why we have the oil lamps throughout our homes for night use.''

''That sounds fine. Hey look, I don't mean to be uncooperative, but there're a few things I've got to think about.''

''I see.'' Fatimah looked down at the floor. ''Felicia, Na'im is not the easiest man to understand, but he is good in here.'' Fatimah placed her flat palm in the middle of her breast. With a brief smile, she left Felicia alone.

Felicia walked into the bath that adjoined her bedroom. It was modernly equipped, with an added eastern flavor. Mosaic tile adorned the floor and the area surrounding the bathtub. Double doors guarded the entrance to the walk-in closet, which was filled with an array of dresses and accessories.

Felicia wanted to show Na'im how much she didn't appreciate his not telling her the truth about his family. She thought about refusing his hospitality and demanding that he take her to a hotel. But what would that prove? Then she would not be near him.

What was wrong with her, anyway? Most of her friends back home would die to be able to say they'd spent the night in a sheik's palace. She guessed that was the reason she was worried. She knew she was in danger of losing her heart. Felicia sat on the edge of the tiled tub and shook her head.

Who was she kidding, anyway? She'd already lost her heart. One more day wasn't going to make that big of a difference. Plus, it had been such a long time since she'd had a nice, long, hot bath. Especially one in a bathtub.

Felicia emerged from the water feeling wonderful. She stepped out of the tub and wrapped herself in a rose-colored bath towel scented with myrrh. The warm water made her sleepy. She laid down on the soft spread that covered her bed. Shortly afterwards, she fell asleep.

Felicia dreamt she heard laughter that ended abruptly, then a man's voice sounding stilted and commanding. Felicia opened her eyes. It was Na'im's voice she was hearing, and she had not been asleep, but at the point where dreams and reality are sometimes confused. Half asleep, Felicia entered the sitting room and found Na'im's face in a mask of anger.

"What was that all about? At first I thought I heard someone laughing or giggling. And now, here you sit looking as if you could tear down a couple of walls or something."

"It's nothing. I just had to make sure some of the servants have the proper understanding about you."

"About me? Did they come in here to look and laugh at me? What were they saying, Na'im? That the sheik has his little American plaything stored away in a special wing of the grand mansion, and let's go see what she looks like?"

"I am not the sheik, *aros al bher*, my father is. And they wanted to see what an African-American woman looks like."

"Oh. So if my ethnic background is a curiosity to them, what will your parents think of 'your African-American female scientist' staying in their home." Felicia tightened her towel around her. "Just forget I said that. Maybe I should just find a room in a hotel."

"This is my home as well, *azizi.* And this entire west wing is mine to do with as I please. My parents will not question my motives for having you here."

"Yes, having *me* here they may not question. But what about a woman they'd consider worthy of your marrying?"

"Yes, she would be invited here as a guest as well."

Na'im could see the disillusionment that had settled on Felicia's proud features, and searched for a way to dispel them. He did not want to be separated from her again.

"I understand you need a place to complete your work. I have the ideal space here on our grounds. I have camels and I can get you anything else that you would need from my country. It would make no sense for you to stay in a hotel. We have space enough here to accommodate you and your research team many times over. So why don't you think about that and let's eat before the food gets cold."

Felicia knew Na'im was trying to squelch her frustrations, so she gladly put the issues behind her to enjoy her moments alone with him.

The meal was most fulfilling. Eating Egyptian style—plenty of fruits and vegetables, and very little meat—was no problem for Felicia, whose palate was accustomed to that kind of diet.

Even though Na'im hardly spoke during the meal, his eyes were constantly on her as she sat with her legs tucked beneath her on the couch. Whenever Felicia reached for food, Na'im's eyes tried to catch a glimpse underneath the large bath towel. This made Felicia moist with expectation. They both knew it would only be a matter of time.

Na'im wore white silky pantaloons that ballooned at the ankles. His bare chest and golden skin were such a contrast against the material.

"Egyptian air can be harsh on skin like yours that is not accustomed to such temperatures," he said to Felicia. "I have an oil that would feel wonderful on your skin and make it glow like the richest mahogany."

"Sounds like the kind of invitation a girl would find hard to refuse."

Na'im rose to his feet and crossed to an adjacent door. Opening it, he bowed as he motioned for Felicia to go inside.

She was astonished when she stepped into a massive bedchamber, twinkling with tiny oil lamps. Metallic wall hangings reflected the lights, creating an impression of unearthly surroundings.

"You didn't think I'd allow your room to be too far away from mine, did you, *habibi*?" Na'im asked as he closed the door behind them.

Large warm hands removed the towel that encircled her body and pulled her back against a hard, powerful frame. Na'im wrapped his arms completely around her as he bent and whispered Arabic phrases in her ear; words she did not understand, but felt the meaning of through his tone and embrace.

Na'im spread the towel out on his king-sized bed, telling Felicia to lie on her stomach with her arms relaxed at her sides.

Powerful fingers rubbed, fluffed and feathered her skin in ways she could only have imagined. Na'im paid close attention to the areas he knew would relax Felicia and bring her the most pleasure. She could feel the smooth texture of Na'im's bare skin against hers as he pampered her, and the hardness of his desire frequently touched her. Felicia wanted Na'im to know how much she wanted him.

As he turned her over to complete his task, Felicia reached up to embrace him. A groan escaped his lips as her supple fingers massaged his spear to its fullest height. Na'im's body trembled with delight, then turned as still as death as her mouth engulfed him.

Over and over again she deluged him until his body cried to be inside her. No longer was he the gentle lover with manipulative hands. Felicia's moist assault had sent him beyond the threshold of need, and she was ready to accept the consequences.

Na'im plunged inside her like a man with the heat of the desert in his soul. Felicia's voice was in his ears, spurring him on. Time and space meant nothing to them as they catapulted themselves into absolute ecstasy, only to come back with eager lips and hands ready for another journey.

▲

Felicia awoke with Na'im on her mind, but he was no longer beside her in his bed. She hurriedly got up, went to her room, bathed and dressed for the day ahead of her.

"May I come in?" a voice called from the door. "It's Fatimah."

"Sure. You're just in time to help me decide what I should wear."

"You are welcome to wear any of the dresses that fit you. Most of these were just brought in from Al Kharijah. Na'im had sent word ahead to prepare for your arrival."

"Goodness, there are some pretty color combinations here. You know this really is a lot of fun. It's almost like dressing for some kind of costume party. You know, like Halloween or the Mardi Gras."

"I have heard of this Halloween. But I thought people dressed in clothes that made them ugly to the eye when honoring it."

"No, not all of the time. You can be anything you like on Halloween. From a princess to a beggar."

"Halloween sounds very similar to a local festivity that we have amongst the smaller villages. It is called '*Awya*', meaning '*yes*.' It is called Dance of Yes or the Challenge Dance. This is when a woman has been chosen for a man, but has not been taken in marriage. She challenges him to say 'yes' and set a date for their becoming one. He must state his true intentions at that time. Everyone dresses in their best for this occasion, many times with masks and extraordinary clothing.

"Wow, that sounds dangerous. Kind of like putting the guy on the spot, huh?"

"It is serious. But with the festival, it can be so much fun."

"How about this peach one?" Felicia held the garment in front of her. "I think I like it. And look at these hand embroidered slippers to match. Boy, Phillip would get a kick out of this.''

''Who is Phillip?''

''He's the head of our research team.''

''Oh, that reminds me. A message has come for you. Maybe you would like to read it at breakfast. I will be taking my meal in the sunroom. Would you join me there?''

''Sounds wonderful to me. Be there in a minute.''

Felicia sat down at the table across from Fatimah, beneath a white awning. A screened partition separated the dining area from where the birds were allowed to fly free. From here they had a spectacular view of the foregrounds, the massive estate and its immense front doors.

''Phillip says everyone's doing okay, and they were awfully afraid something had happened to me,'' Felicia read. He says they were flooded out of the campsite at Al Uqsur and are now in Cairo. He also says because they didn't have the serum, there wasn't much they could do. And now that I've found them, they've got to cut their little vacation short.''

Felicia toyed with her bowl of fruit as she read the rest of the note. Looking up, she could see two camels approaching the entrance gate to the building. Each carried a woman, while three men accompanied them on foot. One of the men beckoned to Kareem, who had been polishing the brass door knockers on the front doors. After speaking with the man, the young boy sprinted back to the house and slipped inside.

''Kareem sure does seem excited. I wonder what's going on?'' Felicia remarked, as the camels advanced further into the yard.

Felicia noticed the way the woman on the first camel carried herself, as if she were the main attraction in a passing parade. She held her head high, tossing her long, dark brown hair like a prize filly. Her long skirt had been pushed high up on her slender thighs to accommodate the camel. Felicia thought she saw the woman shimmy her shoulders, making her off-the-shoulder top even more revealing.

"It looks to be Waheedah Faruuk of Khartoum. They must have found them and brought them back."

"Well, she sure is showing more than your average Egyptian maiden usually shows, don't you think?"

"Waheedah is somewhat different. She is well educated and comes from a family of status. She has also been trained in the fashion of *ghazeeyahs*, what you would call belly dancers. She does not always follow the traditional guidelines for women when it comes to dress."

By now, Na'im had emerged from the house with Kareem at his side. One of the men assisted the second woman off of her mount, but the one who Fatimah had pointed out to be Waheedah reached out her arms for Na'im to help her descend.

Felicia was flabbergasted to watch as this woman who had displayed such a strong back on her way through the gates became as limp as paper. Her body seemed to liquefy as it came in contact with Na'im's. Even after her feet were on solid ground, she still gave the impression that she could not stand without Na'im's support.

I've seen better acting at some of the elementary school programs back home, Felicia inwardly fumed.

"Who is she?"

"She is someone in whom Na'im's father has shown great interest."

"She seems to be showing a great deal of interest in Na'im," Felicia countered.

"Felicia, please do not put me in what you would call an awkward position. Maybe this is a subject you should take up with Na'im."

"Oh, I see."

Several servants came forth, and Na'im handed an unwilling Waheedah over to one of the females. Na'im motioned out his instructions. The women entered the house, while Na'im and the men followed Kareem as he led the camels around the east end of the building to the back.

An uncomfortable Fatimah sat quietly for a moment. "Would you like to see the building that Na'im says you can use as your laboratory?"

Felicia could feel her blood boiling inside, but she took Fatimah up on her offer. She wasn't quite ready to face Na'im or this Waheedah.

The Rahman's land went on for acres and acres. Felicia was surprised to learn that most of it was fertile. Fertile enough for Na'im's family to be one of the largest cotton producer's in their area.

"My family has been in the cotton business for the last fifty years. Before that, they traveled as nomads; bedouins who herded camels and made homes in many parts of north and central Egypt. Na'im's grandfather, Sheik Sadat Rahman, was the one who decided he no longer wanted to be a nomad. It was because of Aneesha (A-nee-sha), his wife, who had become deathly ill, that he had made such a decision."

"He must have loved her very much to change his entire lifestyle. And evidently the people in his tribe trusted him as well, or the settlement could not have grown so big in such a short time."

"He was their sheik. And a sheik is chosen as the head of his tribe because of his wisdom and age. It is a position of high reverence. Usually a man is not bestowed such an honor before he reaches the age of fifty. Then it can be quite a weight on his shoulders because the entire tribe looks to him for guidance."

Felicia and Fatimah had come upon several rows of mud and brick homes. Even though they were quite a distance from the larger structure, Fatimah said they all belonged to the Rahmans.

"This is where many of the workers live. Sometimes families who have come upon hard times in the village stay here as well, but mainly people who work for the Rahmans tending cotton or herding the camels. That is why it is so quiet right now. Everyone's working. This is the time when the cotton has been loaded into carts and taken to Al Kharijah. It takes all workers to accomplish this."

"That hay that's on top of the houses...I've seen the same thing on many houses in Egypt. What is it for?"

"It is fodder. Many workers have cattle of their own. So they store fodder on top of their houses because there is no where else to put it. Na'im does not like it. Sometimes it causes fires."

Fatimah reached out and opened a door to one of the houses. It was larger than the others; an additional room had been added onto the main body.

"This is where Kareem and his grandmother used to live before she died. It is hard to get other families to move in; they fear she is still here even in death. She was a different kind of woman. Many people sought her when sick, but only when they needed her real bad."

"Why were they so afraid of her?"

"Because after Kareem's mother died while giving birth to Kareem, she never was the same. She blamed herself for her daughter's death. She always wanted her to marry someone of station and she forbid her to see anyone who was not. But Tahillah (Tah-hee-luh) fell in love with one of the workers, and when she became pregnant she was afraid to let her mother know. She harmed herself by keeping her belly tied down so she would not notice. When she gave birth, the sack had become attached to her spine. It burst inside of her. Only the child could be saved."

"Why does Na'im feel so responsible for Kareem?"

"Because Kareem's grandmother always thought Tahillah would marry him. He feels he could have told her the truth; that there was no chance of them marrying."

"Why wasn't there?"

"Na'im's father had already made clear that he could not marry Tahillah. He said she was not of the right family bloodline."

"So is that so very important to Sheik Rahman? That Na'im marry someone of the proper bloodline?"

"I can only say what I heard. But Na'im was much younger then, Felicia. Now he is a man with his own mind. I do not believe anyone can speak for Na'im."

Felicia could see the pity that Fatimah held in her eyes as she looked at her. Felicia was not someone who liked to be pitied. She had gotten where she was in the world not by pity, but through knowledge, strength, hard work and pride. Many people back home didn't believe she would amount to anything, but she had proven them all wrong. Felicia was a believer in making the impossible possible. So why did her heart ache with every word Fatimah spoke?

Felicia tried to make light of the conversation. "Well, I guess that's why I'm glad my father was a production worker. With that kind of background, I can marry whomever I wish," she chided. "I think this place will be just perfect for the lab, Fatimah. There's plenty of space. We have access to water, and even though there is no electricity, that won't be a problem. We've brought our own emergency generators. It needs some cleaning up, and I'll start working on that this afternoon."

"That is not necessary. I will send one of the servants from the house to take care of it."

"No, that's alright. I need something constructive to do to keep me out of trouble. Plus, I need to make a preliminary layout of how the lab will be set up. So don't bother. Everything will work out just fine."

Felicia returned to the house with Fatimah, borrowed one of the servant's outfits, and spent the rest of the day clearing out the small house. The physical work gave her a channel through which she could vent her frustration and confusion. Tomorrow she would do the scrubbing and then the lab would be ready when Phillip and the others arrived with the equipment.

The sun was setting as she walked back to the house. She could see the servants preparing the dining room for the evening meal. She was too tired to dress for dinner, so once again she decided to eat her meal in the privacy of her own quarters. Felicia knew Waheedah's presence had something to do with her reluctance, but she didn't want to even think about why.

Chapter Sixteen

Felicia had finished her meal and was sketching a rough layout of how she thought the lab should look, when Fatimah came up to her room. Her heart began to quicken as she heard the footsteps on the tiled floor in the hall. She had braced herself, willing herself to be the picture of poise as Na'im walked through the door. When she heard Fatimah's voice call from the other side, she could not help but be disappointed.

"Ilyas just told me that Na'im will not be coming back to Karib tonight. It seems they ran into some problems trying to turn Shabazz and the others over to the authorities. Hassan's word is the big power in Falam where he is the sheik. Rumor says that Sheik Hassan's son, Abdul, is running things now. We believe he is the backbone of terror that is hitting our villages.

"Na'im knew he could not take them back to Falam, but he did not know that the nearest township would refuse to take them as well because of Hassan."

"So where are they now?"

"They are camping right outside the village. Ilyas says it is most dangerous, but they are not able to return to Karib tonight. It is more than a three-fourth day's journey. They will get back by late afternoon tomorrow."

"How did Ilyas find out about this?"

"Na'im sent a rider with a message to Al Kharijah. Ilyas says they also had trouble getting cotton to the market because of a few of Hassan's men."

"There's got to be a way to appease Hassan."

"I wish it too, Felicia. He is angry at Na'im for taking us back and determines to get back at him anyway he can. He knows that he cannot actually fight Karib because we are the bigger sheikdom; more men and resources. But he is like a pest; over and over he causes small problems until he feels better. I will go now. You sleep well."

"Good night, Fatimah."

Felicia pulled out another sheet of paper and began writing. Quite a bit of time had gone by before she completed the letter. She sealed it and put it by her bedside. She'd have Kareem take it to Al Kharijah in the morning. It should reach Mauritania within the next few days.

Felicia got up early the next morning; she was eager to get back to her work in the lab. As she entered the kitchen, the smell of fresh *baklava* filled the air. She packed some of it, along with an orange and some hot mint tea, in an earthenware pot shaped like a canister with two handles. She returned the servant's clothes she had worn the day before and requested another set.

It was difficult communicating with the servants because they spoke no English. Felicia felt as if she was becoming a professional with hand signals, motioning out what she wanted to say.

She found Kareem munching on a mango right outside the kitchen door and gave him her letter. He wiped his hands on his *galabia* top and placed the envelope in a large pocket in his pants, smiling all the while.

The walk to the small house was refreshing. Some of the women who lived in the houses nearby were still about. Felicia greeted whomever she passed.

"*As Salam-Alaikoom.*"

They did not seem to find her of interest, returning her greeting but continuing on with whatever they were doing without a second glance. Felicia knew she could easily be mistaken for one of the house servants, and her anonymity pleased her.

She found the scrub brushes, soap and containers she'd requested inside the house. After making sure they were there, she pulled one of the wooden chairs outside under a lone tree and ate her breakfast.

The heat began to build within the would-be lab as Felicia cleaned windows and scrubbed floors. The white scarf-type wrap slid to the middle of her head as it bobbed to her arm's rhythm. Closing her eyes and sitting back on her heels, Felicia tried to cool herself. She constantly plucked at the top of her dress, creating a nice sensation of air on her breasts.

"So you are the one they call Felicia, are you?"

Felicia's heart leapt at the unexpected intrusion of a woman's voice. Her English was clipped with a sultry sound to it. There standing in the doorway, and blocking the only fresh air that Felicia had, was Waheedah Faruuk.

"I am."

First of all, Felicia was irritated that her initial face-to-face meeting with Waheedah would find her on her knees. Secondly, she didn't like the way the woman spoke to her. Like master to slave.

"You don't look like a scientist to me."

"I don't remember asking your opinion as to what I look like. And if you don't mind, you can move out of the doorway. It's hot in here."

Felicia rose to her feet and removed her head cover. *At least I can take this scarf off my head.* Nevertheless, she knew her appearance paled beside Waheedah's, with all her elaborate dress.

Waheedah moved just inside the doorway, turning her nose up to show her distaste for the room and Felicia.

"How long will you be staying in Karib?"

"As long as I need to."

"Since your only true purpose here is to finish your project, I guess you should be gone in a few weeks."

"That is one of the reasons why I am here, yes. And if I have any other reason for being here, I don't think it's any of your business."

"Na'im is my business. And your room is in the same wing as his. I suggest you move your belongings into the guest portion of the house."

"Wait a minute. I don't know who you think you are, coming in here and telling me what to do with my things. Na'im invited me here. He decided what room I should stay in. And since it is his house and not yours, I think I'll stay just where I am."

"Oh. Pardon me if I seem a little...what would you call it...rude. I'm simply trying to spare you a little heartache. You see, the house and Na'im will soon be mine. I simply hate to see another woman being used as Na'im's temporary convenience. That's all. Or didn't you know that Sheik Ahmed Salim Rahman has chosen me to be Na'im's wife?"

"No. I didn't know anything about it. But I think Na'im is old enough to make his own decisions."

"This has nothing to do with age. In my country, when a woman has been chosen for a man of Na'im's status, it is more a matter of tradition, money and influence. But since you are a foreigner, and ignorant of our ways, your misunderstanding can be forgiven."

"I don't need you to forgive me for anything. It's obvious that you are the one seeking understanding or you wouldn't have walked all the way out here to find me. Yes, Na'im and I are lovers, but you can believe I'm getting as much satisfaction out of it as he is. So you don't have to worry about me. I think you should be concerned with your relationship as it stands with Na'im."

"Well, I've done what little I can. If you insist on making yourself available to him until he announces the date of our joining, that's up to you."

Felicia watched as Waheedah turned and walked through the door. She no longer felt like cleaning. The knowledge that Waheedah had been chosen as Na'im's wife had immobilized her.

Felicia childishly stomped on the servant's uniform as it fell to her feet. There had been no need for her to stay at the lab. She couldn't have worked another moment if she'd wanted to.

Waheedah had completely upset her. But she was proud that she hadn't shown her how she really felt. As she rehashed the confrontation she'd had with the uppity Egyptian beauty in her mind, her old adrenalin started to flow. *I'll show her and everyone else around here. They don't know who they're messing with, do they?* She could just see the servants gossiping and telling Waheedah all about the foreigner who slept in Na'im's quarters.

She stepped down into the tepid water that filled the sunken bathtub. It wasn't very large, but definitely large enough for her. As Felicia lathered her body, her mind conjured up images from her past.

Felicia had always loved dancing. As early as the third grade, she'd gone to the library and checked out one of those do-it-yourself books on ballet, and from it she taught herself plies and jetes. By the time her mother had decided to allow her to take dance from a former dance student, Felicia had trained and practiced to such an advanced level her instructor felt she was ready for point work. Yes, there had always been a side of her that wanted to shine. But that had its down side as well.

She was one of those girls who the other's never liked. The older she got, the worse it became. "She thinks she's cute," they'd say. All the time, she wished they'd only get to know her. She wanted friends so badly, but they all tended to keep their distance. Until she met Deesha.

Deesha knew where she wanted to go and what she wanted to be–an actress. Through Deesha's eagerness to explore life, Felicia began to blossom as well. Plays, recitals, contests and academic endeavors–she tried them all, and succeeded at most. The more she succeeded, the less popular she became. But it taught her something–to hold her head high when adversity struck. If they must talk, give them something to talk about. And that's exactly what she planned to do tonight.

There were many outfits to choose from in her closet, but there was only one that would fit her needs tonight.

Felicia sat in front of the dressing table not far from the bathtub and turned on all the lights she could find. She stared at her image in the mirror, and thought of how she could transform it. Actually, Felicia derived pleasure at times like this. It was like an actress putting on her makeup for her greatest performance. Everything would have to be just right.

She opened the tiny drawer to her left and found an assortment of makeup–bases that would fit any shade of brown, blushes from light peach to dark plum, eye shadows designed to bring out the best in skin with color.

Felicia took a small section of hair and tied the rest back in a ponytail that clung to the nape of her neck. She considered her face as an artist would a blank canvas, and with the makeup she created the image she wanted to present.

The base gave her deep brown skin a matted finish, revealing not even the smallest imperfection of her skin. A rich magenta blush accented her cheeks and brought the contours of her facial structure alive. High cheekbones bespoke of a heritage synonymous with royalty. The gentlest of violet and royal blue made her eyes the focal point of her face, with kohl that traced their almond shape back to a past known only in the Orient. Full lips, colored like wild berries, whispered the old saying, "The blacker the berry, the sweeter the juice." Felicia smiled when she thought of it. Deesha never liked that saying. Her skin was a creamy yellow with gold overtones.

Felicia piled her midnight black braids high on her head and let the massive ringlets fall as they may, only arranging those that needed it. Her hair echoed her free spirit, but one she knew how to direct.

Long, melodious earrings donned her ears. Now she was ready to slip on her dress.

Felicia felt it was a masterpiece in femininity. Never before had she seen material like it. It was a shimmery white with rosy incandescent flecks throughout; so light, even the slightest breeze would send it into motion. A high draping collar graced its neckline, followed by an oblong slit that showed the slightest hint of chocolate skin beneath it. Its full length sleeves clung to Felicia's arms like kidskin gloves. The garment laid against her shapely frame as if it had been made for no one else, molding her breasts, waist and hips into smooth alabaster.

And now for the finishing touch–tiny, pearl-embossed handmade slippers.

As Felicia gave herself one last look in the mirror, she liked what she saw. Purposefully, she sauntered off to Fatimah's room, feeling good about herself.

Felicia found Fatimah finishing her hair.

"You look wonderful," Fatimah said, with true admiration in her voice.

"Thanks. I thought maybe you were ready and we could walk down together. I didn't want to face the opposition alone."

"Sure we can. Just give me a few more minutes. Did you know Na'im is back? He had some business to take care of in the library, but he should be in his room dressing by now."

Felicia could feel the excitement building in the pit of her stomach. She was as ready as she'd ever be to tackle Na'im and Waheedah together, no matter what happened. If he announced the date when they would marry or simply ignored her because of Waheedah's presence, her self-confidence was at its peak and she could handle whatever they dished out.

Anxiously, Na'im entered the sitting room that joined his bedchamber with Felicia's.

"*Aros al bher.*"

Last night had been long and cold without Felicia's warm body next to his. He had regretted getting up so early the previous morning and leaving without saying goodbye. But he hadn't known that his business outside of Karib would take so much time.

He knew that Shabazz and the others would be released as soon as he left the village, but there was nothing he could do about it. He would have taken them to another township that wasn't under Hassan's thumb, but he had the appointment in Al Kharijah with the Office of Economic Development the following day. The paperwork had already been delayed a day after his problem with Hassan.

The sheik would be pleased when he found out that Na'im had found a way to secure them government subsidies. Yet Na'im knew in his heart that was not the only reason he had offered their estate to Felicia for the research project. Even if she had decided against it, he would have found a way to keep her in Karib.

Na'im stepped inside Felicia's bedroom and called for her once again. Disappointment settled on his handsome features when he realized she was not in.

Tired from hours of riding, he eagerly bathed and dressed. He too chose white for this occasion–a white pantaloon suit with billowy sleeves and pant legs. The jacket crossed at the waist, permitting wide expanses of Na'im's muscular chest to be seen as he moved. He made quite an alluring picture as he made his way to the drawing room.

Waheedah wasted no time in crossing to meet Na'im as he walked in. She had been waiting alone, sipping a sticky, dark sweet tea laced with ginger. She was pleased with her luck to have a few moments alone with him.

Na'im, on the other hand, was frustrated to find the drawing room empty except for Waheedah. But he could tell by the welcoming smile she gave him that she was pleased with their unsolicited privacy.

She was quite attractive in a tantalizing black dress revealing much of her shoulders and bustline. Diamonds highlighted her throat and ears. Her hair was placed in a classic chignon.

"*As-Salam-Alaikoom,* Na'im."

"*Alaikoom-Salam.*"

"It is good to see you back safe and unharmed."

"It is good to be back."

"I also want to thank your family for showing me such hospitality. I have found my stay here quite nice, though I think I would have been more comfortable in the west wing. You see the sun rises directly in my window and I find it hard to sleep to my normal waking hours."

"I will make sure the servants put darker colored drapes on your windows, Waheedah. We cannot have our guests inconvenienced in even the slightest way."

The corners of Waheedah's pretty mouth showed that was not the answer she expected. It perturbed her even more because she knew Na'im was aware of her implication, but he preferred to feign ignorance.

"I understand there will be scientists milling about the grounds for a couple of weeks. Do you have any idea how long they will be staying? I'm used to my privacy, you see, and quite unaccustomed to being in such close quarters with foreigners."

"I don't think Na'im can answer that. As I told you before, this project involves so much, it would be hard to predict a time frame."

Na'im and Waheedah both turned as Felicia, Fatimah and Ilyas strolled into the room. Felicia looked to be the epitome of calmness as she glanced first at Waheedah and then Na'im. A smile began to pull at the corners of her mouth, but she fought it. Obviously, Waheedah had expected her to come to dinner in one of the servant's uniforms, her face showed such great surprise. Na'im, standing by her side, appeared a little stunned, though he recovered quickly. Felicia felt as if she had struck a direct hit against her enemy in their silent little war.

"I must agree with Felicia. I've never been a man to disagree with anyone who looks as perfect as she does tonight," Na'im smiled approvingly.

The awkward silence that followed was broken by the servants serving tea. Waheedah insisted upon dominating all of Na'im's attention after he had openly complimented Felicia. Felicia, in turn, felt more at ease conversing with Fatimah and Ilyas. Actually, Fatimah served more as an interpreter, since Ilyas spoke very little English.

Occasionally, Felicia felt Na'im's magnetic eyes upon her face. His look smoldered with more than the heat from the small cup of tea.

One of the servants entered the room, excused herself, then spoke briefly with Na'im.

"It seems we will be having guests for dinner," Na'im announced.

No sooner had he spoken than three men were shown into the drawing room. The ambiance immediately changed from restrained and quiet to an exuberant display of old friends being reunited.

"Fil-ly!" Phillip exclaimed as he hugged and kissed Felicia, nearly picking her up off the floor. "Let me look at you. You are *tres magnifique.* Egypt agrees with you," he proclaimed in English accented heavily by his native tongue, French. "I expected to find you scrawny and sad looking, not looking like a princess."

Felicia hugged Phillip for dear life. She hadn't realized how much she'd missed him. Tears came to her eyes as he held her at arms length, still chiding her.

"Ooh la la. Had I known you'd miss me this much, I would have stayed away from you sooner," he grinned.

Dear Phillip. Being nothing but his old devilish self and meaning no harm. When she had first met Phillipe Moncharde, they became very good friends. His fun-seeking personality made it easy, but after awhile he'd made it known that he wanted to be more than friends. Felicia had just broken up with Alvin, and she was not ready for another relationship. At the time, Phillip said he understood. But from time to time, in his playful manner, he still reminded her of how she had rejected him.

"Hello, George and...William Ashley, isn't it?"

The older man nodded his compliance. In her jubilation at seeing Phillip again, Felicia had completely forgotten her manners.

"Oh, excuse me, please. Phillipe Moncharde, I'd like to introduce you to Na'im Raoul Rahman. His family owns the estate here where we will be working. Na'im, this is George Mercer and William Ashley, the other research team members."

Na'im responded graciously to the introductions, but Felicia detected a hint of resentment in his eyes as he shook hands with Phillip.

Everyone else was introduced after that, and in good time, because dinner was ready to be served.

Numerous wall sconces were lit in the informal dining room, which featured an eight piece dining room set with gilded armchairs. They were informed by Fatimah that the formal dining room could seat as many as fifty people. Everyone appeared to be duly impressed, except Waheedah.

"It is customary in our country for families with status such as the Rahmans to be prepared to entertain visitors from other sheikdoms. We are a people rich in more than tradition."

Na'im was seated at the head of the table, with Felicia at his right and Waheedah on his left. By now, Felicia had made up her mind that the less attention she gave Waheedah, the better off she'd be. She found the woman to be completely annoying and stuck on herself. And if Na'im intended to marry her, good for him.

Several dishes were placed in the center of the table.

"So what do we have here?" Phillip inquired, pointing at a pastry-type substance.

Na'im sat back quietly, forcing Fatimah to play hostess.

"This is called *tahini*. Sesame seeds are ground into a paste for this dish. And this is *hummus*, made from finely ground chickpeas. They are both very good."

Felicia and the others watched as the natives dunked their pita bread into the liquid concoctions, and then proceeded to imitate them.

"It is so kind of you to allow us to complete our research here on your grounds. I can't imagine how Felicia has convinced you to do it. Providing housing and food for four strangers is really rather noble. And seeing that you're getting nothing out of it, I must commend you."

"Well, I wouldn't say I'm getting nothing out of it, Mr. Moncharde. A true businessman always finds a way to benefit from everything. Besides, I have found Felicia to be very resourceful in many ways."

Na'im turned a dark, veiled glance in Felicia's direction that revealed little, but his words had implied much.

"By the way, is the site for the lab actually in the main part of the house?" Phillip asked.

"No, it is not," Naim responded. There are several smaller structures on the property. The lab will be housed in one of them. And you will be given another for sleeping."

"Well, Filly, how do you like the idea of having to share sleeping quarters with us fellows. You've often talked about how messy I am, and believe me, George and William aren't any better."

"Felicia will not be sleeping on the grounds with you," Na'im informed him. "She will sleep where she's always slept. Here in the house."

Phillip shot Felicia a sideways glance that posed all the questions he wanted to ask, but couldn't. It was Waheedah who decided that this was her golden opportunity to make a point.

"I do know a little about teamwork, Na'im. From what I understand, building comraderie among a team's members helps them to work together better."

"I think Na'im is right. Felicia should remain in the house. She is the only female in the group. And she has already settled here. I've just begun to enjoy her company," Fatimah interjected.

"I must say, I enjoy being the center of attention, but as you all know, I can speak for myself. I think I should be the one to decide where I will or will not sleep, to be totally honest with you."

The multiple clatter of castinets erupted in the dining room, as the next dishes were brought in to be served. The smell of spices filled the air, as stuffed swordfish and pigeons stewed with vegetables were placed on the plates of those who desired it. The meat was complemented by *fava* beans, prepared in a variety of ways.

The conversation changed after the food was served, to more general topics. Egyptian customs and foods.

Religious beliefs. Music. Fatimah and Waheedah provided the majority of the information that Phillip and the others sought, while Na'im remained unnervingly quiet.

A dignified matron of massive proportions joined the dinner party. Na'im informed them that she was the head cook and wanted to know how they were enjoying the meal. Everyone voiced their compliments. Phillip was the most vocal.

"I have never partaken of a more succulent meal. It pains me to think that it is over."

"Not quite, Mr. Moncharde," Na'im chimed in. "My favorite portion of the course is yet to come."

The huge cook snapped twice, curling her fingers in a snake-like manner. "*Kadin budu,*" she announced.

Servants appeared with platters of plump, puffy pastries filled with an assortment of sweets.

Looking directly at Felicia, Na'im interpreted the desserts' names in a most seductive voice. "We Egyptians are known for showing our appreciation for feminine charms. Take these soft, moist treats for instance; well named, ladies' thighs. I myself find them simply irresistible. My favorites are filled with chocolate."

"And what are these called, or should I ask?" snickered Mercer, the youngest of the male research members.

Na'im's explanation had caused quite a blush on Fatimah's face.

"These extremely sweet, small swirls are *olm aly*, or ladies' navels. Quite a resemblance, don't you think?"

By this time, Felicia and Waheedah were both fuming; Waheedah, because of the attention Felicia was receiving; Felicia, because she felt Na'im was being far too brash. Only the men seemed to be thoroughly enjoying themselves. Felicia had little to say during dessert. She made a point of not looking or speaking to Na'im.

On the other hand, Phillip, who admired jewels, gave Waheedah quite a compliment on her earrings and necklace. That was all she needed to appease her wounded honor. She spent the rest of the meal elaborating on her extensive jewelry collection, which had been in her family for generations.

Time couldn't pass fast enough for Felicia. The quicker she could leave the dining table, the better off she would be.

Finally, Phillip and the others began to excuse themselves, citing a day full of travel and a need to rise early the next day to get started in the lab.

Felicia walked them to the door, but Na'im insisted that Kareem show them where they would sleep. Actually, Felicia didn't mind. She couldn't imagine herself walking that far across the grounds dressed as she was. But Na'im's outward display of dominance infuriated her, so she was glad when she was able to return to her room and lock her door.

Na'im was not far behind.

Chapter Seventeen

"Open the door, Felicia."

She refused to answer him.

"You have made me a promise. And you will open this door now!"

Felicia flung the door open. She crossed to the opposite side of the room, fastening the belt to her robe.

"I've got one thing to say to you, Felicia. As long as you remain in my house, you will only have a working relationship with Phillipe Moncharde. If I find out you have disobeyed, you will not be able to conduct the remainder of your research project here. Do you understand me?"

"Do I understand you? I'm sorry to say I really do. You want me here in your bedroom at your beck and call, while your wife-to-be stays chaste in another wing of the house."

"This has nothing to do with Waheedah. Your actions are what I am speaking of tonight. I am not a man to be crossed, Felicia. You have only seen one side of me. Do not make me show you the other."

"Are you threatening me, Na'im. Just what are you going to do to me, if I disobey you? Beat me? Pull my fingernails out? Or do you plan some other primitive way of torture that probably runs in your family?''

''There is one way I can torture you, *aros al bher*, that is worse than all others. It is the one I would most regret.''

Na'im locked Felicia's bedroom door behind him. ''Now come here before me and remove your robe.''

Felicia couldn't believe her ears. ''What do you think I am, that you can turn me on and off like a faucet.''

''I know what you are. You are my woman. Not Phillipe Moncharde's or anyone else's. And now I am going to remind you of that.''

Na'im crossed the floor, ridding himself of his clothes as he walked. He stopped right behind Felicia, his body barely touching hers. With nimble fingers, he untied the belt to her robe and slipped it off her shoulders.

Felicia stood there holding her breath, afraid to breathe. She feared if she did, her body would give in to the feelings that were beginning to stir inside of her. *Damn it, I won't do it. I won't give in to him.* But she knew her determinations were in vain.

Na'im's hands explored her breasts, as he pulled her back against him.

''You are mine, *azizi.* Even now when you don't want to be. I am in your blood. Just as the sand and the desert are inseparable, so shall be your need for me.''

Passionate kisses rained down Felicia's neck and shoulders, kindling a fire inside that only Na'im could quench. Strong arms turned her to face him, lifting her off the floor in their ardor. One hand sought her out and found her ready for the taking. Fiercely he impaled her, sending ripples of pleasure throughout her. With savage fury, they sought to exorcise their need for one another. Again and again, Felicia cried out as if a woman possessed.

And she was. Possessed by Na'im. Her body...his. Her mind...his. Then, at last they exploded in a frenzy of sexual bliss.

Satiated, Felicia and Na'im both fell onto her bed, her sweat mingling with his, the scents of culminated lovemaking in their nostrils.

As Na'im stroked her hair, a deep feeling of despair began to build inside her. She knew her body was no longer her own. As long as Na'im wanted her, she would be his.

Morning came too soon. Felicia's body felt as if she could sleep forever, a natural protection from the mental humiliation that assaulted her once she climbed into consciousness.

Na'im was no longer in the bed. She could hear him, though, in his bedchamber preparing for the day's activities. It was still early. Felicia knew that she should get up, but she didn't seem to have the motivation.

The smell of mint tea and pastries played their part in seducing her out of bed. But the thought of Phillip and the others were the real reason she found herself up and running bath water.

From the doorway, Na'im watched as Felicia stepped timidly down into the scented water. "How are you this morning, *aros al bher*?"

It was hard for Felicia to look Na'im in the face. "As well as could be expected."

"Because of all the things that were going through my mind last night...forgive me if I was a little rough with you."

"It is not my body that hurts, Na'im."

"I probably will be away from Karib for the majority of the day. The last haul of cotton is being taken to Al Kharijah and I'm going with the workers. I don't want any surprises from Hassan."

"Alright."

Felicia could feel Na'im's reluctance as he turned and walked away. It was not that she wanted him to feel bad. She really didn't know what she wanted. All she knew was that she was beginning to feel trapped. She was in love with a man who would never be her husband. That was bad enough, but to know she had an uncontrollable need for his lovemaking was the ultimate degradation. Her body was a traitor to her. She, who had always prided herself in applying the philosophy of 'mind over matter'. Felicia the intellect. She felt as if the entire foundation upon which she had built her life was crumbling.

One of the servants appeared at the bathroom door carrying a brown paper package. Impassively, she set it down on the floor beside Felicia and handed her a slip of paper. Without a word, she retreated from the room.

Felicia held the note, assuming it and the package were from Na'im. But when she saw Phillip's untidy handwriting, an involuntary smile came to her face.

Dear Filly,

Even though I loved your outfit last night, it brought to mind how badly you'll need these to work in. I hope they're not too small. I picked them up in Cairo. - ME"

Felicia tore away the brown paper and pulled out a pair of jeans. Actually, the package held two pairs of jeans and two shirts. Moments after taking her bath, she donned the mint green shirt and a pair of jeans.

Appraising herself in the mirror, Felicia had to admit the jeans clung to her well-formed hips in a way that only designer jeans could. This brought up feelings of home, giving her a sense of grounding. Strange how something as simple as a pair of jeans could do that. Felicia fixed her braided hair in a ponytail. She'd stop and grab some fruit from the kitchen, and then go straight to the lab.

William Ashley was the first person she saw as she stepped into the kitchen. He wore a tee shirt saying "People who have the most birthdays live the longest." He smiled once he saw Felicia. There was such an eagerness about him as he held the basket that the servant had filled with fruit, almost as if it were hard for him to stand still.

"You're late, Felicia. We've been up since sunrise and we finished cleaning the lab. The guys sent me up for some nourishment while they went to get the equipment."

His enthusiasm was contagious, and Felicia was glad when she began to feel it infect her.

"Well, make sure there's enough for me in there," she grinned.

As they walked across the grounds, Felicia showed William her layout drawings for the lab. She told him about the tables and chairs that were on order, but were expected to arrive no later than tomorrow. They talked of the work that had to be done and the challenge it presented.

Felicia learned from William there was a time frame set for completion of the project. Six weeks. Phillip and William were scheduled to be in Australia after that to meet obligations they had committed to long before this project began. Now, because of Felicia's accident and the loss of the Phase I serum, they would have to work doubly hard to make the deadline. But they had their notes, so it wouldn't be too difficult to redevelop the serum.

Phillip and George drove up beside them in an antiquated truck, just as Felicia and William approached the row of houses.

"Good morning, blue jeans. I can tell by the way they fit that they're just a little bit too small. But that's the way I like them," Phillip beamed, his head and arm hanging halfway out of the truck's window. "Now we're going to really put that beautiful bod of yours to work. We've got to unload all this stuff, *mon chere.* And, as you know, every man, woman or child has to pull his own weight around here, even if they stay in the big house."

But today Felicia didn't mind Phillip's teasing. In the beginning, they got into heated disagreements over what she called his "sexist attitude". But as time passed, she realized he really meant no harm. He treated her ideas and input with the same amount of respect as he did her male counterparts. As a matter of fact, she welcomed his teasing. Being a part of a team again would give her something to do and think about other than Na'im.

It didn't take them long to remove the boxes of test tubes, microscopes, syringes and other necessary tools from the truck bed. Some of the animal cages were awkward, but the heaviest equipment by far was the emergency generator. Little attention was given to organizing the boxes. Once they got all of the furniture in the lab, plenty of time would be spent on taking inventory and making sure the proper devices were close at hand.

Lunch was brought over to the lab about noon. It consisted of lamb and pita bread, pistachio nuts and plenty of fresh fruit. They decided to eat in what they now termed "the dorm".

After lunch, William decided to ride out to where Na'im's camels were kept. They'd need no more than two or three for the project, but he wanted to see what was available anyway. At the last minute, George decided to go with him, expressing an interest in seeing more of the grounds.

Phillip kept Felicia amused with his stories of belly dancers in Cairo, and trying to find an Egyptian restaurant that served something a bit more ethnic than bacon and eggs for breakfast. But soon Felicia found herself consumed by her own thoughts; thoughts filled with Na'im, Egypt and how much her life had changed since her arrival.

"I know you have never been interested in me, but this is ridiculous," Phillip said, as he waved one hand in front of Felicia's blank features.

Brought back from her daydreams, Felicia assured him the problem was her and had nothing to do with him.

"Phillip, you can't imagine some of the things I've been through since I almost drowned and Na'im saved my life. Just thinking about it, I can't believe some of it actually happened. It's like a movie or something.

"Well, I gotta tell you, Filly. I could feel a lot of stuff going on last night during dinner. I wasn't quite sure what it was, but I knew a lot of it had to do with that Na'im."

Felicia looked down at her hands in her lap and let out a long sigh. "Na'im Raoul Rahman," she repeated his name more for her own benefit than Phillip's. "I think I'm in a worse fix this time than I was with Alvin. At least when I found out the truth about his being married, I had the strength to let him go. But I'm afraid I can't find it when it comes to Na'im."

"Maybe you don't want to find it. You ever thought about that? Obviously the guy likes you, or he wouldn't have made it so plain to all of us last night. His tactics may have been a little different, but we surely got the point."

"That's part of the problem, Phillip. I know he wants me. But it's not a good feeling knowing you're dispensable."

"Oh, Filly, every woman feels dispensable until a man sticks a ring on her left hand. You're paranoid, that's all."

"What I'm feeling is not just paranoia. Didn't you ever wonder about the dark-haired beauty who was constantly making eyes at Na'im, then rolling them in my direction?"

"Don't tell me that was his wife. My God, does the fella have any respect?"

"She's not his wife, Phillip. But she might as well be. Na'im's father has chosen her to be his wife. You know, arranged marriages. Ancient customs and all that stuff."

"Look. I know I don't know this guy, but he didn't seem like the kind of fella that could be told what to do. His vibes just didn't say that, Filly."

"This has nothing to do with vibes. And even if it wasn't Waheedah, it wouldn't be me. I don't come from the right family line."

"It all boils down to karma, Filly. Now you've known me long enough to know I'm a scientific man. But because of all the logical searching I've done and all the illogical things I've found, I had to conclude one thing: there's one law that permeates everything. It's the law of cause and effect. Maybe in a previous lifetime you were a 'husbandizer,' the kind of woman who disregarded whether a man was married or not. Evidently it didn't mean a hill of beans to you. So now, it's like the big payback. You're reaping what you've sown, Filly. Who knows, maybe a true apology to the man above will wipe your record clean. Or a few thousand '*Nan-myoho-renge-kyo's*.'"

"Goodness, thanks a lot, Phillip. You sure know how to make a girl feel better."

"At least I'm giving you some explanation as to why you always tend to fall for the wrong men. Of course, if you were smart, you would have taken me up on my offer."

"Well, I didn't. And if you don't stop picking on me, I'm going to tell your scientific colleagues that you're really an undercover guru and they're wasting all of their scientific knowledge in dealing with you.''

''That's what I've always said about women. They'll find out all the data they can about you and use it whenever they find it beneficial. And please don't let her be a scientist.''

Chapter Eighteen

"I just don't understand what's wrong with him, that's all." George threw up his hands in a sweeping motion. "She didn't do anything wrong that I could see."

Felicia and Phillip were deep into discussing the notes from Phase I when George and William returned.

"It's something we have to be careful about over here, not knowing the customs and all that," William replied.

"Well, obviously, she didn't think there was any kind of problem."

"Who didn't think what?" Phillip interrupted, his head turning from George to William like a pendulum in a grandfather's clock.

George picked up the last piece of fruit, took a bite out of it, and started to explain.

"The young woman, Fatimah. She didn't think she'd done anything wrong. You see, as we strolled down the road near the main house, we spotted Fatimah. Naturally we stopped and spoke to her, telling her how we'd enjoyed dinner last night and what we were about to do. She asked us if we knew where the camels were kept. We told her we had a good idea, having seen them earlier, but we'd appreciate having her come along, which she did."

"She rode all the way in the back of the truck, while George and I sat up front," William added. "And she was quite a help with the herders, interpreting for us. Everything was going quite well until we ran into that other guy who had dinner with us."

"You mean Ilyas?" Felicia asked, looking up from her papers.

"Yes, Ilyas. He was standing out in the front of the house when we got back. And boy, did he look furious when he saw us. I had decided to ride back on the truck bed with Fatimah. William and I both thought it would be the gentlemanly thing to do. Evidently we were wrong. I jumped down and attempted to assist her in getting off the truck. Suddenly I felt a hand placed, if I should use such a gentle term, on my arm. The next thing I knew, this Ilyas fellow had almost snatched the poor girl, and started pulling her back toward the house. I couldn't understand a word he was saying, but it was plain he was chewing her out."

Phillip cut his eyes in Felicia's direction. "One thing is obvious. These Egyptian men are serious when it comes to their women."

"Is Fatimah his wife?" George asked, looking at Felicia.

"No, she's not. But he's made his intentions plain to her family. It seems that arranged marriages have become a thing of the past."

Felicia placed her hands on her hips and turned toward Phillip, who'd just emitted a scoffing sound.

"*Except* in some cases where the families have rank, and the heads of the family want to make sure their heirs marry worthy of their positions."

"Well, I think he could have handled it a little better," George insisted.

"Look George, I saw the way you were eyeing her last night. But we're in Egypt, not Canada, though I think you Canadians are a little stiff compared to we native Frenchmen."

"Most people wouldn't know you were a Frenchman, Phillip, if you didn't throw in a few *s'il vous plaits,* here and there," Felicia berated him.

"It's because I was an international exchange student. I spent quite a bit of time in your country. You know--the land of the free and the home of the brave; meaning you're free to do whatever you want to as long as you're a citizen and you're brave enough to try it."

"George and Phillip found this immensely funny and laughed until Phillip had tears in his eyes. William shook his head as he thumbed through a folder of papers that he held in his lap.

"William, I'm sure glad you're here. You're the only one who seems to have his head on right. Maybe it's the heat or something," Felicia said, shaking her head. "Alright you guys, do you think we could possibly review all of our notes involving Phase I, so that we can be ready to get started tomorrow once the furniture arrives."

Out of breath and wiping his eyes, Phillip nodded his compliance.

They spent the rest of the afternoon reviewing and analyzing their records in preparation for the following day. Time passed quickly. Soon the tiny homes nearest the lab were budding with household activity. Most of the workers had returned, their work day over, and they were ready for the evening meal. Various scents floated in the air, the products of numerous dishes being prepared Egyptian style.

Phillip's face turned a bright red as his stomach grumbled out its protest for everyone to hear, as they waited impatiently for George to return from the main house with their dinner.

"My goodness, don't you think George should be back by now? He's been gone over half an hour. Pretty soon my stomach's going to start begging some of our neighbors to share their dinners if he doesn't hurry up."

"Hey Phillip, I'm like the mounted police. I always arrive on time." Two baskets hung on George's arms, as he made his entrance. But not for long. Phillip swiftly descended upon them, taking one, placing it on the table, and inquiring about its contents.

"I don't know what half of this stuff is, but it sure smells good and that's good enough for me."

Sunset had just begun when Felicia stepped outside the crowded room. She was the first to finish her meal, since she didn't have much of an appetite.

Children were playing in one of the yards nearby and a group of men had gathered under a lime tree. Soon the team members joined her, and out of natural curiosity they found themselves migrating toward the Egyptians.

Felicia stayed her distance from the group. There were no women among them, so she figured this was an Egyptian facsimile of the "olden" days, when the men retired to the drawing room after dinner and no women were allowed.

She was intoxicated by the heavy scent emanating from the lime tree under which the men sat. She found herself feeling very content as she sat on the ground not far away, partaking of the tree's fragrance and the beauty of the western sky.

Felicia could also see the lights at the main house, so

many of them sparkling. She couldn't help but wonder if Na'im had returned to Karib. Part of her wanted to go find out. The other half, her logical side, made her stay away as long as she excusably could.

Na'im found himself sitting and staring sightlessly at the pages of the book he held. Dinner had been served hours ago. This time there were only four participants–he, Fatimah, Waheedah and Ilyas.

Waheedah was visibly delighted with the foursome. Had it not been for her animation, the table's atmosphere would have been quite glum.

Fatimah was unusually quiet, and Ilyas' countenance reminded Na'im of a puppy who'd been kicked and had run away with his tail tucked between his legs. Na'im could tell his long face had a lot to do with Fatimah.

None of this seemed to bother Waheedah, who bubbled on. She said the dinner provided her with the perfect opportunity to make her announcement. She would be returning home on some special business, but she would be back in about four weeks.

Fatimah expressed her surprise, and told her she hoped it was not because of bad news.

"Oh no," Waheedah responded. "Actually I think what I've planned will benefit us all," she said, giving a cunning smile.

Na'im thought about how glad he'd be when his father returned. Then maybe he could clear up some of the confusion that had mushroomed with Waheedah's return from her captors.

He walked over to the window and peered into the darkness outside. That was where Felicia found him when she entered the sitting room. Silently, he watched her.

Standing by the couch, Felicia turned and faced Na'im.

"Hi."

"Hello."

"We've got things pretty well set up in the lab. All we need is the furniture that will be arriving tomorrow and we'll be ready to get started."

"That is good."

Felicia was not unaccustomed to this monosyllabic Na'im. It reminded her of the days when they first met. It also made her feel guilty, as if she'd done something wrong. But she hadn't and she wasn't going to allow him to make her feel that way.

"Well, I guess I'll see you in the morning," and she started for her bedroom."

"It is so late, *aros al bher*. Will your work keep you occupied to this hour of the night every night?"

Felicia looked over at Na'im's masked face. It didn't reveal anything. Was he angry? Hurt? Or just irritated? Suddenly all of the energy seemed to seep out of her, like a deflated balloon. She didn't feel like arguing with Na'im. She just wanted to be left alone.

"Na'im, I'm tired. I just want to go to bed. Alright?"

Searching gold eyes regarded her for a few moments.

"Alright."

Felicia climbed beneath the lightweight cover. Closing her eyes, she tried to will sleep to overtake her, but her mind's eye was full of images of Na'im. Short spurts of sleep finally came. As she awoke from one of them, she could feel Na'im's warm body behind her. His arm was wrapped around her waist and his breathing was steady, even. She fell back asleep. Now she could sleep peacefully.

Chapter Nineteen

Fatimah's eyes sparkled with curiosity as she walked through the lab. Felicia had given her one of the white coats that William Ashley liked to wear, just to make her feel a little more official.

Actually, neither Felicia nor Phillip found the coats necessary, but William wouldn't be caught dead in the lab without one, at least not in the two days since they had started running some of the tests necessary to complete Serum Phase I.

The men were out back in the field. One of the camels had been tranquilized. Fatimah had watched until George began to insert a catheter into the poor animal, and that was enough for her. It didn't matter that the animal was unaware of what was happening to him.

"Why is it necessary to do that to the animal?" she asked Felicia while examining an empty flask.

"Basically, because we need to run some tests on the camel's urine, but it has to be as clean as it can possibly be. Therefore, we insert the catheter in order to eliminate as many germs as we can."

Fatimah's studious face reflected her deep thoughts on the subject. "How will it help you?"

"Well, camels can store water because they have the ability to control the amount of water in their bodies. It's almost like a built-in thermostat. They can adjust to whatever is needed. We know it has a lot to do with their physical structure, the humps and all that, but we're trying to find out if their urine is also more concentrated; if it consists more of something called uric acid than water. Then we're going to break that down, do some extractions, and so on and so forth."

"It's exciting to me how much you seem to know, and how your life is so much your own. Not like mine. Though my family probably would not mind my finding a job, I think Ilyas would not like it so much."

"Yeah, I can see what you're saying. Is it definite that you're going to marry him?"

"At first I was very sure. But after what happened a few days ago with Mr. Ashley and Mr. Mercer, I don't know. Ilyas is good, but he has deep religious and traditional beliefs, especially when it comes to women. He was not educated as I was, or Na'im. And he does not know how others live throughout the world without such strict beliefs. When I try to discuss it with him, he does not want to listen. He says it is evil, and not the will of Allah."

"Well, maybe you can show him how your being a little more independent can be helpful. I don't know. Start doing something around here. Maybe a little school for some of the workers' children. I'd be glad to provide supplies for small science experiments, things like that."

"Do you think I could? Start a school, I mean. I've only completed secondary school."

"Fatimah, I think your education is enough to help the children here who cannot go to the village schools in Al Kharijah. It is better than nothing."

"Yes. You are right. I will go to Na'im today and talk to him about it."

"Sounds good to me. Go for it, girl."

"What did you say?"

"Oh. It's just a saying we have back home."

Fatimah hugged Felicia in her excitement, as she hurried out the door. Felicia couldn't help but feel a little excited too. She liked Fatimah. It made her feel good to think she may have suggested a constructive outlet for her problems. A song automatically came to Felicia's lips as she worked. "*Caught up in the rapture of love. Nothing else can comp-a-are.*"

"Tell me, is what you sing true?"

Na'im's large frame filled the doorway, as he stood leaning against the border. A rare smile was on his face, and Felicia's heart reacted in a flutter. It warmed her to see him in such a good mood.

When she awoke that morning, he had gone, so she assumed he was attending to business outside of Karib. Evidently she'd been wrong.

Felicia couldn't bring herself to answer Na'im's question, so she dodged it by changing the subject. "Well, hello. This is the first time you've visited the lab, isn't it. Come on in so I can give you the grand tour."

Na'im squinted his eyes, aware that Felicia had intentionally ignored his question. He let it pass, enjoying the lightness of the moment.

Felicia walked from table, to desk, to shelves, explaining the equipment, their purposes, and whatever else she could think of, with Na'im listening intently as he walked beside her. He asked a few probing questions, showing Felicia that his interest in the project was more than superficial. They talked about how the results would benefit those people who lived in dry climates with little rainfall. It was the first time Felicia and Na'im had talked to one another like this, and they both were reluctant to let the rapport end.

"I guess I've got to go. There are so many things that need attending to."

"Right. I'm sorry if I just rattled on and on."

"No. It's okay. I enjoyed it."

Na'im looked over his shoulder as he was leaving the lab. "There's a circus coming to Al Kharijah today. Their performance will be tomorrow evening. Maybe if you need some extra supplies or whatever, we can go there and take in the circus afterwards."

"Why sure. I can think of some things we need. And I haven't been to a circus since I was a little kid. Are the circuses in Egypt like the one's in the United States?"

"No, *aros al bher*. Our circus reflects the magic and the mystery which is Egypt."

"Who-oa, sounds interesting."

"It will do more than interst you, *azizi*. It will make you realize you are in a land whose people are powerful. They are powerful because of their knowledge which has come through many generations. Things about the universe that our ancestors knew and experienced can only be physically revealed through acts like the circus."

"Well, this I've got to see."

Chapter Twenty

Felicia tried to see how she looked from the back in the tall gilded mirror. She'd asked one of the servants to make some alterations to one of the dresses in her closet. It had been cut to a midi length, and matching pants had been added underneath. She didn't want to upset Na'im by wearing her blue jeans that she loved so well, but she simply couldn't see herself wearing a *melaya* or long dress to a circus. Also, she wanted to please him and she felt this emerald garb would do it.

She gave a final tug to her belt in the back and patted her creative headpiece. The emerald and lime-colored turban crossed at the top of her forehead, but left an opening through which her braided ball showed, giving the effect of a crown.

Fatimah tapped softly on the bedroom door and bounced inside upon Felicia's request. She looked marvelous in her more traditional, sky blue attire.

"I have made a list of all the things I think I'll need for the school." Fatima spoke at a slower pace. Yesterday, she had told Felicia about her determination to speak better English, since she was going to be teaching the children.

"Na'im says money is not to be considered when buying supplies because we do want to use the best that Al Kharijah has to offer. Can you think of anything else that we will need," she inquired, passing the writing tablet to Felicia.

"Not right off hand, but we'll have plenty of time to discuss it on our way. Is Ilyas going with us?"

"At first he said that he would. But then he decided he had some things to do that were more important than going to a circus. It is that kind of thinking that hurts us. It could have been time that we could spend together. He is so strict with himself and with others."

"Don't worry about it. We'll have a good time, anyway. So are we ready?"

Nodding her head with eyes smiling, Fatimah's look reminded Felicia of the little dolls she'd seen as a child while riding along in the back of her mom and dad's car.

"Did you know that Waheedah has left?"

"No. When did she leave?"

"Yesterday."

"There's no chance that she's gone for good, is there?"

"I am afraid not. She will be back in about three and a half weeks. She says her family is planning something. She was really rather secretive about it."

"There's no telling with the great Waheedah."

"She will be returning around the same time that Na'im's parents are expected back."

"My-y. A double whammy, huh?"

"Sometimes, Felicia, you speak so strange I do not understand."

"Oh, it's a sort of slang. You know, like when a certain group of people have words they use to express certain feelings."

"Like the Moslems' '*inshallah*'?"

"Yes. Something like that."

Laughter filled the hallways as the two women searched for Na'im and Kareem. Both were extremely happy. This was the first time Na'im had ever asked Felicia to accompany him anywhere. It did nag at her a bit to think that he may have asked her because Waheedah was no longer there. But she wasn't going to let that spoil her fun. A date was a date.

Fatimah was ecstatic because Na'im had accepted the idea of a school for the workers' children. Now she felt like she had a special purpose, and going into Al Kharijah to shop for supplies made it all the more real for her.

They found Na'im and Kareem standing outside waiting beside the truck. Kareem's face beamed as he stood straight and tall in his new outfit. Felicia could tell he was beside himself with pride. She brushed his shiny black hair back from his face with her hand.

"Good morning, ladies," a voice called from the other side of the truck. George Mercer erected himself from where he had been stooping beside the vehicle. Smiling, as he dusted off his hands, he asked if everyone was ready.

"I guess you two ladies can sit up front between Na'im and myself, it it's alright with you. Kareem can ride in the back."

Kareem's small nose wrinkled in disgust at the thought of having his new attire covered by dust from the sandy roads.

Felicia looked at George with amusement. "Mr. Mercer, when did you decide to grace us with your presence on this trip?"

"Actually, Felicia, I thought about how awful it was that with three men on the team, the one female team member had to ride all the way to Al Kharijah to search for and load supplies onto the truck. Felicia, you know that I'm a gentleman, so I knew you wouldn't mind my tagging along. I talked to Na'im here, and I made a deal with him. I told him that if he wanted to, I'd take the truck, making it easier on all of us. So here I am."

"And you're telling me that the Egyptian circus had nothing to do with your wanting to go?"

"Well now that you mention it, I thought it would be an interesting experience. Yes, I did."

Felicia looked at George's sparkling blue eyes. "Well, George, since you put it that way...sure I'm glad to have you come with us."

Felicia and Fatimah talked incessantly throughout the trip, trading ideas for the school. George also contributed some things he thought would be helpful, and Felicia noticed how his eyes became more tender each time he addressed Fatimah.

But it was Na'im who astounded her. He was more relaxed than she'd ever seen him. Cracking jokes about how Fatimah would look as a teacher, he created an even more jovial atmosphere.

They passed many people with carts and camels on their way. Na'im said it was because of the circus. It was a time when everyone could forget about the heavy woes of daily life and get lost in its magic.

It didn't take Felicia and George long to complete their shopping, once they arrived in Al Kharijah. Fatimah's search for school supplies was more tedious and consumed more time. It was only an hour before the circus began when they finally finished.

Felicia could hear the exotic music before they came upon the big top, made of tawny canvas. They shuffled along among the crowds of people, all seeming to be headed for the circus.

Activity picked up as they neared the center of excitement. Vendors peddled their wares in boisterous voices. Women wearing bras and gauzed rags tied low on their hips beckoned to them with serpent-like arms and fluid hands. Painted eyes in soft dark faces surrounded them, giving a preview of things to come.

Na'im bought a bag of toffee for Kareem, who sucked on it noisily, taking it in and out of his mouth until his hands were sticky.

As they walked, they gazed upward at large drawings of performers displaying their talents, which were mounted on tall wooden stakes. Sabir Hamid Rammah (Sab-ear Hom-eed Ram-muh), "The Rubber Man," able to bend his body so effortlessly, it appeared to be boneless; "The Brave Amin" (Ah-meen), Master of the Trapeze; Sutannah (Soo-tan-nuh), "Mistress of the Serpents," all looked down upon them as they entered the circus grounds.

Na'im handed the attendant a fifty pound note to pay their way in. She was a toothless crone, who wasn't the least bit embarrassed to show her decrepit dental condition. Grinning all the while, she greeted the steady flow of patrons.

Strategically placed torches could be seen through the large tent. Because it was still daylight, they had not been lit, but sat ready for the time when they would become necessary. Pennants of gold, green and red were visible at the end of the rows of wooden chairs, dividing them into sections.

Na'im had secured four seats only three rows from the

front. They squeezed by countless knees before they were comfortably seated in the best section of the house.

Kareem's small dark eyes could not contain their excitement as he turned this way and that, watching the scores of people. There were children and adults. Some carried babies, others gooey treats dripping almonds and cream. All the while, Kareem's bow-like mouth continued its suction on the toffee.

Felicia too was amazed as she watched the sea of people. "Does the circus come here often?" she asked Na'im, who was seated beside her, noting the huge crowd that had turned out for the event.

"From time to time. But this is only a small group of performers from the Egyptian National Circus, which has a permanent site at Giza. Historically, circuses were held to honor anniversaries such as the birth of the Prophet or other religious holy men."

Lively music began, and clowns dressed like dancing girls with enormous swiveling hips entered the center ring. Explosions of laughter filled the air as they danced to a tune played by dwarfs on toy flutes. The tune reminded Felicia of the cat in the old Mighty Mouse cartoon being enticed along in midair by some hypnotic fragrance, his body as limp as a rag as he floated along to an exotic beat.

Robust figures collided together as they imitated the classic belly dancers of old. All of them prostrated themselves in the end, with huge, touching rumps forming a circle. Felicia laughed until tears ran down her cheeks at the "dancers" whose faces could barely touch the floor in reverence because of gigantic breasts.

A young camel proved itself to definitely be a beast with a burden as it brought in the clowns' object of worship. She rode on what Felicia concluded to be a large sled.

Elephantine legs and thighs were crossed in her best semblance possible of queen of the Nile. Rolls and rolls of flesh jiggled with the motion of the sled, as she was drawn to the center of the ring.

Oohs and aahs emanated from the crowd as this gargantuan Cleopatra rose onto her elbow. She threw her head backwards and opened her blood red lips for the grapes being fed to her by one of the clowns. Fanning the clowns away, amazingly tiny hands flipped a massive black cloud of hair away from her face, which had been made up in the most extravagant fashion.

Once again the dwarf musicians resumed their tune, and to a dumbfounded audience, this "beauty of Egypt" commenced a dance where each limb performed solo. Like instruments in an orchestra, each mound of flesh contributed its part to the awesome performance. George's mouth remained in a perpetual "O" until the lusty beauty had been removed from the ring.

Now the entertainment took on a more serious tone. The Master of Ceremonies welcomed everyone with expressive gestures, bowing over and over again, the semiprecious stones surrounding his headpiece glittering in the light. Felicia and Na'im's heads touched as he generally interpreted the ringmaster's words.

There was a constant flow of animals in and out of the ring, with beautiful women and ravishing men. The excitement mounted after the introduction of the contortionist, Sabir Hamid Rammah. The crowd watched in hushed silence as he bent and twisted his body into positions that one would not have believed possible for a human being. At the climax of his eye-popping act, Rammah, a full grown man of normal proportions, folded his body up to fit in a box no bigger than a large suitcase.

When he emerged from his small cage, thundering applause rained down upon him.

Felicia, in her excitement, rose to her feet in a standing ovation. Then Na'im joined her, and Fatimah, George and Kareem. Soon the entire audience was on its feet shouting their praises to the great "rubber man".

"I can't believe it," Felicia exclaimed. "How was he able to do that?"

"It is the power of the mind, *aros al bher*. But it is also the ability of the mind to tap into the power of the universe, making them one. The physical is no longer the dominating factor. It is a slave to the mind's commands. Rammah is the perfect example of this."

Sutannah, Mistress of the Serpents, was next. She was a beautiful woman with copper-colored skin. A golden band, highlighted in the front by an intricately-colored cobra, adorned her forehead. Jewelry decorated her lower and upper arms, neck and the waistline of her sheer skirt that hung low on her hips.

As she entered the ring, petite cymbals that were attached to her fingers created an enticing tempo. Similar cymbals with small tassels were perched on the tips of her full breasts.

Throughout her undulating exhibition, a tall reed basket remained balanced on the top of her head and four others were brought in by a slender man dressed in the traditional *galabia*.

George, who sat on the opposite side of Fatimah, called down to Na'im. "Ooh, I know I'm not in Canada now. The closest thing I've seen to anything shaped like her, was a poster picture of a girl in Hawaii. I don't think I could take it if one of those center cymbals should happen to fall off."

"If you think this is something, I'll have to take you to a place called *Ya Noor El Ein*, meaning Light of my Eyes. There you will see the cream of the crop, all trained in the vanishing art of belly dance."

"I'm going to hold you to that."

"My word is my bo—"

Felicia's sharp elbow made contact with Na'im's rib before he could finish.

"If these women are so irresistible, why don't you have one of them staying in the west wing at Karib," she complained in a voice that only Na'im's ears could hear.

"With these, should I say 'ladies', there is no need to bring them home. One can sample their assets without all that, and might I say, for a reasonable sum." One naturally-arched eyebrow lifted with a hint of mischief, and Na'im chuckled under his breath at Felicia's disconcerted expression.

By now, Sutannah had placed her woven container on the floor in front of her and removed its top. A cobra with its colorful hood expanded wavered back and forth inside.

Sutannah had removed the cymbals from her delicately curved fingers, which seemed to enthrall the reptile. Moments afterwards, her entire body appeared to be a hypnotic instrument, as she bent over and curled herself around the "king", who continued his movements, seemingly to the rhythm of the accompanying music.

Next the enchantress was up on her feet, enticingly making her way to each of the reed baskets that had been placed around the ring by the flutist. She flipped back each lid with a flick of her foot or the flounce of a feather-like hand.

Once all of the containers had been uncovered, Sutannah began a personal dance, a serenade for each of the king cobras that had emerged, hoods expanded, from their lairs. Each performance culminated with the reptile allowing her to coil its hooded body about one of her limbs, lastly her waist.

Once again, George felt provoked to speak his feelings about the remarkable performance.

"I've got to say what I heard a bunch of the boys say back in the States–she's too much woman for me. And they weren't even looking at anything like this. This lets me know I just need a simple girl to meet my needs." He glanced at Fatimah, who blushed, but kept her eyes focused on the center ring.

Several acts followed Sutannah. "The Brave Amin" was infallible on the trapeze, followed by tightrope walkers and animal acts.

By now, the torches were burning brightly under the big top, illuminating the satisfied expressions of just about everyone in attendance. The ringmaster was basking in the admiration of the crowd as he announced "Bakkar (Bahkar) of the Blades".

The mesmerized audience watched as Bakkar swallowed torches aflame with fire and maneuvered swords of various lengths down his slender throat. Faster and faster, to music similar to "The Sword Dance," his beautiful assistants passed his swords. Then Bakkar demonstrated his unique ability to actually swallow blades, regurgitating them back up at will.

This brought forth booming applause from the astonished audience who begged for more. Bakkar mounted a small podium near the front of the ring, spoke briefly and began to look around in the audience. Felicia didn't understand a word Bakkar had said. Just as she turned to Na'im for an interpretation, he rose to his feet.

"What's going on?" a bewildered Felicia asked as she tugged at Na'im's pants.

"Bakkar asked for a volunteer from the audience for his next act. Nobody seems to want to do it. So I'm volunteering."

Felicia's face was struck with confusion. "Volunteering to do what?"

"I'm not sure yet. But I guess I'll find out in a few minutes."

Applause rang out again as Bakkar acknowledged Na'im, who was making his way toward the center ring.

Felicia watched as Na'im was greeted by one of Bakkar's female assistants, who led him over to a large board held steady by wooden braces. Next, his arms and legs were tied spread-eagle to the makeshift dart board, and a blindfold was placed over his eyes. His golden brown chest gleamed under the torchlights, as it heaved evenly with every breath. His glossy brown hair was slightly pulled back from his face because of the blindfold, giving him the appearance of a Native American.

Everything was happening so fast that Felicia didn't quite know what she was feeling, until one of the women placed a blindfold over Bakkar's eyes. Then Felicia knew. Cold fear gripped her, as she watched Na'im standing blind and helpless. Before she knew it, Felicia had reached out and grabbed Fatimah's hand.

Bakkar began to swallow two short blades at a time, each time bringing them back up with such force, they became projectiles that landed at various points near Na'im's taut frame.

Felicia covered her mouth, willing herself not to scream as she watched the exasperating ordeal.

At long last, Bakkar projected the last blade, which

landed at the top of Na'im's head. Snatching off his blindfold while his assistants removed everything that restrained Na'im, Bakkar walked toward him and raised his arm high as the crowd shouted and clapped their approval.

It was a smiling Na'im with sparkling eyes who seated himself next to Felicia, who felt as if the wind had been knocked out of her. What was he so pleased about? Didn't the fool know he'd just put his life on the line for some stupid circus act?

Kareem was the first to voice his opinion. "Na'im, you are so brave. I want to be like you when I grow up," he announced in his best boyish voice.

Na'im rumpled Kareem's hair as he looked at Felicia, who had not looked his way.

"That was quite brave of you, my cousin, but I do not know if it was wise. In your father's absence, you are the head of Karib and should not risk your life without real cause."

"Fatimah, that is only the female side of you talking. You know that all of our lives are governed by a source higher than ourselves. I will die when my work is completed. Not before."

Silently, the group found their way out of the tent. Felicia could not find her voice to say anything. It had only taken that short period of time, seeing Na'im at the mercy of Bakkar's sightless blades, to make her realize how much she loved him.

They made their way into the darkened streets of Al Kharijah. Na'im could feel Felicia's unrest, so he chose not to taunt her. He wasn't sure why she was so quiet. As a matter of fact, she was quieter than he had ever seen her, except for the first silent days of their acquaintance. Maybe she felt he had shown off by volunteering. No matter what he had first thought about Felicia, he now knew in her heart she was a true humanitarian; one who very much valued the gift of life, and who was actively seeking ways to help prolong it.

George and Fatimah were the first to reach the rambling bazaar that dominated the section of town through which they now walked. Even at nighttime, the booths teemed with activity.

The bazaar at night was much more alluring to Felicia. Numerous candles lit rows of booths, adding a mysterious quality to the scene. She reflected on all of the lives that had touched hers since she had come to Egypt. Najid and his family, Aisha, Shabazz, Na'im.... She didn't know if she'd ever truly understand these people born in the place that many considered the cradle of civilization.

Haunting voices drifted from the colorful booth to their right. Three men were playing an oboe and two string instruments that Felicia did not recognize. In front of them, a man and a woman sang a sort of ballad. Their dress was different from what she'd seen since her stay in Egypt.

The man wore clothes similar to the nobility in the movie, "Jason and the Argonauts." The woman's clothing was of a lower class, simplistic but with the grace only ancient Egypt could bestow. The man's voice and motions portrayed feelings of remorse and longing for this woman who was obviously below his class. She, in turn, would reply in a voice reeking with sorrow, pain and disappointment. The sounds the duo brought forth were so sad.

"He sings of his love for her. But because of his station

he cannot marry her. He can only take her into his household as a servant, never to be given the respect due the position of a wife,'' Na'im's voice spoke near Felicia's ear.

''But she is a woman of pride,'' Fatimah added. ''Even though she loves him, she says she would rather die than live so close to him, knowing they can never really belong to each other. She could belong to him like a cow or camel. But never as two people who love each other.''

''It is so sad that we as human beings have complicated life so much,'' Felicia reflected. I don't believe that love should be treated as a business deal, but as the highest human emotion that we should function from.''

Na'im's face clouded at the solemnity of Felicia's words. He was glad that the cover of night kept the entire group from seeing how Felicia's every mood had a definite effect on him. He no longer knew if he had been truthful with himself about his feelings for her. He'd told himself he was attracted to her because of her beauty and a sincerity he found rare in most women; especially if they had a career that allowed them the leverage that Felicia's allowed her.

He hadn't thought twice about putting her in a room so close to his, and making his estate available to her research party in order to keep her close. But how long would that last? Another four to five weeks? Then what?

Everyone had noticed how sedate Felicia was since leaving the circus, even Kareem.

''Songs too sad. Let's go to games tents. Play. Have fun,'' Kareem whined as he tugged at Felicia's hand.

It wasn't long before they approached a booth where rings were being tossed at wooden pegs. Kareem waited his turn in line, holding his twenty *piasters* given to him by Na'im, tightly in his hand.

"I'd like to try my hand at this," George piped up.

"I bet I can beat you," Fatimah chided. "I'm the best ring tosser in Karib. Am I not, Na'im? At least I was when we were younger."

"She's right, George. I think you have a real adversary in Fatimah when it comes to this."

"Me too," Kareem's injured voice broke in.

"Both of you are on. I'm going to show you how the people in my hometown do it. The set up isn't exactly the same, but it's the same principle."

Kareem was the first to try his hand, emitting joyful squeals when he got one, and low grumbles of displeasure when he missed several in a row. Everyone had gotten caught up in the excitement. Except Felicia.

The flap to the booth next door lightly brushed the back of Felicia's head as it was opened by someone inside. A young woman, bowing her thanks with a look of apparent satisfaction, walked past them as she exited the small tent.

Felicia had thought the booth was closed because both flaps were down and there was no sound coming from its direction. Now she could see two tiny lit candles on a small table inside.

Walking forward to get a better look, she met face-to-face with a man who looked about fifty years old. He didn't wear the traditional *keffiyeh*, but a large turban with a shiny stone in its center.

"Oh, you scared me," Felicia gasped, placing her hand over her chest.

"I am sorry," the man spoke with a resonant voice, but otherwise impeccable English.

"I am Tahlil (Tah-leel). Most people call me a fortune teller. I prefer to be known as a visionary. Would you care to have me look into your life, to help you prepare for the things yet to unfold?"

"I don't think so."

"Why not. Why be afraid of the future? The present is a reflection of the past, and the future a reflection of the present. It is now that you have the most power over your future. Would it not be better to know what you have already shaped, so if it is not to your liking you can remold it?"

"I think I'd be more prone to let you do it if you weren't so serious," Felicia attempted to lighten the moment.

"But life is serious, little one. Everything that we do is recorded on our life's record. This does not mean one should not live their life happily. Happiness and seriousness are not opposites. They can complement one another."

Felicia regarded this gentle man, who was so full of wisdom. Once she'd thought about having her future told when she was in California. But she had changed her mind when she realized there were literally hundreds of people claiming to have the ability. It wasn't that she didn't believe there was something to it. Actually, she believed in the power of the mind; that it is our conditioning and limited beliefs that hinder it. But here in Egypt, where the greatest of intellectuals were still seeking to understand the mysteries of the ancient civilization's abilities, she felt it would be different.

Felicia looked back at Na'im, who had begun to listen to her exchange with Tahlil.

"Well, what do you think?"

"It's up to you, *aros al bher*."

"Alright, then. Well, why not."

"Do you want me to come with you?" Naim looked down at Felicia.

"No-o, I don't think so. You might hear something that I don't want you to hear."

With that she and Tahlil entered his booth.

Tahlil's white turban was the only imposing thing about him. Felicia now saw that the shiny stone gracing its middle was a large amethyst. Other than that, he wore a simple white *galabia.*

Though his eyes were extremely dark, appearing to be pitch black, they were not hard and piercing. There was nothing significant about his face, but Felicia could see that he lived what he taught. Despite his serious expression, the lines around his mouth echoed a perpetual smile.

Felicia was surprised that there were no tarot cards or crystal balls on the table or in the room. As a matter of fact, it was rather bare. There was one table and two candles, two stools upon which she and Tahlil sat, and another stool sitting alone in the corner.

Tahlil placed one of the candles on the vacant stool. Then he returned to the table, seated himself, adjusted his turban, and asked that Felicia sit forward with both arms outstretched toward him. He then pushed the other candle to Felicia's far right.

"Now...I want you to concentrate on the flame of this candle and listen to my voice."

He gave Felicia these instructions as he caught both of her hands in his.

"No, I do not use other aids to help me with my task. I use you, the main source and channel, as the vehicle to help me tell your future. I will tune into the energies in your life force. They will be transmitted to me, and through the gift of my foresight, I will be able to vision your life."

Felicia tried to relax but it wasn't easy.

"Don't worry. You are doing fine. Relax. Become one with the flame. Let its light burn within your mind and your heart. Let it engulf you, blocking out everything but its enlightenment and wisdom. See yourself walking into the flame. You are no longer separate, but one with the light. Now close your eyes, continuing to see you and the flame as one."

Felicia felt serene and at peace as she waited in silence for Tahlil to speak.

"You have long been an entity known to help others. This you will accomplish again. It will be done through your bringing together people of unlike cultures. It will also be done through your intellect in a field that you have studied in more than this lifetime. This is very clear for me to see.

"Your personal future is vague. It is because you have not determined what you really want. There is love in your life for a man, but you do not feel within your heart he is yours. I see anguish and torment. I feel the heat of destruction. But because you are a powerful being, like coal turns to diamonds under pressure, your life force holds the key to your happiness."

Felicia's eyes involuntarily flew open at the ominous words that Tahlil spoke of her future with Na'im. She wanted to withdraw her hands, but she felt unable to.

Tahlil's pupils seemed to have all but vanished behind his eyelids as he channeled Felicia's energies, focusing on his third eye crowned by the amethyst.

With Felicia's break of concentration, Tahlil's eyelids closed, and when he looked at her again, his eyes were soft with compassion.

"Remember, you are the one who shapes your future, but one must determine what future they want before they can build it. Now go, and may peace go with you."

Felicia nodded numbly. "How much do I owe you?"

"As much as you care to give."

Felicia thought of Aisha. She and Tahlil had a similar feel about them–Aisha accepting no money from the villagers, Tahlil accepting whatever patrons thought to give him. She gave Tahlil five pounds before leaving.

George's voice was the first thing she heard when she stepped outside of the visionary's booth, crying out his discontent over being beaten by Fatimah.

"Let's play just one more game. Just one more."

"George, this is three times that you say that. I beat you. That's it," Fatimah replied, dusting off her hands to add finality to her words.

George began to shake his head in dismay. Kareem was the first to notice Felicia as she emerged from the booth. He ran over to her, the excitement of the entire day apparent on his face.

"You be rich? Fortune teller say you be rich?" he echoed, his body bobbing up and down.

"Not quite."

"Don't tell me," George kidded. "You're going to marry a handsome waiter, and live happily ever after over the restaurant in which he works."

Felicia playfully swiped at George's head, missing him by inches as he ducked away, pulling Fatimah in front of him.

"Well, aren't you going to tell us what he said?" Na'im queried.

"I don't think I will. Some things a woman has to keep to herself."

"Aw-w, spoil sport," George whined. "It couldn't have been all that great, anyway."

"Maybe so. Maybe not. You're just mad because Fatimah beat the pants off you at that game. Don't try to put your anxiety off on me, George Mercer."

Na'im tilted his handsome head to the side. Raising one smooth eyebrow slightly, he further pressured Felicia. "So you're really not going to tell us, are you?"

Squinting her eyes while posting her own Mona Lisa smile, Felicia answered him with a firm, "No."

Chapter Twenty-One

It had been two and a half weeks since the lab started operating. Felicia and the others were deep into Phase II of the project. Initially, they felt the project would require at least four stages of development. But after a lot of discussion and revamping of methods, a three-phase plan was developed.

Felicia was more than pleased that they had managed to reproduce the serum needed in Phase I so quickly. Now tests were being carried out on lab animals to see if gene transfers would be a feasible method to reach their goal.

Having always been an animal lover, it still bothered Felicia when experiments resulted in the death of some of the smaller rodents. Kareem hadn't helped with this sentimental problem one bit. He had named just about every single lab animal in the place.

Felicia could hear how his English had improved tremendously over such a short period of time. And since he seemed to enjoy the lab so much, she put him to work. He was responsible for feeding the animals and keeping their cages clean, but only the ones who were not being used in testing.

A couple of times, Felicia let him help her when weighing animals that had been injected with various levels of a saline solution. These tests were being conducted to see how salt could be beneficial, and controlled in helping to store fluids.

Kareem's small face was serious as he placed the little animals on the scale, making sure they remained as still as possible during the process. Felicia could see why Na'im had grown so attached to the boy, aside from what she knew about his mother.

Her contact with Na'im had become limited to their nights together. She carried the impact of those nights with her throughout the day. Rivulets of pleasure would pulsate through her, as her mind conjured up images of the night before.

Both of them seemed to have called a truce, neither one bringing up the future, but only living for the present and the passion-filled nights they shared together. Their lovemaking was so consuming, all that could be thought about was the rhythm of their insatiable bodies. They were constantly reaching for one another, feeling, touching, even in the midst of sleep.

Felicia no longer went to her bedroom at night. Since the night of the circus, she'd slept with Na'im in his bed. She would wake up with this satisfied feeling in the pit of her stomach, but with the slightest movement from Na'im's hard body, her desire for him would make itself known. He seemed to know this instinctively, and would come to her prepared to fill all of her needs.

Their lovemaking in the morning light was a revealing thing. There was no way for anything to be hidden with the bright sunlight finding its way through slits in the curtains and along the windows' sides.

Na'im took full advantage of this. His eyes seemed to consume her as he took her, watching their bodies join together, and once done, he held her eyes with his as he brought them both to ecstasy.

After their morning sessions, Na'im would play with Felicia's braids, which hung in wild, hanging locks of curls. She, in turn, would pull his shoulder-length hair back from his face and up on his head, telling him what a handsome woman he would make. This always resulted in his reminding her that he knew she was glad that he wasn't a woman, accompanied by an onslaught of tickling.

Laughter would ring out in the early morning hours in the west wing. Felicia laughed because almost every part of her body was a tickle zone, and Na'im because it amused him to see her laugh with such abandon.

Rarely was Na'im on the estate for dinner. Many times Felicia and the others had their dinner in the lab or outside near the building, hashing over the day's activities.

Word spread quickly that Fatimah would be opening up a school for the workers' children. Many of the mothers offered to make things for the small classroom, housed in the building next to the science lab.

It took a couple of days for crude, but usable tables to be fashioned out of pieces of wood, and for all the finishing touches to be added; but with so many pitching in, class was scheduled to start the next day.

Fatimah's interest in the school appeared to have added life to her. She was always bustling around in the classroom. This day she seemed especially excited.

More than once she'd burst in on Felicia, frantic that she'd forgotten this or that. Felicia took the time to calm her, and assure her it had already been taken care of.

"Fatimah, what you need to do is calm down. Now

you've been over that list I don't know how many times, and if you ask me, 'Did I buy chalk?' one more time, I'm going to scream."

"Is she making a pest of herself, Felicia?" George entered the lab, smoothing his blond hair back from his face.

"She certainly is. And I wish someone would just take that list from her."

"Alright then, I'll do better than that. I've finished with everything I'm going to do today. So, Fatimah, if it's alright with you, I'll go over the list and double check it to make sure you have done everything, and you have everything you need."

"Oh, Mr. Mercer, you don't have to do that. I am fine."

"Oh, no you're not," Felicia butted in, in frustration. "Now if the man is going to help you, pu-leeze let him do it."

"And how many times have I told you not to call me Mr. Mercer? You make me feel like an old man."

With the two of them ganging up on her, Fatimah had no way of getting out of it. So she and George went back next door for a final checkover of everything.

Fatimah liked George's company. She'd thought about him a lot since their travel to Al Kharijah for supplies, and to see the circus. He'd been so lighthearted and carefree that day, making her feel the same. George seemed to be always full of conversation. She'd caught him looking at her several times in a somewhat whimsical way, but she had pretended not to notice.

Fatimah was fascinated with his ash blonde hair. It was the color of desert sand, and such a contrast to her own. And to Ilyas'. She'd told herself it wasn't fair to compare him to Ilyas. And why should she compare them? Ilyas was the man who had expressed his intentions toward her. She had accepted that one day they would be married. This is why she found her preoccupation with George disturbing, and tried to stay her distance from him. But it wasn't only that. Since then, whenever she saw George, her pulse seemed to race, and she felt all tingly inside. It was for this reason that she had rejected his offer to help.

Now, in looking down at his silky head, she felt the urge to touch it, as he knelt counting tablets and then books in a large crate.

"Fifteen, sixteen, seventeen. Alright, we can check these off. Now what's next?"

Fatimah bent to look into the next crate just as George decided to do the same. She nearly knocked him over in the process. George grabbed onto her arm, trying to balance himself. His weight pulled her down toward him, and dark brown eyes stared into sky blue ones.

George rose to his feet, with Fatimah standing not even an arm's length away.

"I am sorry. I did not mean to knock you over," she stammered, searching for any place to look except George's face.

"It's okay," George managed in a raspy voice. "Fatimah, I..." Impulsively, he planted a light kiss on her lips.

Fatimah wanted to wrap her arms around his neck and pull him close to her; to rub her face against his; feel the texture of his hair. Instead, she turned away. She heard Ilyas call her name, as George reached for her hand.

Chapter Twenty-Two

Felicia was feeling exhausted from the day's activities. As she slowly moved around the lab tidying things up, she was startled to hear loud noises coming from the schoolhouse.

Rushing from the lab, she found Fatimah using all of her strength to restrain Ilyas. Speaking to him in rapid Arabic, and louder than Felicia had ever heard her, Fatimah spoke in a commanding tone.

George's face was flushed with color and his pulse throbbed visibly at the temple.

Ilyas' voice was ragged with emotion as he addressed Fatimah. She, in return, turned to George and asked him to let them have some time alone.

"George, I am sorry this happened. But it would be better if you left now."

"I am sick of this guy coming and ordering you around like he owns you. I could just knock his..."

"No George, please. Just go. You don't understand. Ilyas wants an excuse to kill you. Please go. Now."

George hesitated for a moment, turned and walked briskly past Felicia, who was standing just outside the door. Felicia decided to follow him. She could see that Ilyas' anger was targeted at George, and that Fatimah was not in any physical danger.

Felicia caught up with George as he reached the lime tree where the men gathered in the late evenings.

"Are you alright?"

"I'm fine. But something is just not right about that relationship between Fatimah and Ilyas." He turned frustrated blue eyes toward Felicia. "Felicia, I know she likes me. I can feel it when I'm around her. I think she's something special and should be treated like it. I wish I could take her out. Go dancing, to the movies. You know. I just wish things were different."

"Well, have you said anything to her to let her know how you feel?"

"I haven't had an opportunity to. She's been avoiding me ever since that last trip we took to Al Kharijah. And I know it's because of this Ilyas guy. Are they engaged? Or what's the deal between them?"

Felicia felt obligated to ease a little of George's pain, but she determined she would not play go-between for George when it came to Fatimah.

"No. As far as I know, they are not officially engaged. Fatimah has not told me a lot about the situation. You're going to have to talk to her. But George, I'm going to give you some advice. We're not back in the States or in Canada. We are in Egypt, and the ways and thoughts of these people are quite different from what both you and I are accustomed to. If you choose to get involved with her on a personal level, I think it would have to be all or nothing. You can't come half-stepping. It just wouldn't work over here. You're going to have to make up your mind about what you really want. Ilyas is serious. This is not a game for him. What Fatimah told you was a warning and not a threat. So just be careful, okay? I think we both need to be careful."

"Yeah, I hear what you're saying."

The sun had already started its slow descent in the western sky. Felicia felt as if it were a sign; telling her that time was running out for her to make up her mind about Na'im.

Often now, she caught herself daydreaming; visualizing herself confronting Na'im and telling him no other woman, including Waheedah, would ever have him. She knew she was playing it safe by not facing the facts of their relationship; that another woman had been chosen to be his wife; that her stay in Karib was only temporary. It was her deep need to be with him that made her such a coward, but she knew it would not last for long. She had been turning her back on her pride and convictions she claimed to be her own.

"Did you know that Egypt is sometimes known as the land of the sun?"

"No," George replied, stubbing his foot against a clump of grass.

"Well, it is. The sun shines so brightly in its skies that everything is clearly defined for you. The trees. The hills. Everything. It is for this reason that many artists come here to paint. They say, where else in the world can you go and there is not even a hint of a shadow in miles and miles of landscape. It's an artist's dream. I think things have been made clear to us too, George. It's just that we are afraid to step out in the sunlight and see the truth as it is, without shadows."

A wistful look crossed Felicia's face as she smiled with resignation. She knew in George she had a comrade; someone like herself who had been smitten by the mystery of this land and its people, and had to make up his mind as to what direction to take.

Chapter Twenty-Three

Felicia watched as Na'im dressed in a white *galabia* with magenta and silver thread edging the borders of its hem and sleeves.

They'd spent extra time together this morning. Na'im had some business to attend to that would keep him away from the estate over the next three to four days.

There was no way for Felicia to hide the thoughts and feelings that had resulted from George's clash with Ilyas. Even though she did not speak of them to Na'im, he knew something was different and their lovemaking reflected his uncertainty. It was slow and, oh so tender, having a feeling of reverence and spirituality. They held each other close throughout the night, and after making love again in the morning, they just laid in each other's arms, silently.

Felicia's watchful gaze disturbed Na'im. There was no laughter or lightheartedness in her eyes. Only something that resembled a distant pain. When his eyes would meet hers, bountiful eyelashes would come down to block him from seeing what he needed to know.

Glistening black waves of hair cascaded over her shoulders, nearly hiding the dark brown tip of one breast, while the other sat up boldly.

The rich purple coverlet that encircled her trim waist, called to him to come and lay his head in her lap. He wanted to please her and make her happy. He had thought until last night she was. Na'im was his happiest and most fulfilled when he was with Felicia, and he had thought she felt the same. Now he knew that was not true.

Na'im stepped over to the bedside, bent down and placed a kiss on Felicia's lips. "I'll see you when I get back."

"Alright. Be careful, Na'im."

Felicia knew that Na'im had not solved his differences with Hassan. No matter what happened between the two of them, she couldn't stand the thought of Na'im being harmed in any way.

After Na'im left, she took a long, pacifying bath. She was in no hurry to get to the lab today. Phillip and George had scheduled extensive testing this morning that involved the renin output and kidney physiology of some of the lab animals. They didn't need her for that, so she planned to go out later on and share the results of some of the experiments she'd conducted in the area for which she was responsible. Not only that, it was the first day of school and she wanted Fatimah to feel she had complete control of her class. Without Felicia in the lab, Fatimah would know there wouldn't be a well-wishing, impromptu guest popping in.

The servants had become accustomed to Felicia and Na'im taking breakfast in their rooms. One of them had brought a tray overflowing with pastries, fruit, tea and coffee. Felicia chose an orange that had been peeled and partially separated.

The corner of an envelope caught her eye beneath one of the plates. She pulled it out, and saw it was addressed to her from Nouakchott, the capital of Mauritania. She had almost forgotten about the letter she had written over two weeks ago.

The envelope was quite thick, so Felicia knew it contained several pages. Tearing it open, she sat back in the chair to read its contents.

Dear Felicia,
I was surprised to find out that your work has brought you back to Africa so soon. I am happy to know you are continuing the research you started here, that will hopefully someday cut back on the sufferng and pain that is paramount in my country. I had to speak to many government officials and others in the social service area before I could even start to address the proposal you set before me. At first, all of the military leaders were skeptical about such a plan, but after a friend of mine who is a social worker convinced one of the lower representatives to tour several crowded shelters and buildings, he was able to carry the banner for our cause; bringing out the unusual circumstances under which these women now live, and how life in Falam, despite its troubles, would be heaven compared to this. It has been agreed that twenty women, some with children, some single, will be transported to Al Kharijah for the purpose of living in the village of Falam. All of the women volunteered to go, just as you mandated. I guess because you had worked so closely with some of these people during your stay, you knew the proposal you presented would be welcomed by them. We have made sure the majority of them are Moors, so there will be no problems with language, but three

of them are Black Africans and speak the tucolor language. I, along with one social service agent and two government personnel, will accompany the women and children to Al Kharijah. But I must insist that you meet us there on April 27th. The government is providing an old military plane as a means of transportation. I hope you will have everything prepared for our arrival by that time. This was not easy for me to arrange, Felicia, so I hope your end of the project has been taken care of. See you soon.

Your Compatriot,
Imam Anwar Jabar''
(E-mam An-wahr Jah-bar)

Exhiliration filled Felicia as she completed the letter. The priest had done it. She knew he would. She'd seen how well respected he was in that community, in and out of his masjid as well. And now, twenty women would be traveling here to be joined with Hassan's village.

So many thoughts began to run through Felicia's mind. She hadn't told Na'im of her plan to help bring women to Falam, but she hadn't thought Imam Jabar would work so quickly. She only had six days before the group would reach Al Kharijah. Six days to bring Karib and Falam to a point where they would sit peacefully together and listen to her solution. Felicia knew that was impossible. She had to figure out a way to do it without them.

Felicia threw on her jeans and a long top she'd had made especially to wear with them. As she dressed, she knew she would need help in carrying out her plan.

The first person who came to mind was Fatimah. She felt she could trust her to keep quiet until it was time to let everyone know. But who could be the negotiator between Falam and Karib?

Felicia ran her fingers through her braided hair while gazing in the mirror. Her mind came up with every possible solution it could. Then Najid Mu'adin came to the forefront. Najid worked in Al Kharijah. He knew many of the people who traveled back and forth from their villages to the oasis. And he knew Sheik Ahmed Hassan.

Anticipation sparked Felicia as she crossed the grounds to the area where the school and lab were housed. She knew Na'im would not be happy when he found out she had taken it upon herself to make decisions that concerned his village, but she felt the risk was worth it to solve the problem with Hassan.

Felicia knew her motivation stemmed from something deeper than Na'im's problem with Hassan. Her stays in and out of battered women's shelters as a child had instilled in her a deep need to help women in similar situations. Some might think it cruel and presumptuous for her to initiate a project such as this, but only those who had lived a life similar to hers would truly understand the value of a chance for a new life.

Now Felicia was somewhat glad that Na'im would be away for the next few days. There was so much to accomplish in such a little time; letters to be sent, and maybe even trips into Al Kharijah.

Fatimah thought about why Felicia had invited her to her room after dinner. She had been so upset with how the first day of class had turned out. After the first two hours, most of the children began to squirm in their seats, playing with their pencils or flipping the pages of their books and tablets. She knew the experience of just sitting and listening would be new to them. But if today was a sample of how every day was going to be, they were not going to learn much of anything.

Fatimah found Felicia with numerous papers and envelopes spread in front of her on the cocktail table. She held a ball point pen in her hand.

"Fatimah, I'm glad you're here. I've got something I need you to help me with. I know you've just started the school, but I think this is something that could really end up being a good thing."

Fatimah sat down on the couch and gave Felicia her full attention. Felicia told her what she'd done, and about the letter she had received from Mauritania that day. She told her that she planned on getting Hassan or his son, and maybe a few key men, to Al Kharijah when the women arrived.

"This sounds like a very dangerous plan, Felicia. Hassan wants nothing to do with anything involving Karib. They will not come, even if you told them it involved some women who want to come to live in their village. They will think it is a trap."

"But I won't tell them that. I will have a friend of mine, who works at the American Consulate, take the letters that we're going to write to the message center. He will inform the clerk there that officials from Mauritania are on their way to the States and asked him to deliver their letters to the center. So when Hassan hears about it, it will be the message center telling him the letters came from Mauritanian officials."

"It may work, but Hassan's son, Abdul, will be skeptical."

"It's got to work, and that's why I need your help to make the letters look more authentic. The documents have to be in Arabic and I need you to write them."

"I wouldn't know what to write. I don't..."

"That's alright. We'll decide together what goes in the letters tonight, and then tomorrow you can translate them into Arabic. The next day, I plan on making a trip into Al Kharijah to visit my friend and ask if he will help us."

"You know Na'im will not like this."

"Why? Because I'm a woman? And women aren't supposed to take on such large responsibilities?"

"You know that's not the reason, Felicia. You did not include him. You should have asked him what he thinks about all of this."

"I was planning to, once I got a feel for what Imam Jabar would be able to do. I didn't want to come to him with an empty idea. I wanted to wait until I was pretty sure my plan would work. When I got the letter from the Imam this morning saying everything was set up, Na'im had already left. He's going to be gone three or four days, Fatimah. If I wait for him to return, we won't have enough time. Besides, you said Abdul doesn't want anything to do with Na'im and your family, so it could be even more dangerous for Na'im."

"That is true."

"You've got to help. If my plan works, it will solve a major problem; one that has been a threat to several villages, including Karib. We could put an end to it. So will you do it?"

"I will do it," Fatimah gave in, throwing her hands in the air. "I just hope we're doing the right thing."

Chapter Twenty-Four

When Felicia stepped into the reception area of the American Consulate, it brought back all kinds of feelings. That day seemed so long ago, and all the events surrounding it seemed like a dream. Actually, it had only been one month since Na'im had saved her from drowning and brought her to the consulate to seek help. How things had changed since then.

Felicia's memories were jolted further when Najid emerged from a door not far behind his desk. He glanced at her briefly before he shut the door. Then recognition set in, and he whipped around with surprise and pleasure.

"Is it you, Felicia?"

"Yes, Najid, it is me."

Tears of joy streamed down her face as she hugged the small, brown man who was shorter than herself, all the gratitude that she felt for him and his family in her embrace.

"It is good to see you again. We got your letter, and were glad to know that you were doing well."

"How is everyone–Majidah, Jamillah, Sana and Ali?"

"They are all doing fine, and will be pleased to know

that I have seen you with my own eyes and you are fine as well."

"Najid, this is not just a social visit. I've become involved in a project that will be good for all the villages in this area. But I'm going to need your help."

"You know I will help you, Felicia, if I can. It is the way of my family."

Felicia knew she could count on this man who'd shown her such kindness. Excitement began to mount in her as she described what would take place over the next few days, and the role she wanted him to play in it.

"Now, this is the letter I received from Mauritania. So when you tell the clerk at the message center that Mauritanian officials left correspondence to be given to Hassan, there's some truth in that."

"I see. I can be an instrument to help bring peace to my people. Their happiness is my happiness, Felicia. I will do what I can to help."

Felicia was glad William had driven her into Al Kharijah. Initially, Phillip wanted to drive, saying he had business to take care of in town. He would have noticed reticence, and tried to persuade her to talk. But her contemplative mood didn't bother William in the least. From time to time, he would begin a brief conversation, but for the most part their journey back was a quiet one.

Once they entered the estate, William dropped her off in front of the lab and drove off, saying he was going to assist George with the generator, which had broken down the day before. If George had already repaired it, they'd load it onto the truck and bring it back to the lab.

Felicia had worn a bright yellow *pagnes* and head wrap to Al Kharijah, mainly because she didn't want to call attention to herself. This was accomplished with no problem, but coming back to the estate was completely different. Almost everyone had become accustomed to seeing her in jeans and long tops around the lab. Seeing her in her colorful attire caused quite a stir, especially with Phillip.

"Well, my, my. What do we have here? A mustard-colored desert flower? What's the occasion, Felicia?"

"Nothing in particular. I just felt like becoming one with my environment today. You should try it, Phillip. One of those blousey-sleeved tops that show your chest and a pair of pantaloons might suit you well. You'd probably look quite sexy."

With Najid agreeing to deliver the letters for Hassan to the message center, Felicia was feeling quite pleased with herself, and up to giving Phillip a little of his own medicine.

"Oh I would, would I?" Moving closer to Felicia, Phillip put on one of his best James Bond looks. "And would that mean you'd find me just as attractive as you find your Egyptian 'Denzel Washington'?"

"Why Phillip, I've always told you, you are an attractive guy. It's just that..."

"Don't play with me now, Felicia. I've been out here in the middle of nowhere for four weeks now without a woman. If you give me the slightest provocation, I might just show you how badly I'm in need of one."

Felicia heard the joking lilt in Phillip's voice, but she could also see a hint of seriousness in his eyes.

"Now Phillip, you know we have been friends for a long time. Let's not mess things up at this point."

Just for a second, Phillip's eyes clouded over with a hurt look, and Felicia realized she could have been softer with her rejection. Placing her arms around his neck and giving him a brotherly hug, she whispered in his ear. "Phillip, we are friends. We'll always be friends. I don't want to hurt you, but you can't let our close working relationship misdirect you regarding your feelings for me."

Very softly, Phillip agreed with her, and they spent a few moments in comforting friendship.

Felicia opened her eyes as she released Phillip, to stare directly into Na'im's golden ones, overflowing with anger.

"Na'im!"

"So you couldn't wait until I got back? Or have you two been using the lab I provided for you as your meeting place all along?"

Before Felicia could respond to his accusations, Na'im disappeared out the door.

"Oh, sh--! I hope he's not another hothead like Ilyas," Phillip groaned. "I heard what happened between him and George."

"Is that all you can think about–yourself? Why didn't you say something?"

"I was caught off guard, just like you were. Do you actually think he was going to stand there and listen to me make excuses about why I was hugging his woman. He'd only think I was lying."

"Well, you could have at least tried. I was trying to comfort you and your horny butt, remember?"

"Do you want me to go after him? I will if you want me to."

Felicia had always known that Phillip's bark was worse than his bite. For him to even offer to try to explain to Na'im was more than she expected from him.

"No. That's alright. I'll wait until he calms down and try to talk to him while we're having dinner. Maybe then he will be in a better mood.

Relief flooded Phillip's face. "Yeah, that sounds like a good idea. Put some of the old female charm on him. He won't be able to resist you."

Felicia wrapped the floor length, sheer nightgown about her feet, as she glanced at her watch for the umpteenth time. She'd had dinner delivered to their room as usual, but one thing was missing–Na'im.

The goat dish, simmered in sesame oil with okra, red peppers and onions, looked hardly edible. It, and the *molokiea*, an opaque green soup, had been sitting for such a long time, both dishes had grown cold and taken on a congealed look.

Felicia had no appetite. Her nerves were on edge and her ears strained for every sound that might be Na'im approaching the sitting room. They had been apart for four days and three nights now, and she had missed him terribly.

When Phillip had suggested that she use her feminine wiles to persuade Na'im, she thought it was a bad idea. But as time passed, and the look of anger and mistrust in Na'im's eyes kept playing over and over in her mind, she had decided to use any method she could to get him to listen to her.

She was forcing down one of the dates that made up the small fruit dish, when she heard footsteps in the hallway. She felt a breathlessness come upon her and her stomach muscles began to contract. She didn't know what she had expected when Na'im walked through the door, but it was not the solemn, aloof person who confronted her.

Suddenly she felt embarrassed about her near nudity. Na'im's eyes held not even the remotest spark of desire or feeling for her. They were golden orbs devoid of anything nearing emotion, and that frightened Felicia more than anything had in a long time.

"Hello, Na'im." Felicia waited for his reply. But there was none. He just looked at her.

"Won't you give me a chance to tell you what was going on?"

"If you can tell me the truth."

"I've never lied to you before, and I don't intend to start doing it now."

"Alright. You've got your chance."

Felicia instinctively felt repulsed by the business-like tone of Na'im's voice, but she told herself this was not the time to show it.

"I was simply comforting Phillip."

"Oh. It appeared to me that he had you backed into the corner between two tables and the two of you were 'comforting' each other."

"No, not really."

"Why were you comforting him?"

"It all started when he commented about my wearing the yellow *pagnes*. And then he..."

"What did he say about it? He didn't like the idea of your looking good for him?"

"That's not why I wore it, Na'im."

"Well, why did you wear it? You usually wear those jeans he bought you that show far too much, but at least you had the decency to wear a long top. What made you wear that today, Felicia?"

"I just felt like wearing it today. Na'im don't be angry with me." She knew it sounded flimsy, but she could think of nothing else to say. She couldn't tell him the truth about why she had worn the dress without revealing to him her visit to Al Kharijah.

Felicia had never seen such contempt on anyone's face as she saw on Na'im's.

"You think you can dress like that and seduce me into forgiving you for your tramp-like actions? You think that I only need to see your naked body and I will be blinded to your indiscretions? I am not a slave to your passions or to mine, Felicia. I told you once, do not rile me to the point where I would find it necessary to punish you. Then, I felt your punishment would be my own. But now I no longer feel that way. It is obvious to me that despite your other activities, you are still willing to go to bed with me. But that's something I don't plan to do."

The sound of Na'im's harsh words echoed in Felicia's ears as he closed the door to his bedroom behind him. Tears of anguish and hurt flooded her eyes, but she wiped them away as swiftly as they tumbled down. How dare he think those things about her! Felicia felt as if she'd been stabbed in the stomach with a knife, the pain of Na'im's rejection was so strong. Through a veil of tears, she made her way to her bed. Flinging herself across it, she cried until she could cry no more. Her pillow was wet with her sorrow. Before she drifted off to sleep, she pushed it aside, falling into slumber with her knees curled upward toward her belly. Never before in her life had she experienced such emotional pain.

Sleep was the one relief that Na'im sought, but it would not come. Out of his jealousy, he'd said things that he knew had terribly wounded the person most important to him. He'd tried to listen to her. He wanted her to give him an explanation that would take away the betrayal he felt. But instinctively, he knew she was not telling him the complete truth.

It had angered him even more to think she thought him so weak for her that he'd be able to forget the sight of her in Phillip's arms and still make love to her. All of his life, Na'im had been known as a man full of pride. His pride had meant more to him than fame, wealth, or even love.

Na'im closed his eyes to hurry the peace of sleep, but it was as if his body felt the heat of Felicia, knowing she was so near. Those four days away from her had felt like an eternity. That was the reason he had returned early and gone to the lab. He couldn't wait to see her. He had wanted to spend the rest of the day with her, behind closed doors, and discuss the future.

He knew her career was important to her, and that living with him at Karib would virtually bring an end to that. But he had felt he could convince her that his country needed people like her; that there would be special projects she could work on...once they started a family.

Now, Na'im feared there was a side to Felicia he had refused to acknowledge, the one thing he had warned himself about from the very beginning. She was an American, and he had experienced a pattern of infidelity and dishonesty among American females.

When Na'im had first arrived in the United States, beautiful, wealthy females were plentiful. He had been with all shapes, colors and sizes. Being an Egyptian and the son of a sheik, he was thrown into the jet set crowd, and women were available in droves.

In the beginning, he had enjoyed the wild gatherings

and the different women each night. But soon it became monotonous. He began to notice the little games the women played. Some would feign coyness, playing the sweet virgin scheme. These women were looking for a man who could take over their lives and fulfill their every fantasy. Others came on strong, straight to the point, stating what they wanted, when and how they wanted it. But there was no depth to these affairs; only superficial relationships with superficial people.

He hadn't gone to the United States to look for a wife. He had gone to learn more about the culture, but deep inside he had also felt an intelligent woman brought up in that country could be an asset as a wife.

Felicia had appeared to be different, maybe because of the circumstances under which they had met. She had shown herself to be a sensitive, giving person, with brains as well. Na'im felt he could trust Felicia, until Phillip came along.

No matter how much he mentally battered himself with Felicia's betrayal, his body longed to be with her. Her nude, dark brown body had stood out underneath the see-through white gown, and the faint scent from her need of him, mixed with her perfume, had floated enticingly about his nostrils when he came near her. It was his physical urge to take her regardless of the circumstances that had fueled his anger.

Finally, the ache in Na'im's loins compelled him to go to Felicia's bedside. A panel of light from the moon illuminated her shape upon the large bed. Na'im could see that she was asleep. He could also see the tear stains that marred her velvety complexion.

He craved to reach out and take her in his arms, no matter what she had done. His thirst for her was paramount in his mind and body. He stood there, watching, for an endless amount of time. With resolution, he hung his head, accepting that his manly pride would not allow him to do it.

Not even for the woman he loved.

Felicia found the short note Na'im had left her on the nightstand near her bed the next morning. It simply said he would be gone for the next few days.

She didn't feel like eating breakfast, so after bathing and dressing, she headed for the lab. She could hear excessive laughter coming from the schoolhouse. She wondered what was going on.

The last time she had talked to Fatimah about the school, she'd talked about how discouraged she was. Classes had been in progress for at least a week, and she had not been able to really get the children to listen. They'd shown no real interest in their lessons, or in Fatimah's method of teaching.

Another outburst of laughter emanated from the small building as Felicia passed by. She could see and hear Fatimah explaining something in Arabic, but the children's eyes were all riveted to the opposite side of the room.

As she walked further, she caught a glimpse of George noisily acting out the role of a monkey. It was George's actions that were bringing the guffaws from the children.

Fatimah opened up one of the children's textbooks and started to read, pointing to George as an example. Then she had them all repeat the word "monkey" in English. Felicia was pleased to see Fatimah looking relaxed and satisfied. Evidently George's presence had worked wonders for her as well as the students.

William was the only person in the lab when she arrived. George showed up moments later, gratified with his role in Fatimah's progress. They only had a week and a half left to complete the research project, and things had gone pretty well up to now.

They'd determined that gene transfers or saline solutions were not the answer to dehydration, but a sugar substance known as trehalose might be. Many tests had been conducted on what was known as the desert resurrection plant, because of its ability to survive an unbelievable period of time without water.

Next the experiments advanced to tiny animal life. Nematodes were brought to the lab from some of the desert water holes. Felicia was amazed to see how these tiny invertebrates could lose more than fifty percent of the moisture in their bodies, appearing as dry as dust, and then revive totally when they were put back into water.

The substance that increased in the nematode's body during these dry periods was trehalose. Trehalose was the key. And that's where the problem began.

Their experiments to help lab animals produce this substance had failed, and the animals died. William, Phillip and George were spending long nights trying to solve the dilemma. Felicia worked with them, doing her share during the daylight hours, but now that the Mauritania proposal was so close to completion, it had put a damper on her input.

None of the team members complained about it. Actually, they felt their late night hours were overtime, and something they chose to do voluntarily. She knew all of them, including Phillip, wanted to give her an opportunity to spend time with Na'im. She couldn't bear to tell them that Na'im hadn't been in Karib on many of the days they'd let her leave early.

▲

Felicia was scheduled to meet Imam Anwar Jabar in two days in Afrah El Jabel, a large, noisy crowded place in the middle of Al Kharijah. Najid had suggested this as the meeting place. It was a place known to all the nearby villagers. It would be a good place to meet because it was never empty during the day or night. He knew the owner of the spot, and had convinced him to let them use a large room in the rear of the building.

Everything had been prepared. The letter stating officials from the Mauritanian government had chosen Hassan's village as a special place for recognition had been delivered to him. Word of his tragedy had traveled far.

Hassan was told not to leak this information to anyone, for the other village heads were sure to be jealous and could possibly cause trouble. He was told to bring several men, along with camels and carts. Hassan had replied as he'd been asked to. He stated he would be there at the appointed time.

Once Hassan's message was received, the clerk contacted Najid, who then informed him the Mauritanian officials would be returning to his office in a couple of days. At that time, they expected to pick up all their correspondence. Everything had gone just the way Felicia had planned, up to this point. Everything was set.

Phillip showed up at the lab shortly after George. He tried to joke with Felicia, but seeing she wasn't in the mood, he left her alone and got to work.

After her ordeal with Na'im the night before, and his leaving without saying goodbye, Felicia found the tedious lab testing a welcome relief; one that she buried herself in over the next two days.

Chapter Twenty-Five

Felicia's eyes burned with the strain of reading by candlelight. William and Phillip had already quit for the evening, and were in bed in the adjoining room. George said he had some other things to tend to, and had left an hour earlier.

The men had placed a piece of canvas up to the doorway, separating the lab from their sleeping quarters. Felicia had chosen only one candle to work by, so as not to disturb them.

Her back and shoulder muscles ached from sitting on the three-legged stool, balancing her upper body over the small table to take full advantage of the light. She stretched her arms far over her head, yawning with sheer abandon. Boy, was she tired. She stacked up her papers, put them back in the file, and blew out the candle.

The moon shone brightly above in the blackish indigo sky, as she made her way back to the main house. Everything was so quiet as she crossed the grounds. Felicia had decided on these nights that she worked so late, she'd use the back entrance. She didn't want to disturb the servants who might feel obligated to ask her if she were in need of anything. As she approached the door, she could hear what sounded like voices coming from the garden.

Felicia walked quietly over to a hedge of wildflowers that bordered it, and the voices became louder. Once she reached them, she could tell it was a man and a woman--George and Fatimah.

Without making a sound, Felicia made her way back toward the house. Her mind only dwelt on the two young people sitting on the stone benches in the garden for a few moments. She wished them well. There were too many other things to think about: trehalose, Mauritania, Hassan and Na'im.

"You were wonderful with the children today, George. Have you ever thought of becoming a teacher?"

"Yes, I considered that at one time, but my father talked me out of it. He said I wouldn't make any money. So, I guess I let greed guide me instead of my conscious. Being a research scientist isn't bad, though. I get to do a lot of things that could help humanity as a whole."

Fatimah reminded George of the beautiful women he'd seen in National Geographic magazine as a child. He had never known anyone like her, and he was glad she'd accepted his invitation to meet him in the garden.

They had to wait until after dinner because she had to take care of several other duties. He had gobbled down the *sitt alnoubeh*, a sweet chicken stew with purslane and pastilles of aloe, and hurried to the appointed spot.

George had waited an abominable thirty minutes before Fatimah appeared between red and white blossoms that filled the garden hedge. She had already changed her *pagnes* before dinner, but this was the first time he had ever seen her long, waist length, dark brown hair undone.

Behind one ear, she wore a golden lotus flower hair ornament which set off her brown skin wonderfully.

George rose when he saw Fatimah. He was speechless as he gazed upon her beauty under the moonlight. She smiled at him, but this time it was not a timid smile. It was the smile of a woman who knew what she was doing.

Fatimah could tell that George was more than a little nervous as he rubbed his hand over his moonlit hair. Purposefully, she sat on the bench where he'd sat before rising to greet her. But having risen, he moved to the bench right beside it.

"My life has changed a lot since you and Felicia arrived. I see things a lot differently now."

"Do you think that's good or bad?"

"It is good in some ways and bad in others. It is good for the side of me that has always wanted her freedom, to do with my life as I please; to dream of more than living as a wife and a mother, where I am worth not more than the work or children I produce; growing physically old before my heart is ready. Even though I am the niece of Sheik Rahman, Na'im's family will not be able to protect me for long. But it is bad as well, because I am an Egyptian woman who will probably marry a man whose roots are deep in tradition. It is not the religion that causes the problem. Some of the customs intrinsic to this land would be my enemy, customs that in time smother the female so that she can no longer grow."

Fatimah inhaled the gentle scent of one of the flowers in the hedge behind them. "And so she withers, as this blossom that I have plucked from its place of nourishment will wither with time."

"But you're a teacher now. You're showing how valuable you can be to Karib and this community."

"How long do you think that will last if I marry a man like Ilyas? He will not want me to work. He will say my proper place is in the home, not out in the public taking care of the children of others, but taking care of my own."

"So it's decided, you will marry Ilyas?"

"It was something that was decided a long time ago, before I came to Sheik Rahman's house. My mother was the sheik's sister. I loved her and my father very much, but when she died from a sickness, my father remarried. His wife was my age, and she did not want me to live in their house. My father asked the sheik to take me in, and they moved away to another village. But before my father made me the sheik's ward, he told him he would not have to be responsible for me long, because I was promised to one of the villager's sons. Ilyas. I was young at the time, and did not think much of it. I only knew I was coming to live on the lovely Rahman estate and I was happy. I actually thought it was a compliment for a man to want me. And Ilyas is not a bad man. He is not. It wasn't until you came that I felt I might be making a mistake."

George reached over and touched Fatimah's face. The feel of her skin sent tingles through his fingertips.

"Fatimah, I would marry you tomorrow if you would have me, and if I had the means for taking care of you as I would like to."

"Material things do not make happiness. I believe with all my heart I would be happy with you, no matter what you have. What do I have now, George? Would it not be better to be at the mercy of the man you love than one you have just learned to tolerate?

George's soft, but firm lips descended upon Fatimah's.

This was the first time she had ever been really kissed. Involuntarily, her bountiful lips parted as she tried this new experience. Cautiously, George slipped his tongue inside, tentatively touching hers. Fatimah's large brown eyes flew open in surprise, but closed again as marvelous sensations began to surface inside her.

She placed her arms around George, and her hand brushed up the back of his neck to the silky hair at its nape. George's heart began to pound inside of him. He could tell all of this was new to her. So slowly, with passion held in check, he drew her completely into his arms.

"There's no way I'm going to lose you, Fatimah, now that I've found you. We'll work it out somehow."

The soft-spoken words were music to her ears, for she felt the same way too!

Chapter Twenty-Six

Felicia worked the first half of the day in the lab. The night before, she had felt she was close to finding a solution to the trehalose problem, so she had come in early to try and find the piece of the puzzle that would make the experiments successful. Her efforts were futile, however. She couldn't concentrate. Her mind was centered on the transaction that would take place at Afrah El Jabel that afternoon.

Fatimah had stopped by during the children's lunch break to wish her success. Felicia had never seen her look lovelier or more content. It was obvious that she loved George and he loved her. He had whistled the entire morning as he worked in the lab, waving a gallant goodbye to Felicia as he went to conduct some field tests.

She'd received word from Imam Jabar that he and the women would arrive about six that evening, so she had plenty of time to get there.

Borrowing the team's truck had posed no problem. She told the men she had some personal business to attend to, and she didn't need their help. She planned on parking the truck behind the American Consulate so as not to bring undue attention to herself.

Najid had promised that he and Ali would meet and help her. That was a blessing. She knew her Arabic had improved over the past month, but not enough to accomplish this feat alone. With Najid and Ali along, she could keep a really low profile, since she felt a man like Hassan might not be interested in doing business with a female.

Once again Felicia chose what she planned to wear with care. A simple plum *pagnes* would serve her purpose well. Najid had mentioned Afrah El Jabel was quite a "live" spot, and a woman dressed in a black *melayah* would seem out of place. She decided to keep her jeans on until she arrived at the oasis. Then she would change. Felicia had never seen an Egyptian woman from the villages driving a vehicle. A woman in traditional dress driving one would be very conspicuous.

The ride to Al Kharijah was long and hot, but it provided Felicia with plenty of time to think; something she was doing a lot of lately. It wouldn't be long before her stay at Karib was over. The time alloted for the project would end, and there would be no reason for her to stay in Egypt.

It was so hard for Felicia to picture her studio apartment back in Memphis, Tennessee. She had settled there during a research project for St. Jude Children's Hospital. Life in Memphis was simple and pleasant; nothing like the sights, sounds and smells of Egypt. And, of course, Memphis did not have Na'im.

Felicia pitied those tourists who traveled across the ocean only to see the Sphinx or the Great Pyramid. Yes, they were a part of Egypt, but she knew the magic of Egypt could be felt more through its people.

The streets of Al Kharijah were busy as usual. She remembered her first time visiting the oasis and how out of place she felt. Today her mind and eyes cherished the sights and sounds, branding the scenes in her heart as if this would be her last visit.

Najid had advised her to arrive after the representative had gone home for the day, thereby giving her access to his office as a dressing room. It was a comfort to see his smiling face, and once again she told him how grateful she was for his help.

"So much praise will make me grow in arrogance. We are all here to do Allah's will. And my Majidah says it must be the will of Allah for women and children to have homes, and a man, a woman and a family. This should be done without violence, but with compassion and love."

Najid's soft, brown eyes sparkled as they always did when he spoke of his wife.

"Ali has gone over to the place where the plane must land. I told him to come and inform us when the plane has arrived. I will go now. Maybe Hassan and his men have already come."

"What does Ali think of this?"

"He is a good son. He is a Mu'adin. He does not question his father," Najid said, as he left.

Najid returned before Felicia finished changing her clothes. He said Hassan had not arrived. He'd brought back several street snacks, saying Felicia should eat after her long ride. The two of them devoured the food in silence, washing it down with mint tea.

Felicia glanced at her watch and saw it was five forty-five. Najid suggested they go to Afrah El Jabel to wait for Ali and once again look for Hassan. At this time of evening the streets were a sea of people, so their progress across town was slow.

Finally, they approached a large, mud and brick

edifice that sat near the end of one of the main roads. Felicia assumed the Arabic writing scrawled across its top was Afrah El Jabel. She could hear the loud wailing music coming through the large, wooden double doors.

Another building sat next to this one, directly on the corner. It was obviously well kept, and had been painted with dusky red paint. Gold letters stood out boldly on it, bearing its name. Beneath the building's awning sat a massive woman, with eyes painted like an Egyptian idol. Felicia watched as a group of men, who stood between Afrah El Jabel and the red building, tried to make up their minds which building they should enter.

The woman was also looking at the men. Pulling her large frame up from the chair, she began to make her way majestically over to them. Felicia had never seen an Egyptian woman dressed like this one. More than a yard of material trailed from the back of her garment, edged by lots of fringes, leaving a sweeping pattern in the sand.

"I haven't seen anyone else with a dress like that," she remarked.

Felicia didn't catch the subtle change in Najid's expression as he answered.

"The dress is a custom of some of the women who live here in Egypt. It is designed to sweep away their footprints in order to make it difficult for *Schaitaan* to follow them. I think in your language you call him Satan. But a dress alone will not be able to keep him away from her. She is the mistress of the house of sin, *Ya Noor El Ein*, 'Light of My Eyes'."

Once she reached the men, the woman smiled seductively, running one well-kept hand down the side of a large breast, past her waist, to rest on a heavy hip. In no time at all, the woman had the men following her hulking gyrations inside the building.

So that is where Na'im goes when he wants the "cream of the crop" as he called it, Felicia mused. She smiled to herself as she and Najid turned to enter the dimly lit, noisy tavern. She took pleasure in the thought that the large, painted creature was Na'im's epitome of womanhood.

Felicia had thought the streets of Al Kharijah were crowded, but they were nothing compared to this. Sultry music pulsated loudly as she attempted to keep up with Najid.

From the moment she stepped through the door, she could tell the people who frequented this establishment were Al Kharijah's pleasure seekers. Hordes of men and women stood around, while the luckiest of the group were able to sit at the tables and chairs provided for them. A woman laughed lustily in Felicia's ears, as the man beside her grabbed one cheek of her hefty bottom through a skintight, floor length dress.

Occasionally Felicia could see Najid's short head between the people in front of her. Systematically, he would pause, giving her a chance to catch up.

"We are almost near the door to the back room now."

Felicia nodded her head in understanding before he started on his way again.

The sound of chair legs scraping against the wooden floor, followed by a crash and loud voices erupted to the right of her. Despite the lack of space, the crowd began pushing away from the area of the commotion, pinning Felicia's backside against a short, stocky man with horrible breath and a lascivious smile. Another man was caught between Najid and Felicia. Everyone's attention was centered on the disturbance now in front of them.

A very thin man with leathery dark skin seemed to be the focus of the uproar. He was holding onto a wooden chair that he had obviously snatched from beneath a burly fellow. The big guy was having a difficult time righting his generous body, as he shouted the closest thing to Arabic obscenities Felicia had ever heard.

There was something very cruel about the smaller man's face, which was shrouded by a white *keffiyeh.* He had a wildness about his eyes that Felicia had seen in the lab rats as they scurried around their cages as if running from death itself. A sneer crossed his narrow face at the fallen man's anger, and as quick as a blink, he'd produced a knife large enough to disembowel a large animal.

Several gasps rose from the women in the crowd as he made his way purposefully toward his prey. A soft-spoken voice stopped the man in mid stride. Then another man, equally as tall, stepped forward. He was impeccably dressed in a white *galabia* and head wrap. There was a remarkable resemblance between he and the man holding the blade, even though he was much older. There was also an air of submission about him.

The larger man breathed a sigh of relief as he got up on his feet. The elderly gentleman offered what Felicia assumed was an apology.

By this time, Najid had eased his way back through the crowd to her side.

"That is Sharif Hassan."

"My goodness. As violent as he is, I don't know if we're doing the right thing by bringing the women here."

"Hassan is not the angry one. He is the one who stopped his son, Abdul, from attacking the Berber."

Felicia looked at Hassan again. She had not expected this mild-mannered man to be the leader of a ring of men abducting women from their homes.

"I just can't picture that man doing anything cruel or aggressive. Even now he shows he is not a violent man."

"It is Abdul Hassan who is behind the abductions. After the sheik lost Abdul's mother, he lost his love for life. He no longer cared if he lived or died. He took no interest in what went on around him. Maybe now, with renewed life in his village, he will become himself again."

Abdul's eyes gleamed like a madman's while the sheik offered his apologies to the Berber. At first, it looked as if he was about to put the large knife away, but something changed his mind. He shouted several words at the sheik. His voice held contempt as he spoke to his father and spat at his feet. He began to wave the blade high over his head while pounding on his chest with his free hand. He mirrored a man out of control.

First he struck at the wooden table near him, causing the knife's shaft to stick in its surface. It took both of Abdul's hands to extract the weapon from the table's hold, giving the sheik enough time to draw his weapon, a small revolver.

The sheik's tone was calm but ominous when he spoke to his son. Felicia could hear that his voice revealed the sound of a warning. Obviously, everyone heard it except Abdul, who swung his blade with the intention of decapitating his father.

Felicia, along with the others, let out a blood-curdling scream. The screams were accompanied by the sound of a shot from the sheik's gun. The bullet pierced Abdul's temple, and he dropped to the floor–dead.

A pregnant silence followed. The sheik knelt down beside his son with tears flowing freely. He closed his son's eyes, looked up at the crowd and began to speak slowly and deliberately. His speech lasted only a few moments, and even though Felicia could not understand every word he said, she felt she understood the message. The sheik was apologizing for the grief his son had caused, and now his son was out of his misery.

Several men helped the sheik remove Abdul's body from the tavern. Najid followed them outside, pulling Felicia through the crowd, grabbing an abandoned chair as he went.

"You will be safer sitting near the door. That way you will be near if you are needed, but not in the middle of the transaction. Ali or I will let you know when the women come. Now I will go and talk to Hassan."

The music commenced again and the people went back to whatever they were doing before the trouble broke out. Felicia was shaken by the scene that had occurred only moments before. Somehow she felt responsible for what had happened to Abdul.

A few minutes later Najid emerged from the crowd, followed by Hassan and three other men, one of whom was Shabazz. He did not acknowledge Felicia's presence as they passed by and went into the back room.

It was hard for Felicia to see her watch in the faint light provided by what appeared to be oriental lanterns. She thought it read ten after six.

Ali had not returned, or at least she didn't think he had. She began to wish she knew what was going on inside. Najid had said he'd tell her when the women arrived. It was so hard for Felicia to sit and try to act normal, with all that had happened and what was supposed to take place on her mind. She felt apprehension building inside of her as her mind conjured up all kinds of images. What if the plane had crashed? What if Hassan had changed his mind after experiencing such an awful ordeal? What if the government officials decided to change their minds at the last minute and not let the women come?

Felicia's thoughts had taken her far away from what was going on inside the tavern. As she became aware of her surroundings again, the man with the lustful smile was standing by her side. She realized that looking up at him was a big mistake, because he construed it as an invitation to make conversation. Felicia met the man's words and gestures with the only thing she could–silence. He took that for acceptance. Getting down on his haunches, he slid a club-like arm around her shoulders, pulling her closer toward him.

Just at that moment, the door to the back room opened. Felicia slid from beneath the man's arm, hoping the man emerging from the back room was Ali. It had been such a long time since she'd seen him, and their encounter was so brief, she didn't quite know if the man was Ali. His face was averted, and she couldn't see it because of his headpiece. What if it were Shabazz instead of Ali? Her heart beat a fast tempo as she lifted her arm to tap him on the shoulder. Then he turned toward her...it was Ali. He clutched her hands enthusiastically.

"They are all here. Your friend Imam Jabar expected to see you at the airstrip, but I explained to him that we all thought it best that you remain here. I came back with them instead of going ahead so they would feel welcome and comfortable. My father was waiting for us outside the door in the rear of the building."

Felicia couldn't contain the excitement in her voice. "So what are they doing now?"

"One of the Mauritanian representatives is reading an official paper from his country."

"And the women, do they all look well taken care of? Are any of them sick?"

"Everyone is fine. Some of the children were crying

because they were afraid of the airplane. That is all. Once everything is taken care of and Hassan is ready to take the women to Falam, I will come for you so that you can talk with the Imam."

Ali disappeared back inside the door. Felicia was glad to see the bothersome man had left. She supposed she could thank Ali for that.

It wasn't long before Ali appeared again, beckoning Felicia to step inside. The bright sunlight coming through several windows was a harsh reality after the tavern's dark hues.

Imam Jabar was the only person remaining in the room. Outside, she could see Ali running to catch up with the group of women and the others.

"Felicia Sanders. It is good to see you again. Egyptian style dress becomes you."

Imam Jabar's smile was a flash of white in his ebony face. When Felicia had first met him, she'd thought she'd never seen anyone with skin so dark. It reminded her of an African statue she'd seen at Bayside in Miami, Florida. Smooth, shiny and black. Beautiful in its own right. A product of his Nubian heritage.

Imam Jabar's English was slurred by his native tongue, the tucolor language. Felicia remembered him saying once that he preferred speaking English to Arabic. He found it easier to pronounce.

She embraced the minute man. Funny how men so small in stature like the Imam and Najid could be so large in heart.

"It is so wonderful to see you. I don't know how to thank you enough for what you've done."

"It is our country and Hassan who should thank you for seeing a need, and taking the initiative to fill it. It is unfortunate, Felicia, that you are not claiming credit for this good deed. They think I am the one who is responsible."

"It doesn't matter who gets the credit. We'll always know we did it together. You, Najid, Fatimah and I. I just hope we did the right thing, with Abdul getting killed and all."

"Yes, that for sure is to be regretted. But hopefully, with time the pain and sorrow will go away and the sheik, along with the villagers of Falam, will be able to forget. The sheik has given his commitment to protecting the women and children with his life. He said they will have the best life his village can offer," the Imam reflected. "It is a shame, Felicia, that our visit must be so brief, but it is already time for me to head back to the plane."

"Let me come with you. It is fine now, everyone has gone."

Felicia accompanied Imam Jabar down the streets of Al Kharijah past villages and booths. Cafes dotted the colorful avenues, the aroma from their foods calling to all who came near. A rather large group of people had gathered at one of the more expensive establishments. The men's headpieces blew in the wind, resembling sails in motion on the sea.

"Could it be Anwar?" a masculine voice questioned with disbelief in its tone.

Imam Jabar turned when he heard his name, looking for the person who had spoken it. A well-built Egyptian with laughing eyes rose from his seat to single himself out from the crowd.

"It is I who have called you, Anwar. Ahmed."

"Ahmed! I cannot believe my eyes. It is you! Well, Allah be praised. It has been such a long time, my friend."

The two men embraced heartily, the tiny priest and his towering friend looking quite awkward.

"What brings you to Egypt? Why did you not tell me you were coming? I could have offered you the comfort of my home during your stay."

"Do not worry. My visit here has been a very brief one. I just arrived today and I am now on my way back to the plane to return to Mauritania. Felicia, I would like you to meet an old friend of mine, Ahmed. Felicia is the reason I am here. Because of her, your villages are now rid of a major threat to your homes. No longer will you be troubled with Hassan or his son. The poor fellow killed his son while defending his own life."

Looks and hushed words of shock passed between the entourage of people with the tall Egyptian.

"A group of women and children from my country in need of a home were transported today to Falam. I accompanied them, along with some government officials."

"Well, this is a surprise! I am so grateful to you, your country, and this young woman. You remember my wife, don't you? Yasmin?"

"How could I ever forget someone so beautiful, physically and otherwise. It is so good to see you both."

Felicia couldn't believe her luck. These people couldn't be Na'im's parents. But as she looked at the two of them, she had a sinking feeling they were.

"This is Felicia Sanders."

"Hello," Felicia managed to choke out.

"Felicia Sanders, my wife Yasmin."

"It is a pleasure to meet you. It is impossible for me to express to you how grateful I am personally for what you have done. My gratitude goes beyond words."

Gold eyes the color of Na'im's showered her with thanks as his mother addressed her.

"We must be on our way now. It is so good to have seen the two of you again. We must write each other, Ahmed. There are so many things we need to share."

The two men hugged once again. Jabar then took Yasmin's hand and said goodbye.

"Why did I get the feeling, Felicia, that you were not happy to meet my friends. Have I caused some problem for you?"

"No Imam Jabar. You have done nothing wrong."

There was no need to burst his bubble. They had accomplished what they had set out to do. Now she would have to face the music back at Karib once Na'im found out what she had done without his knowledge.

Chapter Twenty-Seven

The household was buzzing with activity when Felicia returned. Everyone was preparing for the sheik's arrival.

The ride back had given Felicia time to psyche herself up for anything Na'im might say. She told herself she had done the right thing; something that was good for everyone concerned, and if he didn't like it because she didn't consult him, it was just too bad. Now if only she could keep this vein of confidence flowing until she actually had to deal with Na'im.

Fatimah came out of Kareem's room, just as Felicia was passing on the way to her own.

"You are back. Did everything go okay?"

"Everything went perfectly. At least, almost perfect. The women should arrive in Falam at any time now, and hopefully they'll live happily ever after."

"Well, why do you not look happy, Felicia? It is a good thing that you have done. And now that we have received word that the sheik is in Al Kharijah, there will be cause for celebration."

"Yes, I know the sheik is in Al Kharijah, and that's the reason I don't feel so good. Can you believe I was introduced to the sheik as the person responsible for the whole thing?"

"Oh no! It is not true."

"Yes, it's true. It appears Imam Jabar and Ahmed, as he calls him, are old friends."

"Do not feel too bad. Maybe Na'im's anger will pass quickly once he finds out."

"Fatimah," a small, weak voice called from inside Kareem's bedroom.

"Is that Kareem? Is he sick?"

"I don't know what is wrong with him. Recently he has been having very bad dreams. After the one last night, he seems to have very little energy. He tried to do his work this morning, but one of the servants found him collapsed outside in the garden."

"Maybe it was the heat."

"Karib's heat is not a problem for one who has lived here all of his life. It cannot be so."

"Fatimah, is Felicia there?" Kareem managed with effort.

Felicia entered the small but adequately-furnished room.

"I'm here, Kareem."

Kareem had always been a thin boy, but tucked in under the sheet, his small body looked as if it belonged to a child no more than five years old. Felicia placed her hand to his forehead. His head was not even the slightest bit warm. It was almost cool to the touch.

"How do you feel? You're supposed to be running around pestering everyone while they prepare for the sheik's arrival," she quipped.

"I no feel good. I feel very tired."

Felicia looked up at Fatimah who still stood in the doorway. "Have you called a doctor?"

"He left not long ago. He said he could find nothing wrong with Kareem. He told him to stay in bed and rest, and then he left."

"Felicia, would you bring me one of the animals in the lab to keep me company?"

"Kareem, do not bother Felicia with such unimportant things."

"It's alright, Fatimah," Felicia assured her. "Which one of the animals would you like me to bring, Kareem?"

"The guinea pig with the black eye. He say he afraid to die. Like my mother. She say she afraid to die."

Felicia threw a questioning glance at Fatimah. "Your mother?"

"Kareem says his mother comes to him during his dreams."

"She come to me. I want to be with my mother. She is so beautiful in my dreams. Her voice is like the flutes in the oasis."

Fearfully, Fatimah warned Kareem against saying such things. "You must not speak of joining your mother, Kareem. It is dangerous to want to join the dead."

"My mother not dangerous. She is kind. She like helping others. She say I should help others too. Like Sheik Rahman."

"That is enough of that talk, Kareem. Be quiet now and rest until Felicia comes back with your animal."

Kareem's eyes closed with ease before Felicia could rise from her seat on his bed. Talking of his mother seemed to take a lot out of him. Felicia and Fatimah left Kareem's bedroom together.

It was dark before Felicia returned to the house with Kareem's companion. She had stayed in the lab a while, discussing the next day's scheduled activities with Phillip, William and George.

She lit an oil lamp upon entering the child's room, and placed the cage in a chair she pulled near his bedside. Felicia tucked the sheet around Kareem's narrow face. His breathing was extremely shallow against her hand.

"Kareem?" she called softly, trying to awaken him. She wanted him to know she had brought his pet. Felicia didn't want to admit his shallow breathing frightened her. By waking him, she would be reassured of his condition.

Kareem did not respond to Felicia's voice, nor to her gentle shakes.

"Kareem!" she shouted, panic in her voice.

"What is wrong, Felicia?" Na'im had entered Kareem's room without Felicia's knowledge.

"It's Kareem. He won't answer me. Thc doctor said he just needed to rest, but I know something else is wrong. He spoke of wanting to join his mother. His breath is so weak, Na'im. I'm afraid he's dying."

Na'im knelt and held Kareem's small hand in his. It was extremely cool, as if the warmth of life had almost left it.

"Na'im, I think we need to send for Aisha. There is something abnormal about this. A perfectly healthy little boy turns deathly ill in one day?!"

"Aisha?" Na'im repeated distractedly, his brows knitting together in concern over Kareem's condition.

"She is the woman I told you about who helped me after the accident. She lives in a very small village about three hours outside of Al Kharijah."

"The only village I know of that close to the oasis is Bada, a tiny little settlement where most of the villagers are elderly people. I will send for her tonight. Do you think she will come?"

"I believe she will if she knows she's really needed."

Chapter Twenty-Eight

Felicia awoke in Kareem's bedroom late the next morning. Fatimah was sitting across the bed from her in a chair, sipping cinnamon tea.

"When I came in to check on Kareem last night, I found you sleeping here. I was frightened because I could see he had become worse and I decided to stay."

"I guess I was more tired than I thought. Na'im is back. He is sending for a woman I met named Aisha. She knows about these kinds of things, and I believe if anyone can help Kareem, she can. I decided to wait with Kareem until she arrives."

"Yes, I met Na'im on his way to meet his father, and he told me about her. She has not come yet. I hope she comes soon."

"I'm sure his father will tell him about Hassan and the women that were brought to live in his village. But I told myself I'm not going to dwell on how Na'im will feel about me afterwards. Things haven't been going too well between us lately anyway, so I guess one more strike against me won't really matter."

"I am sure that will be discussed along with several

other things. I understand the sheik received an announcement from Waheedah's parents from Khartoum this morning. Actually, the letter arrived from a special messenger last night."

"Do you know what it said?"

"No. But I believe it has something to do with the proposed marriage of Na'im and Waheedah."

The thought of Na'im marrying Waheedah was like a bombshell. Even though Felicia knew their marriage had been prearranged by their parents, she had always dealt with it in the realm of possibilities. Now Fatimah's words brought it into the sphere of reality. The pain of it was too much to think about, so Felicia changed the subject.

"How are you and George coming along?"

Fatimah recognized Felicia's need to talk about something else. She didn't want to hurt her friend, but she didn't want her to be in the dark either.

"George is wonderful, Felicia. He brings me such joy. Last night he told me he would talk to the sheik this morning about us. But I told him to wait. There will be other business more pressing that the sheik will need to attend to first. George wants to marry me."

Felicia couldn't help but feel a little envious toward Fatimah in her happiness. Everything seemed to be working out the way she wanted it. She nor George cared about the differences in their backgrounds. They loved each other and that was all that mattered.

"What about Ilyas?"

"George wants me to tell him. He said that if I do not tell him, he will. I told him it is not wise to do so. Felicia, I know that Ilyas can be very violent, and it frightens me. I told George he should talk to the sheik first, and then I would tell Ilyas." A look of deep concern crossed her young features. "It was the only way to stop him from going to Ilyas. Ilyas would not dare harm anyone who had the sheik's blessings, no matter what the circumstances."

"Well, definitely, I think you did the right thing."

Felicia rose to her feet. "While you're here with Kareem, I'll go bathe and change my clothes. I have a very important meeting with the guys today. I can't believe how fast these five weeks have gone by. Before you know it, we will be leaving Karib. I'm going to miss you all, Fatimah."

"We will miss you as well, my friend."

Chapter Twenty-Nine

"You look well rested, my father. Your absence from Karib has been good for you."

"Yes, it has been good for me. But it is also good to be back, my son. I hear fortune has smiled on us."

"Things have gone well, yes. But you speak as if you talk of something in particular."

"You do not know, then? Women volunteers from Mauritania were brought to Al Kharijah to live in Falam. But in the midst of this, Sheik Hassan had to defend his life, which was threatened by his son. Now Abdul is dead."

"Is that true? How did this happen without my knowledge? And how do you, my father, know of this when you were only in Al Kharijah one day?"

"Do you remember my friend, Imam Anwar Jabbar of Mauritania? He visited us here at Karib nearly three years ago during a special festival. I saw him in Al Kharijah yesterday. He and a young woman, who I suppose must work with social matters in his country, were responsible for it."

"But how would they have known about the problem Falam faced unless someone here told them about it?

Maybe someone from the Egyptian government informed them. That is good and bad news, my father."

"Yes, it is. But you know that Allah in his mercy cannot always protect us from the karma that we ourselves have created. Your mother does not always agree with me on this. She says we are one with 'The One' if only we would allow ourselves to claim the power."

"Yes, that I know. But what karma do you now speak of?"

"There are two things. First, though I look healthier and feel better, I am not a well man. The doctors in Cairo say that I am quite ill. They say I will need blood transfusions from time to time, if I am to stay alive."

"Well, that should not cause you great concern. Blood transfusions are routine in the western world. It should not be difficult in a major city like Cairo."

"It is not a problem for the doctors in Cairo. It is a problem for me, Na'im. I have a rare blood type that they do not have. It would have to come from someone who is of blood kinship to me with the same type blood."

"Since I am your only surviving relative, it would have to be me."

"But you cannot help me, my son. We have already checked. We sent for your medical files while we were in Cairo. Your blood does not match. It is like your mother's. That is why it is so important for you to decide on the marriage I have arranged between you and Waheedah Farouk. I want to know you are married to an Egyptian woman who will strengthen our bloodline for generations to come before I die. It is also important because she has scheduled an *Awya* in two days. She and her family will arrive tomorrow with an entourage. I received an official announcement from her father this morning. He speaks of the shame his daughter faces because you have not claimed her. She feels performing the 'challenge dance', carrying on the traditions of our ancestors, is the only honorable way to force you into making a decision."

Na'im walked over to the window and gazed out over the wall that surrounded his home, into the village of Karib. The villagers had always looked to his father to guide them and protect them. In his absence, they would look to him for the same things.

"Don't worry, my father. After the challenge dance, I will make the right decision."

Chapter Thirty

"The problem is, we've developed a serum that will only be administered to less than one-fourth of the people who really need it."

During the entire project, Felicia had never seen William so emotional. Lines of frustration creased his forehead as he continued to speak.

"As a liquid, we found it simply evaporated when placed in extremely hot temperatures. As a tablet, the heat simply reduced it to a liquid and then it evaporated. The serum has to be kept at temperatures no higher than forty-five degrees Fahrenheit, and that means refrigerators or coolers of some sort would be a must. These people are not equipped for that."

"That's true," Phillip added, "but even if they were, electricity is a problem here. When the power is switched off in most of these smaller villages, the refrigerators wouldn't do them any good anyway."

"I know," Felicia stated, "I thought about all of this on my way over here this morning. Our problem has been trying to find a form of trehalose that would be easy for the people to use. My mind is full of everything that's happening now–the project, Kareem. He seems to be in limbo. A sort of coma, but a self-induced one. So I thought, what if we could reduce trehalose to a limbo state, freeze-dried state."

"Alright. What if we could?" George countered.

"I catch your drift, Filly," Phillip interjected, his eyes narrowing with understanding. "A freeze-dried state would mean there would be no liquid to evaporate, but the essence of the trehalose would be the same."

"That's right. Say it was freeze-dried into powder form; all that would be needed to activate it is a liquid of some kind, even saliva."

"Felicia," William said, slapping his clipboard, "I think you've got something there."

"Hey, well what are we waiting for?" an impetuous George edged them on. "Let's get started."

George and William patted Felicia on the shoulder, while Phillip gave her a meaningful hug. At that moment their appreciation and acceptance of her meant more than they could have imagined.

Later that afternoon, Fatimah brought word to Felicia that Aisha had arrived. She also announced that they were expected to attend dinner that evening in order to meet the sheik.

"Whoa, so the big cheese is back. It's good that we've just about completed our work. He might not have the same reason to welcome us as Na'im did," Phillip quipped, casting a meaningful glance in Felicia's direction.

"Well I've heard that the sheik's a pretty nice guy. I don't see any reason why he would want to throw us off his property," George countered, defending Fatimah's uncle.

"George, if you heard that from the person I think you did, I know you'd believe anything she told you," Felicia teased.

George blushed with embarrassment.

Well, I think we've done all we can do at the moment. Let's get ready for dinner. And remember, wear your finest, lady and gents,'' Phillip grinned, ''you'll be in the presence of semi-royalty.''

Felicia stopped by Kareem's room on her way to her own. She was glad she hadn't seen Na'im since last night. Somehow it made things easier.

Aisha was seated on the bed next to Kareem with her back turned. Her tiny frame appeared almost as small as the child's. Peaceful slate gray eyes turned to meet her as she entered the room.

''Felicia, my child.''

''It was so kind of you to come, Aisha. Just your presence seems to soothe me.''

''That is good for my heart to hear. But my presence does not seem to help the little one,'' she replied, looking down at Kareem.

''What do you think is wrong with him?''

''I know what is wrong with him, my child. But there is nothing I can do unless I can encourage his soul to want to remain here with us.''

''You mean he wants to die?''

''That is true. Do you know why?''

''All I know is he talked of joining his mother, who is dead, before he slipped into this coma-like state.''

''And that's what he has willed himself to do. His spirit lingers in the doorway between life and death.''

''Is that possible? Well, how do we call him back, Aisha?''

''We cannot. I must convince his mother that she

should encourage him to come back. I have done all I can to call his spirit back to this side. Did the boy speak of seeing his mother?"

"No. He seemed to communicate with her through his dreams."

"Then we must wait until tonight when his mother will be nearest to the portal through which he would join her. I will try to reach her then."

Aisha tilted her silver gray head to the side. "And how are you, my child?"

"Aisha, so many things have happened since the last time I saw you."

"We will talk. You determine the time."

Felicia hugged the small woman and replied, "I will."

The table was more elaborately set than Felicia had ever seen it. Silverware with golden handles lay beside china patterned with ancient Egyptian figures and hieroglyphics.

Felicia was the last to enter the dining room. She had dressed to perfection. A sky blue, floor length dress with a full skirt floated around her as she entered. To herself, she had commended Na'im for his taste in clothes when she saw herself in the mirror. The wide neckline was enticing, showing part of her smooth shoulders, but modest enough to show only a hint of bustline. The bodice resembled a leotard, form fitting and smooth.

She wore her braided hair away from her face. Massive curls tumbled down from the top of her head, and down the center, ending in a profusion of ebony loveliness below her shoulder blades. Large topaz earrings glowed brightly against her dark skin.

"Well done, my dear," Phillip whispered as she seated herself between he and William.

Sheik Rahman nodded his head in her direction and Na'im's mother did the same. Na'im, who was seated to the sheik's right, simply stared.

"I understand there is much that has happened here in my absence, my son."

"Yes, much indeed. These people are members of the science research team that I spoke of to you earlier."

"Yes, you did mention that. I did not know that you had such a strong interest in these things," the sheik said, looking at Felicia. "But after reading the letter we received from the Egyptian government, I commend you for taking advantage of the subsidies program. I believe it does promote international relations, as well as provide an opportunity for villages like ours to increase our economic position."

Turning to Felicia and the others, the sheik questioned them with just the right amount of politeness. "Have you had an opportunity to enjoy any of the sights of our country, or has your work occupied the majority of your time?"

"I was able to get out some, Sir, and so has Felicia," George answered, "but most of our time has been spent on our work."

"I see. So maybe you will find the festival to be held here day after tomorrow of interest. That is, if you can take time out to join us."

Phillip leaned forward, trying not to drop any of the *hummus*, or chick pea puree on his clothes. "What kind of festival is it, may I ask?"

"It is called *Awya*, an ancient custom among our people. It is a challenge dance."

Felicia's dark eyes flew to Fatimah's face and then to Na'im's. The challenge dance! So that's what the special announcement was about. Waheedah was challenging Na'im to make a decision about their marriage. Felicia suddenly felt as if she could hardly breathe. First she hears from the sheik that Na'im had not just offered them the use of facilities for their science project out of the kindness of his heart, and now this!

She took several sips of the warm minty concoction that sat near her plate in an attempt to regain her composure. Felicia's reaction was not lost on Na'im's mother, who sat at the opposite end of the table from the sheik. She'd studied Felicia from the moment she'd seated herself at the table.

"Did the young man say your name is Felicia?"

"Yes, he did."

"You look so familiar. Are you not the young woman who we met yesterday in Al Kharijah with Imam Jabbar?"

Felicia had not had time to recover from hearing about Waheedah's planned *Awya.* Now Na'im's mother had recognized her. There was nothing she could do but tell the truth.

"Yes. I did have the pleasure of meeting you and the sheik yesterday."

"Yasmin, you are right," the sheik confirmed.

"You mean Felicia is the young woman you spoke of, who helped arrange the transporting of women from Mauritania to Falam?" Na'im could barely conceal his astonishment.

The sheik regarded Na'im questioningly, as he heard the current of underlying emotions in his voice. "Yes, she is the one of whom I spoke."

Felicia didn't blink an eye as Na'im looked at her. She no longer cared how he felt about what she had done. He hadn't thought enough of her to even tell her about his government "deal" or to inform his parents about their relationship.

In meeting them at the table tonight, it was obvious that their interest in her was no more than they had in the other research team members. There Na'im sat so quietly while his father announced the challenge dance. She was glad she had something to throw back in his face; to hurt him just as he was hurting her by his silence.

From that point on, the conversation took a turn. The sheik and Yasmin showered Felicia with questions about the transaction and about Jabar. She answered them as best she could. It wasn't easy because Na'im's emblazoned eyes were glued to her face.

After dinner, everyone moved to the reception area. Phillip and the other research members soon excused themselves to work on the project. Felicia walked them to the door and told them she would join them shortly.

Na'im had situated his tall frame against a column that stood between Felicia and the adjoining room. Defiantly, she walked right past him without casting him a single glance.

"Felicia, I need to speak with you."

"You do? I can't imagine why. You didn't think enough of me to mention me to your parents."

"The time was not right."

"When will the time be right, Na'im? After you have married Waheedah and I'm back in the States. I don't know how I've allowed this to go as far as it has. I should have trusted my instincts, and not my body and you."

Standing arrow straight, his voice a hushed tone, Na'im countered Felicia's verbal assault.

"Trust? Felicia, do you really know the meaning of the word? You have never caught me in the arms of another woman, as I have you in the arms of another man. And now to find out that you did not respect my leadership enough to tell me of your plans with Jabar; something that had a great effect on the lives of my people."

"What would you do to punish me, Na'im? What I did was not wrong and I'm sorry if I have injured your pride. But from the way I see it, there were things more important at stake."

Yasmin entered the foyer just as Felicia turned to walk away. She could feel the tension between these two young people when she entered the room.

"Are you about to retire for the evening, Felicia?"

"No, I'm just going to my room to change. We've almost finished the project, so we'll be working pretty late in the lab tonight." Felicia's eyes were bright with emotion as she bid Na'im and his mother goodnight.

"So what are your plans tonight, my son," Yasmin asked when Felicia had gone.

"I may review some paperwork in the library. I have been in the field so often, things have piled up."

"Why don't you relax and take a walk with me in the garden. Your father is feeling tired and has already headed for the chamber. Besides, it has been such a long time since we have spent time together."

Na'im knew this was no casual offer. His mother was never one to waste words or time, so he agreed.

At first they walked in silence, letting their feet guide their way. Na'im noticed how flattering the moonlight was on his mother's strong features. The soft light seemed to melt away the years, making her the beauty she was as a younger woman.

"There is nothing like an Egyptian sky at night. The stars are limitless, bringing many small aspects of light to the darkness. It is like everything else in this world. There can be no light without darkness, and there can be no darkness without light. Nothing is perfect, my son. Even those we love must have flaws. So do we."

Na'im remained silent, nodding his head in compliance to let her know he understood.

"Your father wants you to do what he feels is best for Karib. Your father is a man of wisdom; that is why he was honored with the title of sheik many years ago. But he is no different from you. His wisdom flows from within just as yours flows from within. I believe a wise individual is capable of making the right choices for their own life. Your father is the past. You are the future. Without change there can be no progress; and remember, it is progress that your father truly seeks for Karib. The woman you choose as your wife should be strong and courageous in spirit, for it is from a man's spirit that strength is born."

Once again they stood in companionable silence. In the distance they could see a figure leaving the west end entrance, and crossing the grounds to the workers' quarters.

Felicia held her head high as she walked with a purposeful stride. They both watched her until she was no longer in sight.

"Let us return to the house now, my son. I think I am beginning to feel the effects of my travels with your father. Suddenly I feel very tired."

Chapter Thirty-One

Felicia returned to the main house in the early morning hours. Finally, they had devised a rough formula that would accomplish their goal. A few more tests would be necessary to refine it, but the foundation had already been laid.

Felicia pushed the stray papers that were trying to escape the manila folder under her arm back into place.

One of the servants had left an oil lamp burning for her in the kitchen. After closing the back door, she picked up the lamp to light her way. The entire house was engulfed in darkness, except for a shred of light coming from under the door of Kareem's room.

Felicia placed her ear to the door. Hearing nothing, she slowly opened it and stepped inside. Aisha, who had been sleeping in a large cushioned chair that had been brought in for her comfort, was awakened by the sound.

"How is he?"

"Better."

"Did his mother come?"

"She came. It was never her intention to call him over into the spirit realm. Though she wants him with her, she knows his purpose has not been completed on this side. He felt the great love that she has for him, and that is why he wanted to join her."

Had someone told Felicia two months ago she would believe in the things her experiences in Egypt had taught her, she would not have believed them. She realized how much she had changed since coming to this strange land.

"But why did she decide to contact him now?"

"Those who live in the spirit realm are not restricted by time and space as we are. Though we can tap into the universe with effort and practice, it is a regular part of their existence. Kareem's mother said there is something that Kareem must do. She will tell him once his life force is strong enough. Now he has just started to venture back to this side. By late tomorrow evening, he should be out of danger."

Felicia could see the slight movement of Kareem's small chest beneath the sheet. All they could do now was wait.

"You look tired. But I feel your work is not the real reason for your weariness."

"I just need to go home, Aisha. I do not belong here."

"One can belong wherever one chooses, if it is truly in their heart to do so."

"Well, maybe that's it. I thought, or at least I had hoped that I'd really found something special here. Now when I look back, I've been misleading myself."

"This something special is a man?"

"Yes," Felicia replied, sitting down on the edge of Kareem's bed close to Aisha.

"He does not feel the same way about you?"

"I don't know what he feels or thinks about me. We are so different. Because of his culture, his thoughts and beliefs are sometimes so distant from mine."

"There are no two people whose thoughts and beliefs are always the same."

"The sheik believes that an Egyptian man of status should marry an Egyptian woman of like social standing. The family of the woman he has chosen for his son agrees. So she has scheduled an *Awya* on the day after tomorrow."

"A challenge dance," Aisha's eyes twinkled with amusement. "During your encounter with the `breath of life' you spoke of dance many times. You have a natural love for it?"

"Yes. Maybe I should have become a dancer, and then I never would have ended up here in Egypt in this predicament."

"Nonsense, my child. Because you are one with 'The One', you chose this path, and it will be up to you to get what you want from it. Why do you not challenge the challenger?"

"What? Challenge the challenger?"

"Is this not a challenge dance? Then it is also appropriate for any woman to challenge the union of the woman and the man who is being challenged; to challenge the challenger."

"So I can challenge Waheedah?"

Aisha nodded.

Felicia could feel her heart palpitating. "But why should I? I'm not an Egyptian."

"If you feel this man has feelings for you, you should show your feelings for him in the way of his people. Your life force is strong, Felicia. You have great power because of your closeness with 'The One'. Think on it. Your decision will be right only if it reflects an alignment of the mind, the body, the spirit and the heart."

Before leaving, Felicia promised to consider Aisha's idea.

▲

Felicia could hear the servants stirring, and the sun had begun its ascent in the sky before she got to bed. She was awakened that afternoon by an elated Fatimah, who was so agitated she couldn't sit down.

Felicia was so exhausted when she finally tumbled into bed earlier that morning that she hadn't even bothered to change her clothes. The long shirt she'd worn with her jeans the previous day was wrinkled, and her waist had semi-permanent creases where the jeans had cut into her skin.

Fatimah paced excitedly back and forth, mumbling something about George. "He's doing it now."

"He's doing what now?" Felicia moaned, as she dragged herself to the bathroom.

"George is telling Sheik Rahman that he wants to marry me."

"Oh. I see," Felicia replied, not nearly as excited as her friend.

"Isn't it wonderful? Everything is working out just perfectly. Even little Kareem opened his eyes this morning."

"I am glad things are working out for the two of you, Fatimah."

Felicia's remark was sincere, but it lacked the sound of joy that Fatimah was expecting. Then she thought of the sheik's announcement the previous evening concerning the *Awya* scheduled by Waheedah.

"It is so selfish of me to talk this way when you are not happy. In my joy, I simply was not thinking. You know I would do anything for you, Felicia, if I could help change things. I truly believe you would make a better wife for Na'im than Waheedah."

Felicia smiled warmly at her friend, as she walked over to hug her. "You're a very special person, Fatimah. You deserve nothing but the best of everything, and that is what I wish for you."

She turned to walk away, then stopped mid step. "Wait, there is something you can do for me. You can help me design a costume for the *Awya*. Two can play this game. I'm going to challenge Waheedah tomorrow night during the festival."

"You are? There has not been a female challenger to an *Awya* that I have known of in many, many years."

"Well, you'll just help me make history, honey. So close your mouth and start telling me exactly what's going to happen. And we'll take it from there."

Fatimah sat on Felicia's bed while she bathed, describing the two *Awya's* she'd actually seen with her own eyes, and a third described to her by her mother.

An *Awya* was quite a ritualistic affair, embracing many beliefs from the ancient ones. She rubbed the goose pimples that had appeared on her arms as she told Felicia about the ceremonies.

Fatimah's story was interrupted by a servant, who was sent by Sheik Rahman to summon her. The goose pimples began to resurface as she approached the door to the sheik's study.

She entered the medium-sized room and bowed at the waist to the sheik, who was reclining on a burnt orange divan. George was seated in an armchair facing the sheik.

"*As-Salam-Alaikoum*," Sheik Rahman greeted her, motioning for her to sit on a cushioned stool near his feet.

"*Alaikoum-Salam*."

Fatimah's voice was so soft, she couldn't believe only moments ago she had been animatedly describing *Awya* ceremonies to Felicia.

"I hear from this young man of your desire to marry?"

"This is true, Rahman."

"Fatimah, I realize I have not expressed it well over the past years, but I am very concerned about your happiness. I have tried to raise you in the manner I would raise a daughter of my own. Therefore, I was always of the impression that you would marry an Egyptian. As a matter of fact, your father had already arranged that you should marry Ilyas. That is one of the reasons he was given the position of overseer here on the estate. It was not that he is such an outstanding worker, but I wanted to make sure you were well provided for."

"I am grateful to you for such favor, Rahman."

"That is why I do not understand this sudden change of mind to marry a foreigner. Forgive me, Mr. Mercer, but I must be frank."

"It is very simple, Rahman. I love George. I do not love Ilyas."

"But love is not everything, my child. You are accustomed to an Egyptian way of life. I do feel you are not prepared for a life other than that as a mother and wife of one of your own kind."

"This may have been so until recently, Rahman. In your absence, my life has changed much. I have organized and opened a school for the workers' children. I have found self-respect that flows from more than the knowledge that I am a woman who should be glad that a man would have her. You yourself, Rahman, have said many times that Karib must progress. Karib is its people. I am Karib, Rahman, and I have grown. This man has been good to me, and I know in my heart he will continue to be, if given the chance."

Hearing the sheik's opposition to their proposed marriage, George could not let Fatimah fight the battle alone.

"I want nothing but the best for Fatimah. If you think

it is best that she stay here in Karib and live, I will make my life here as well.''

''A wife's place is with her husband. It should be the place of his choosing, not her's, or her parents or guardian. I will give you my decision after the *Awya*. Now if you will leave me, I will think about all of this.''

Once they arrived at the front doors, Fatimah impulsively pecked George on the lips. Pushing the door open, he smiled his goodbye, almost stumbling over the luggage stacked before him. George caught himself just before he fell into none other than Ilyas, who was standing with another bag in his hands. The two men locked eyes. Ilyas looked up at Fatimah, but he would not move. He continued to block George's way.

''Ilyas,'' a syrupy female voice called, then instructed him to tell his men there were more bags to be carried. Grudgingly, he placed the bag he was holding on the ground and went back to direct his workers.

Felicia had watched from the window as the four white Mercedes Benz' drove into the yard of the estate. There was no doubt in her mind who they carried. As if on cue, the front door on the driver's side of each car opened at the same time. Out of each stepped statuesque Nubian men dressed in identical white pant suits.

One after another, they opened the passenger doors of their vehicles for the entourage until the front yard of the estate was a collage of beautiful fabrics blowing in the wind, each one appearing more fabulous than the other. But, of course, Waheedah's was the most exotic of them all.

Flowing green and gold material hung from the bottom of her turban-like headpiece, the exact length as her dress, which was an olive green with gold motifs.

The entourage consisted of ten people, excluding the drivers. Two women busied themselves unnecessarily, making sure Waheedah's every whim was executed in the style and manner to which she had become accustomed.

There were Waheedah's parents–her father was quite rotund and short, while her mother was as thin as a reed–and a man and woman who were obviously their attendants. Three young men, who were dressed in some of the most colorful *galabias* Felicia had ever seen, were the last to emerge.

Ilyas and two of the workers had expected the cars, and proceeded to unload the luggage as soon as they arrived. They received no assistance from the chauffeurs of the three vehicles, who stood staunchly, staring in the opposite direction of the cars.

Felicia had no idea how long Waheedah and her family planned to stay in Karib, but she gathered from the amount of luggage they brought, it had to be for an extended period of time. She watched as the pile of luggage grew in front of the wooden double doors.

Waheedah waved her arms vehemently, pointing to the luggage that blocked their passage into the house. One of the workers scurried to remove the obstruction, allowing the procession entry.

Felicia stepped back from the curtained window. She knew neither Waheedah nor her family thought Na'im would reject the marriage. Logically, she agreed with them, but deep in her heart she hoped they were wrong. She had not seen Na'im at all today. Her day had begun so late, he was probably taking care of whatever duties needed his attention.

Anyone in their right mind would have had second thoughts about challenging the Faruuks. They were a powerful force in Cairo, and therefore in Egypt. Felicia was no exception. Seeing them in all their splendor made her know what she would be up against the following night. But it didn't change her mind.

Sheik Rahman and Yasmin received the Faruuks in a south side room, whose cream-colored walls were a continuous succession of open arches divided by sky blue columns.

The floor was covered with a rich gold, bronze and black Turkish rug. The furniture consisted of several armchairs patterned in white, gold and blue, along with a solid white couch. All of the furniture was trimmed in gold. The room lent a feeling of being inside, yet outside at the same time.

The greeting between the Rahmans and the Faruuks was very formal. The sheik, beseeching them to treat his home as their own, offered them the customary drink of mint tea. Had their meeting been on more amiable terms, as the preparation for Na'im and Waheedah's marriage ceremony, the atmosphere would have been much less restrained. An *Awya* was another situation altogether.

Jamal (Jah-mahl) Faruuk inquired if the sheik had already started preparations for the ceremony.

"The entire household and sheikdom have been made aware. Food and the necessary ritualistic objects are being brought into readiness."

It didn't matter that Waheedah had initiated the festivity. According to the ancient custom, the male's family was responsible for providing these things. None of this would be necessary if he had already claimed his bride-to-be.

"I understand that in addition to the shame this *Awya*

has already brought us,'' Faruuk continued, ''your son is keeping a woman of foreign descent under your roof.''

Taken by surprise, the sheik denied the accusation. ''I am not aware of this if it is so.''

Waheedah smiled inwardly at the sheik's apparent discomfort. It also pleased her to know that Na'im had not gone so far as to tell his parents about his American distraction.

''Are you saying you are not aware of what goes on in your own home? Perhaps we are making a mistake in trying to bring about a union between my daughter and your son.''

''Mister Faruuk,'' Yasmin interjected, ''we can assure you we are knowledgeable about the activities in our household. For many years now, the west wing has been considered Na'im's own domain. We do not enter it without his permission, nor do we interfere with what he chooses to do there. Should it not be with a man who will soon be making decisions for an entire sheikdom? Should he not make decisions about his own home?''

Yasmin's mind flashed back to the night when she had seen Felicia leave the west wing and head toward the lab. She had not mentioned to her husband that the young woman was residing there, nor had she questioned Na'im about it.

''I demand that she be removed,'' Waheedah pouted. ''It is inappropriate, and I am sure room can be found for her in another part of your home, which is so expansive.''

''Let me assure you, my wife and I want to do everything we can to make you comfortable as guests in our home, but as my wife just mentioned, we have no jurisdiction over the west wing.

''Then Na'im must be asked to remove her.''

The sheik, who was tiring of this charade, put out both his hands in a gesture of helplessness.

"But surely you know, Faruuk, that Na'im is in a day's solitude, as it has always been during the hours before *Awya*."

Faruuk mumbled, "This is true," glancing at a disgruntled Waheedah.

"I understand the research project will be over by the end of the week," Yasmin added in consolation, "so whatever discomfort your family might feel now will be short-lived. Are you otherwise pleased with your living quarters?"

"We have not seen them. But one of my servants informed me that my bedroom is much smaller than I am accustomed to. I hope I will not become claustrophobic."

This time even Waheedah's parents looked a little embarrassed over her attitude.

"We hope that will not happen." The sheik's nerves were frayed to the end. He was not feeling well at all after this exchange, and was glad when the Faruuks decided to take their meals in their rooms and rest for the remainder of the evening.

No sooner had the Faruuks departed than a visually-distraught Fatimah appeared under the entrance arch. Her hands were clinching and unclinching the sides of the skirt to her *pagnes*.

"There is something dreadfully wrong with Kareem, Rahman. He's highly excitable and he says he will not eat a thing until you come to him. I know he is nothing more than a worker's child, but he has already had such a bad time. Aisha says his body cannot stand any more strain. Do you think you can find the time to see him for a few moments?"

"Nonsense. You know Kareem is more than a worker's child. He is like a member of the family. Tell him I will be in to see him directly."

A sigh of relief escaped Fatimah's lips as she turned back into the hallway.

"Fatimah," the sheik's voice halted her in mid step, "who is this Aisha?"

"Felicia told us about her. She is a very wise woman. Very powerful. I do believe had it not been for her, Kareem would not be alive today."

"Very well, I am on my way."

"I will come with you, my husband."

A wide-eyed Kareem with flushed cheeks greeted Sheik Rahman and Yasmin. Aisha, whose chair had been moved further into a corner of the room, nodded her head respectfully as they entered.

"You are Aisha." It was more a statement from the sheik than a question.

"I am."

"We are grateful for what you have done for Kareem."

"It was Kareem who decided to stay here with us. His will is very much one with 'The One'.

Yasmin's eyes lit up with understanding as she listened to Aisha speak.

"So you are also a believer in 'The One', my child?" Aisha asked, looking at Yasmin.

"For as long as I can remember, I have been."

"My mother is a believer in 'The One'." Kareem's large eyes looked down at his hands folded in front of him.

"She was," Yasmin echoed, "but how do you know that Kareem?"

"She tell me so. And she tell me other things too."

The sheik and Yasmin looked from the boy to Aisha,

not knowing what to make of such strange comments from such a young child.

"Kareem has had a very spiritual experience. I was with him, and he speaks the truth."

Kareem felt more confident as he heard Aisha confirm his statement.

"She tell me I can help Sheik Rahman. I am the only one. She say you very sick and I am one who have what you need. She tell me you do not know this and I must tell you. She say it very important."

Sweat broke out on the sheik's brow as he realized what Kareem was saying. Yasmin stood as still as stone. They had told no one of the sheik's illness but Na'im. There was no way Kareem could have known.

Kareem's unnatural message from his deceased mother also revealed that Kareem was the sheik's son and Na'im's brother.

Chapter Thirty-Two

Only once in his lifetime had Na'im heard the repetitious clanging of cymbals signaling the beginning of *Awya.*

He was only five years old the first time, and the cymbals that rang out from the village woke him out of his sleep. His mother had come to his room and explained the custom of the continuous cymbals.

Twelve sets of cymbals were strategically placed throughout the town in households with women of marrying age, but who were not wed. At the appointed hour, one cymbal after another would be struck in succession, symbolizing the protest of all women against men who did not honor a prearranged marriage in a timely manner.

As a child, he'd thought the festival was one of the most exciting days of his life, with the strange customs and the dancing and singing. The entire village seemed to participate with an air of expectancy. He also remembered his disappointment at being sent to bed before the main event began.

He'd heard many stories since then about the *Awya.* The men spoke of it with apprehension, while the women considered it a just means to an end–matrimony.

His mind reflected on Hambir (Hahm-beer), the eldest village councilman, who was chosen to prepare him for solitude. Normally it would have been his father, Sheik Rahman, administering the rights, but because he was the sheik's son, the duty was passed down the line of authority.

First he was instructed to dress in a plain black *galabia.* After that, he was escorted to the village masjid. The Imam led him to the back of the large structure, where they climbed two sets of stairs before approaching a heavy wooden door with a sizeable lock.

Behind them several villagers carried various objects, including a large trunk decorated with intricate carvings. No women were allowed to accompany the group, because a man who was facing *Awya* could not behold a female for twenty-four hours prior to the ceremony.

Na'im could tell the door had not been opened for quite a long time. It took great effort for the Imam and Hambir, who were both elderly, to force it open because of its rusted hinges.

After the villagers had put down the articles they carried, they left with the Imam, leaving Na'im alone with Hambir.

Hambir was dressed in a red ceremonial *galabia.* The ends of his headpiece touched his waistline. It was held snugly on his head by a braided cord of black, gold and red.

Hambir removed a large key from the folds of the clothing he wore. Kneeling on both knees, he bent forward placing his forehead on the top of the trunk. Then he opened it.

In silence, he removed a tiny tasseled cushion, a burgundy book with gold-trimmed pages, an exotic oil lamp carved with numerous poses of nude women, whose base was pure gold, and a package neatly sealed in a square cloth.

Turning to Na'im after placing the cushion under his knees, Hambir opened the book to a page pre-chosen by a silk bookmark.

"Kneel directly in front of me, Na'im Raoul Rahman."

Na'im did as he was told.

Hambir began to recite. "This passage is not for the ears of those with peace of mind. If you are the one chosen to hear this passage or any other, reply *Awya*."

"*Awya*."

"Tonight's vigil and tomorrow should not be looked upon as punishment, but as an aid to one who has shown not the ability to honor the decision of his sire." Hambir waited for Na'im's reply.

"*Awya*."

"The black *galabia* you wear symbolizes the darkness that clouds your mind, inhibiting you from taking Waheedah Faruuk as your wife. As you clean this room with what has been provided for you, you will also wash away the confusion that now blankets your mind."

"*Awya*."

"Only after you have completed your task will you bathe your body and don the purple ceremonial robe. The purple will help magnify your ability to look inward, so that you can know your true mind."

On and on Hambir read, until he replaced the bookmark at the place where he had begun more than thirty minutes earlier. Once he was done, he did not speak again, nor did he look at Na'im. Hambir replaced the book inside the trunk and closed the lid.

Next he unwrapped the white parcel. It contained one purple and one gold ceremonial gown, along with a mask and a golden chalice. He laid them all out on top of the trunk. Picking up the lamp, he placed it on a stone-carved table. Then he left, without a second glance.

It had taken Na'im over an hour to clean the dust-filled room. The blanket on the makeshift bed was covered with it and so was the furniture.

Na'im used a wooden chair to climb up to the high windows in order to open them. The more he cleaned, the more the dust filled the air, until it was hard for him to breathe. He could hear the cymbals through the open windows.

He thought how different Karib was from Van Nuys, California, where he'd stayed for a short time while in the United States. The mystery of the *Awya* would be lost there. Karib had no air conditioners, so the villagers' windows were constantly open, covered only by mosquito net to keep the pests outside of their homes. There would be no way to hear the cymbals in Van Nuys.

Na'im knew it was after midnight. Midnight was the appointed hour the cymbals began.

Hambir had told him during the "opening of the mind" that pita bread and the drink of *Ya Natir*, The One Who Waits, would be brought to him and left outside the door. He waited, listening for the approach of footsteps outside the door for an indeterminable time. He never heard the footsteps. The door was probably too heavy for that. Finally, he heard a rapid chain of knocks and the key turning in the lock. The great door opened wide enough for a tray to be pushed inside, and then it was closed.

Na'im sat on the bed with his back against the wall. He had not eaten since the day before. That, too, was preparation for the ceremony later that evening. His father had told him to eat well. It would be his last full meal before the ceremony.

Na'im could see the new moon through the arch-shaped window as he chewed pensively on the bread and drank the poignant liquid.

Hambir had read that *Ya Nati*r contained many powerful ingredients, including "the sacred man root."

"It will be brought to you three times before the ceremony. Through it, the torture of the body will become one with the confusion of the mind. No man can drink of *Ya Natir* without evolution."

As Na'im drank, he thought of his roots, his people. There was a part of him that had wanted to rebel against this antiquated means Waheedah had chosen to force him into making a decision. But Na'im was a true Karibian, one who respected his ancestors and their wisdom. He could not suddenly refuse their ways. Change would come among his people. But it would be subtle and in a way that everyone could accept.

Chapter Thirty-Three

A groan broke from Felicia's lips as she straightened her back. Circling her head around in yogic fashion, she tried to release the tightness in her neck and shoulders.

Fatimah's nimble fingers continued to work, sewing bead after bead onto the iridescent material.

The two young women had talked for a brief moment before dinner. Both had wracked their brains about the perfect dance costume for Felicia to wear. Looking in her closet, Felicia's frustration mounted. There was nothing she could do to alter any of the clothes she saw there. None of the material conveyed the image she wanted to project, so her resources were limited.

Later, when Fatimah had returned to Felicia's room, she was as fidgety as a child. Then she told Felicia she had something to show her. Taking one of the oil lamps, Fatimah led Felicia outside the house, only to reenter the east wing entrance–the exclusive wing of Sheik Rahman and Yasmin.

Apprehension rose inside Felicia as they entered the hallway and scampered into the second door to their right. The small lamp barely illuminated the large room, casting frightful shadows.

Felicia hesitated at the doorway, but soon followed Fatimah, who was feeling for something behind a heavy set of curtains. Then a tiny click resounded throughout the room. Fatimah had located the door she was looking for. After unlocking it, the two women stepped inside onto a stairway platform. They began to descend the stairs with caution.

"There is another way to come here, but the entrance is far out inside the stables. It is very busy there now. Some of the animals will be used during *Awya.*"

"Where are we, in the basement or cellar?"

"It is actually a large tunnel. Na'im's grandfather built the estate. There was much unrest during that time. Many were seeking power. He built it in case his family needed to escape. At the time, there was no wall surrounding the grounds. Once they reached the stables, there was a good chance of getting away."

"How did you find out about it?"

"While playing in the stable, Na'im and I found the trap door. We called it our passage to the underworld. We used to play here quite often until we were caught and forbidden to come here."

The humidity in the tunnel was heavy; nothing like the air above ground. Felicia had always pictured underground tunnels with rats and bugs of all sorts. Up to the moment, she had not seen any here.

"I wonder if your granduncle ever had to use it."

"I believe he did. And that is why we are here now. Once we pass the next curve, there is a space large enough for a room. It is located in the center of the tunnel between the two openings. As children, Na'im and I considered it our personal treasure room. We took a vow of secrecy not to tell anyone, not even our parents. To this day, I have told no one. I don't know about Na'im. After we got older, Na'im and I no longer played together. I only came to the estate with my mother to visit. I had forgotten about it until today."

What Felicia saw when she rounded the corner was quite a disappointment. To children it may have been a treasure room, but to their adult eyes it was far from that.

There were a few canvas-like bags piled closely together, and because of the years that had passed, they fell apart with the slightest touch from Felicia's hands.

"Well, I guess anything we might have used from these bags has rotted just like they have," Felicia remarked, trying not to sound too disheartened.

"I knew we could not use the clothing that is in the bags, but there may be something else we can salvage."

Fatimah set the oil lamp down on the ground and removed a file from inside her dress. Taking both hands, she began to dismantle the pile of bags. Beneath them lay a large metal case made of heavy copper.

"Felicia, this is what we came for. I do not believe there is anything of great value here or my granduncle would never have left it . Those sacks were full of plain *pagnes* and *melayas*, perhaps for my grandaunt and her servants. This case may have been her's as well. Once Na'im tried to open it with a stone," Fatimah said, pointing to several dents in the rusted lock.

Fatimah struck the lock several times with the metal file. Because of its age, it gave way. It took both of the women to open the lid and lay it back against the wall of the tunnel.

A canvas bag like the ones that were now scattered about lay flat over the contents of the case. Fatimah removed it. In the left hand corner of the case lay several *pagnes* of quality, but the fabric was not what Fatimah or Felicia had in mind. At the bottom of the stack they found a bundle wrapped in goat skin.

"Allah be praised," Fatimah expressed with amazement. Inside lay the most remarkable material Felicia had ever seen. It looked like spun gold and felt metallic to the touch.

Fatimah lifted it out of its wrapping and found it to still be strong and viable. Evidently, the moisture in the tunnel was not able to penetrate the metal, even after all these years.

"This is so beautiful," Felicia remarked breathlessly. "It looks like a dress that was never finished."

"I think you are right. Here are more pieces of the same material that is uncut."

Fatimah held the material against Felicia's dark skin. The contrast of brown and gold was stunning.

"Now this is the material for your costume," Fatimah said with conviction.

Felicia wholeheartedly agreed.

They also found some hair ornaments that were unique, and a small brass container with ornamental beads inside. Several strings that Fatimah said were from a camel's tail were also inside the container. It was evident the beads were intended to be strung into a necklace or a bracelet, using the camel hair as the cord.

It was hard for Felicia to believe her good fortune. Before, life had consisted of only what she could see and touch, and what could be explained through the many branches of the scientific realm. Meeting Aisha had helped to change that. Her beliefs were far from scientific, but they had worked for Aunt Esme, for herself and for Kareem. And now this. For over three generations, this metal case had rested here unopened, as if waiting for the precise time when she would need its contents. Could it be coincidence, or was Aisha right again, that her will was actually one with 'The One'?

Fatimah looked at her friend. "Let us wrap the material and beads and take them with us."

"Alright." Felicia's thoughts at that moment were so profound, that was all she could manage to say.

They did not bother putting the bags on top of the case before making their way back to the hidden door. Fatimah cracked the door before opening it. The room was silent, clearing the way for them to leave the east wing and make it back to Felicia's room undiscovered.

Felicia walked over to one of the bedroom windows, stretching all the way.

"You know, it's funny, I haven't seen Na'im all day. I know I've spent the majority of the day here in my room, but I thought I would have heard something from him." Wistfully she added, "Maybe my challenging Waheedah won't do me any good."

"It is not you, Felicia, that keeps him away. He has been placed in solitude. It is one of the customs of *Awya.* He will not be seen by anyone except the keepers before the ceremony begins. There is something you must do as well. You must find someone to present you when the time comes. I cannot because I am a blood relative of Na'im's."

"Then I will ask Aisha."

"Good. Now we must hurry with the beading. You will need to be well rested for tomorrow."

In the distance Felicia could hear a vaguely familiar noise, followed by another and another, until the clear sound of cymbals was heard coming from somewhere on the estate grounds.

"Were those cymbals I just heard?"

"Yes. The day of *Awya* has begun."

Chapter Thirty-Four

It was nearly two in the morning when Fatimah and Felicia finished her costume. Felicia was exhausted, but it was hard for her to sleep. She awakened early that morning. The excitement and the enigma surrounding *Awya* seemed to dominate her sleeping and waking hours.

Her dreams were filled with the clashing of cymbals. She could see herself twirling around and around like a ballerina doll in a jewelry box. She knew she had slept, but she didn't feel rested.

Feeling the need to talk with someone, Felicia threw on a top and her jeans. She thought she would stop by Fatimah's room for a few moments to bolster her confidence and calm her nerves. Surprisingly enough, she was met by Fatimah who was approaching her bedroom door.

"Good morning, Fatimah. I was on my way to find you. I'm so nervous, I don't know what I'm going to do."

"I think this is natural. So do not worry. I myself am rather afraid this morning. Someone has told Ilyas that George has asked the sheik for my hand in marriage. I believe it was one of the servants. I could hear him talking loudly as I reached the kitchen this morning. When I entered, there was silence. I have seen Ilyas angry before, but never like this. His eyes were like black coals when he questioned me. I thought of George, but I could not deny it. This is not good, Felicia. As you will see, my people's emotions are very high during festivals like *Awya.* I must go and warn George to stay away from Ilyas until the sheik has given his permission. Then Ilyas would be prohibited by law from harming him. George will not like this, I know."

"Yes, I think you better warn George. So much is going on now." Felicia could tell that Fatimah was shaken by whatever Ilyas had said to her, and she felt a little guilty for her calm reaction. "I suppose it seems like I can only think about myself, Fatimah, but you know I'm just as concerned as you are."

"Yes, I know you are," Fatimah smiled apprehensively. Oh–I just left Aisha. She is looking forward to seeing you this morning. She remains in the room with Kareem. You should go right away and talk to her. She also has something for you. I will meet you in your room, later."

Felicia gave Fatimah an encouraging squeeze of the shoulder as they both left the room. Fatimah disappeared out of the west wing entrance, while Felicia continued further down the hall into the interior. As she passed the front foyer, one of the servants was holding the door open, while another threw shredded lotus petals inside and outside the entrance. She also noticed the women were dressed in white *melayas* instead of the customary black ones Felicia was used to seeing.

Roasting spits were being set up inside the wall near the west end of the grounds. Several servants were skewering a goat and mounting it over one of four pits. Smoke billowed from piles of damp wood, while fish from the Nile was placed above it and enclosed in mini-canvas tents.

Felicia could see a large platform being erected in the distance. The faint melodic voices of some of the workers flowed on the wind, reflecting their anticipation of things to come. Felicia, too, could feel the excitement, and tremors of expectation ran through her.

Aisha was alone when Felicia entered the room. It had been rearranged to accommodate the small guest. The sheik had offered Aisha a separate room, but she had refused, stating the length of her stay at that point did not merit it.

Aisha had wound her extremely long braid in a coil on top of her head. To Felicia it looked like a crown of twisted silver. Her armchair had been replaced with a twin-sized bed, and a table with two chairs occupied the only available space that was left. There, in one of the chairs, Aisha sat waiting for Felicia.

"Come and sit, my child. I am told that you and Fatimah worked until the early morning hours on your dress for *Awya*. So, it is correct to assume it was hard for you to sleep?"

"Yes. It was."

"That is why I invited you to visit with me this morning. From my own herbs, I have prepared a special elixir to calm your nerves, as well as strengthen you for the event to come."

Aisha placed a tiny cheesecloth-type pouch, tied with string, into the ceramic cup in front of Felicia. A scent similar to apples wafted up to Felicia's nostrils, and she inhaled deeply the pleasant fragrance.

"Camomile has been used by my ancestors for centuries. They thought it so precious, it was dedicated to 'Ra', the god of the sun. I have also added a touch of ginseng from the Orient. It is the ginseng that will give you endurance."

"You sound like I'm going to run the Boston marathon." Out of nervousness, Felicia attempted to lighten the mood. "I admit I'm somewhat out of shape. I haven't exercised since I came here, but how hard can one dance be?"

"*Awya* is not a single dance, Felicia. Once you challenge Waheedah, it will continue until one of you drops from exhaustion."

"Oh...so that's how it goes. So she has a definite advantage over me," Felicia stated, realization setting in. "She's a dancer, and she has probably been preparing for this for the last few weeks."

"But she does not know that she will be challenged. It is you who knows that."

Felicia sipped the elixir and reflected on what Aisha had said.

"Right now, I just wonder what I will prove by doing this."

"Only you know the true answer to that. It is still not too late to change your mind, my child." Soft silver eyes looked into Felicia's almond-shaped brown ones.

"I won't change my mind. Will you present me at *Awya* this evening, Aisha?"

"I will be most honored to do so."

After returning to her room and taking a nap, Felicia woke up feeling well-rested and exuberant. The camomile had done its job in relaxing her. Reaching on the nightstand beside the bed, she retrieved the pouch of camomile Aisha had given her before she left Kareem's room.

"Add this to your bath, Felicia. It will soothe and relax your muscles. One hour before *Awya*, drink no more than a thumb's length of ginseng tea. It is very powerful in its pure form. You will need it."

The tile felt warm beneath Felicia's feet as she walked to the tub. Turning on the tap, she sprinkled the entire pouch of camomile into the running water. Sitting on the tiled edge, she trailed her feet in its bubbling mass until the water reached an inch below her knees.

The water seemed to enfold her, as she slipped into its wetness, reminding her of the feeling of Na'im's warm arms when he used to hold her.

Felicia moaned as she lathered her body with myrrh scented soap. Her need for Na'im was so strong, even her own hands seemed to stimulate her. She closed her eyes, allowing her mind and its fantasies to ease the pang of her desire. Her thoughts of Na'im were so strong, it was as if he were there beside her. The feel of him, his smell, as real as her own.

Na'im sought comfort in the foaming hot waters that surrounded him no more than two miles away from where Felicia bathed. The heat of the almost scalding water was a welcome balance to the fire in his groin that had plagued him throughout the night.

Hambir had not lied when he said "the drink of the one who waits fires the body making it a tormentor of the mind." Na'im longed for relief, his mind conjuring up many images, but the ones that plagued him most were haunted by Felicia.

A rap on the door and a masculine voice had broken his hours of affliction. He was instructed to stand clear of the door with his back facing it and his eyes closed. Moments later, feather-like hands, scented with citrus, placed a blindfold over his eyes and tied it. He was then led, by unseen hands, down the back hallways of the masjid.

His mind, which had tortured him throughout the wee morning hours, began its onslaught again. Were these women who guided him? Or were they scented boys presented so to cause him more strain. He could tell they were not tall in stature, for they both held the top of his forearms with ease as they guided him through the darkness.

No one spoke as smooth hands removed his robe, leaving him feeling exposed and vulnerable, his desire apparent for any with eyes to see. Then he was led forward to the edge of the tub where pressure was placed on his arms, gently forcing him down. A web-like substance brushed his arm as he complied with the silent demand. It felt heavy, but soft, like the hair of a woman when it's unbound. An involuntary shiver shook him as round soft flesh momentarily brushed against him. Then the web and the scent of citrus was gone.

When Na'im first placed his foot in the steamy water, his automatic reflex was to snatch it back. But as time passed, he was able to place both feet in, his legs and eventually his entire body. The tension in his body drained away as he sat in the water. His physical need seemed to dissipate with the water's heat, but his mind still sought release. "Your mind shall cry out its pain. Its only consolation, fulfillment of the flesh. This only the one who has drank of *Ya Natir* understands."

After his bath, Na'im was taken back to his room by his mysterious hosts, but this time he did not care. His sole focus was to be rid of this torment, to be rid of this pain, for *Awya* to be over with so that he could find peace. These thoughts filled his head as he drifted into a deep sleep.

Chapter Thirty-Five

The music began as Felicia dried herself off from her bath. Festive music, played by anyone who knew the melody and had an instrument to play.

Several songs could be heard at one time, as the estate grounds overflowed with the villagers of Karib. Concealing herself behind the curtain, Felicia continued to look out of her window.

Karib was a small village, but from the mixture of its people, the history of Egypt could be told. Skin tones ranged from that of fair-skinned Arabs to the concentrated black of the Nubian culture.

An impromptu group of Nubian musicians played bongos and blew the clarinet. The clear vibrancy of their voices easily reached Felicia, while their heads bobbed and their feet danced a lively step, raising dust all around them. Felicia's body responded intuitively to the rhythm as she watched the animated bunch.

There was much milling about as families shared their "gift of promise" with others. Fatimah had said each family would prepare a dish, something that could be easily eaten with the fingers, and this they would bring to the *Awya.* These dishes symbolized the family's promise to stand behind any marital arrangements it had already made, or would make in the future. Sharing with everyone made it even more bonding.

Music flowed throughout the crowd and there was much dancing. Traditional dances were being performed by a few couples, but most of the dancers were individuals who began to dance in place as the feeling struck them. Some drew a crowd, but many danced for their own pleasure and release.

It was amazing how a festival like *Awya* brought the ancient roots of the villagers to the fore. For the six weeks that Felicia had lived in Karib, never had she seen anything indicating that the people embraced such colorful traditional roots. Conservatism was in their mannerisms and the way they dressed and spoke. Control of the mind and spirit seemed utmost in their lives. But today, all restraint had been tossed to the wind.

The women were still modestly dressed, but the colors were more vibrant, some more daring than others.

Cyclopean cushions with tassels had been placed around a platform, which resembled a large auditorium stage in size. These were accompanied by oblong tables that could be eaten on with ease while one sat on the huge cushions. A seat in the middle of the cushions rose majestically above the rest. Its base was a cushion similar to the others, but larger. Upon that sat a great, legless chair.

The blinding sunlight reflecting off the chair made it hard for Felicia to distinguish the design that fanned outward like a peacock's tail. Nor could she tell if the flashing colors of gold and blue were painted onto metal or wood.

She noticed several steps had been built, mounting to the center of the platform. A line of servants with flower arrangements and bowls of fresh fruit marched back and forth upon the small stairway, resembling ants carrying food back and forth to their colonies.

Felicia's bedroom door suddenly flew open with such velocity, she didn't know what to expect, as a high-strung Fatimah whirled her way into the room.

"I thought you were already dressed." Incredulity marked Fatimah's normally calm features. "It is less than an hour before the ceremony begins. I will help you."

Felicia crossed over to the finished costume that lay spread out on the end of the bed. Her hands trembled as she picked up the beaded boustier, causing the iridescent beads to shimmer.

The gold strap that supported it gripped her neck snugly as she put it on, pulling her breasts upward to form a natural cleavage. Trio's of strung beads covered the shiny object, quivering with every movement Felicia's body made. The sunlight made the top flash a myriad of colors, as it played back and forth between the gold background and the glittering baubles.

Timidly, she stepped into the bottom half of the costume. The golden skirt they'd found in the tunnel had been evenly shredded into tiny strips all around, creating the illusion of wholeness. The slighest movement from Felicia's toned frame caused it to splinter, revealing glimpses of her chocolate brown skin and the gold-beaded bikini underneath.

Beaded bracelets had been made for her wrist and ankles, and very fine ribbons left over from the skirt had been clustered together with beads, creating ornate earrings.

After Felicia finished dressing, Fatimaah instructed her to sit in a chair she had pulled into the center of the room. It was time to style her hair.

"I want you to lean forward so you can arrange your braids high on top of your head. I have kept this ornamental cone for many years because it was my mother's. I have never worn it. She says it was found in the tomb of Ramses II. I know she would be proud to have you wear it this evening."

When Felicia walked over to the mirror, she could tell Fatimah had polished the nearly six-inch hair ornament to perfection. It was amazing how light it felt upon her head. From the look of it, she had assumed it would be heavier. A profusion of dark curls tumbled out of the cylindrical top, enhancing its scintillating gold tones.

Fatimah watched as Felicia transformed her almond-shaped eyes with black kohl pencils. Imitating to her best ability the makeup of ancient Egypt, she applied a bronze lipstick to her mouth and a raisin brown blush to her high cheekbones.

Looking at Fatimah's reflection standing behind her in the mirror, Felicia's body took on a pose of readiness. "Well, girl friend, this is as good as it's going to get."

"We have done well. You look wonderful," Fatimah grasped Felicia's shoulders in a gesture of support. "I believe Na'im had a black cape with a hood made for you along with the other clothes when you first arrived. You will need that to cover yourself until the proper time. Wait here until I return with Aisha. We will use the west wing door to go onto the grounds."

Chapter Thirty-Six

There was almost complete silence throughout the crowd when the processional music of *Awya* began. The crowd opened up and made a pathway stretching from the front gate to the platform's stairway, wide enough for two camels to walk side by side.

Felicia and Aisha had wedged their way forward so they could see better. It had not been easy, for everyone pushed and shoved to be on the front line. Little attention was given to the two women. All eyes were centered outside of the front gate in the direction of the masjid.

Sheik Rahman, Yasmin, as well as Waheedah's parents had taken their places on the platform. A special cushion had also been provided for Hambir, who would conduct the ceremony. A group of selected musicians settled behind them far to the right.

Standing behind the massive chair in the center of the cushions was Waheedah. Felicia had never seen her look more beautiful. Luxuriant blue and white veils cascaded from the back of her head, framing her slender face and neck. Sapphire and diamond earrings hung from her ears. Her well-made up face was expressionless as she stared outward. She would be the first to see the procession as it advanced onto the grounds. Felicia could not see what Waheedah was wearing; the back of the cushioned chair blocked her body from view.

Now that she was close enough, Felicia could see the flamboyant design on the chair's back was a painting of the face of Isis, the Egyptian goddess of female fertility and love. Her striped headpiece edged the chair's back in black and blue, with thin gold lines between them. Her face, solid gold in color, was dominated by penetrating black eyes, an unimposing nose and bountiful lips. It seemed to intensify Waheedah's cause, and visibly announce the importance of female energy.

Cushions had also been made available for the remainder of the relatives and their attendants, directly in front of the steps. None of them were being used though, for they, like the crowd, were on their feet looking in the direction of the town. Fatimah stood among them. Kareem was not far behind.

A rapid succession of drumbeats broke through the air. An oboe followed, which seemed to answer its demanding beat. Repetitiously, the drum and the oboe spoke as if calling forth the processional.

The blending of hushed whispers slowly made its way forward along with the shining bodies of eight men wearing golden bands around their throats, wrists and ankles. White balloon pantaloons, resembling wraps, rode high above their ankle bands. All were bent forward at the waist, swaying in unison with their arms outstretched slightly behind them.

Next strode Hambir, in a white, gold-trimmed *galabia*, carrying the golden chalice upon a small ceremonial cushion.

The whispers rose in pitch to soft rumblings as Na'im brought up the rear.

Felicia's heart beat uncontrollably as Hambir passed by, for she knew the rousing sounds from the villagers of Karib announced Na'im's appearance.

His broad shoulders seemed to rebel against the golden material of the *galabia* he wore for the *Awya*, as his bare feet marched to the rhythm of the processional music. There was no way to tell what feelings moved inside him as he walked, for his face was covered with a golden mask, giving him a perpetual expression of distress. His reddish-brown hair, that touched just below his shoulders, hung vibrantly about him.

"This is going to be wild," Felicia could hear Phillip's voice no more than a few feet behind her. "Check out the outfits these guys have on."

"Yes, it's impressive," William responded, always the intellectual.

"I wish I could see Felicia's face when she gets a load of this. Where is she, anyway?" Phillip asked, irritated. "We didn't see her at all today or yesterday."

"Maybe she had something to do," George remarked. "We've all been pretty busy trying to wrap things up around here. The project's just about completed. We have the formula written down. We just need to make some samples, and that should be pretty easy to do."

Felicia was glad the hooded cape concealed her face. There was absolutely no other way to hide the alarm that deluged her as she watched Na'im walk by. His back was so straight and stiff. He walked like a man in a trance.

"What is wrong with him, Aisha?" she asked, fear encasing her every word.

"It is the 'drink of the one who waits' that has drained him. His mind is like a dry sponge needing water. Peace evades him now. The 'drink of the one who waits' makes a man know how human he is; how needy he is of a companion. *Awya* makes a man know how empty he is without a mate. And sometimes he makes his decision out of that emptiness. That is why it is good you have decided to challenge. Without it, I believe he would definitely choose the woman from Cairo.''

''It sounds like he's been drugged!''

''The ancients did not think of it as a drug; only as a way of making a man know his need, and reckoning with it according to their customs.''

Staccato flute notes chirped loudly as Na'im climbed the stairs, while the heads of the men who accompanied him circled as if in madness.

Without hesitation, Na'im crossed the platform, taking the seat that awaited him. Waheedah remained behind the massive chair. Na'im gave no indication that he was aware of anything until she removed his mask.

A remote look filled the golden eyes that Felicia knew so well, and a strong urge to protect him grew inside of her. Yes, she would challenge this woman for Na'im. She would challenge anyone for this man who had taught her the true meaning of love.

Hambir, who stood before them all, sang out one phrase before the challenge dance music began. Aisha automatically began to interpret for Felicia.

''Open your minds and hearts to the spirit of Isis,'' she spoke, as if to herself.

No sooner had Hambir finished, did the music begin again, and Waheedah's arms were raised arch-like above her head. Tiny rings were attached to her thumbs, encircling her in a Nile blue cloud that formed from the veils attached to her waist. Repetitiously, she brought her elbows to touch in front of her face, causing the veil to conceal and then expose Na'im as he sat motionless.

With deliberate motions, Waheedah danced her way around the cushions, ending up in front of Na'im. At first the music was slow and enticing, as her rhythmic feet, pointed and pivoted, causing her small waist to swivel and her hips to rise.

Time and time again she raised her arms above her head, spinning so fast her body was nothing but a blur in a midst of blue. She was an accomplished dancer with the grace and agility of a gazelle, and this was her moment of glory.

Closer and closer she danced to Na'im, until his hair blew from the air created by her whirling veils. As the bongo's beat became stronger, the snapping movements of Waheedah's hips pounded with the sound. She was a vibrating mass of flesh from her shoulders down.

Na'im's eyes began to watch her hips, as if mesmerized. Like a cobra following its prey, his head turned as if on a swivel. The music mounted with a frenzied rhythm while Waheedah's body echoed its maddening vibrations.

Na'im's face transformed into the personification of lust, as cord-like tendons flared on the sides of his neck, and his chest heaved until you could see the imprint of his muscles beneath the gold material. His eyes glared with an unnatural light, while his tongue repeatedly licked his usually firm lips that now appeared slack.

Felicia thought the music would never end. She had never seen a man's primal sexual instincts brought so close to the forefront of his conscious mind. It hurt all the more because it was Na'im.

Finally the tantalizing music was over. A breathless Waheedah stood with a detached veil across her face.

Motionless. Showing only her eyes that feasted on Na'im. He, too, had eyes for no other than Waheedah. Felicia's heart seemed to stop as she watched the two of them.

Once again, Hambir's voice rang out loud and clear as he stood before Na'im and Waheedah, holding the chalice up high. Then he turned and spoke to the crowd. The intonation of his voice suggested a question.

"The time has come, my child," Aisha said before stepping forward into a nearly-closed pathway.

At first Hambir did not see the tiny woman as he ceremoniously offered the chalice to the villagers of Karib. Then Felicia heard Aisha speak up in a feminine but piercing voice. A surprised Hambir acknowledged her.

Felicia's legs seemed to move her forth on their own volition, as Hambir and Aisha exchanged words. And then Aisha announced her name.

The crowd opened and backed away, as Felicia removed the hood and cape that covered her. Fatimah stepped forward to take it.

The change of events evoked an astonished reaction from the crowd as the word spread.

"Hey, that's Filly going up there!" an amazed Phillip shouted, rousing even more interest from the villagers.

"Boy, Phil, you're right," an excited George chimed in. "It *is* her."

Sheer astonishment dominated the faces of the people on the platform. Waheedah gasped audibly as Felicia came forward and mounted the stairs on Hambir's command, with Aisha close at her heels. Even Na'im's dazed eyes came to life when they focused on Felicia.

Waheedah's father jumped to his feet protesting loudly, but Aisha interrupted him, suggesting in her quiet but powerful way that English be spoken for Felicia's benefit.

"We are a people of respect. And I am sure a man of your status, Jamal Sutan Faruuk, will show respect for our ancestors by respecting one who wishes to be a part of this ceremony."

Sheik Rahman looked on in bewilderment, but the eyes of Na'im's mother, Yasmin, burned with unadulterated pleasure.

Angered beyond belief, Waheedah attacked Hambir. "You cannot allow this woman to challenge me in *Awya*. She is a foreigner and does not have the right to do it."

Things were moving so fast that the stoic Hambir's composure had crumbled a bit. He did not know if what Waheedah alleged was true.

"Sheik Rahman, you have performed more *Awya's* than anyone here. What does the Book of the Ancients say on this matter?"

"It grieves me to say, Hambir, that I have never led ritual to an *Awya* that involved a foreigner. Therefore, I do not know."

"I know what the Book of the Ancients says," Aisha spoke up. "A foreigner can challenge *Awya* if she is presented by an Egyptian with spiritual leadership such as myself. And this has been done."

"Father, we cannot take the word of this woman who is obviously on the side of the foreigner who challenges me," Waheedah argued.

"No, my daughter, I will not permit it." Menacingly, Faruuk addressed the sheik and Hambir. "I demand that you send to the temple for the Book of the Ancients."

The sheik nodded his head in agreement, and Hambir summoned a runner to get the book, giving him the sacred kcy.

All the commotion had a positive effect on Na'im. He

was still not himself, but Felicia could tell he was becoming more aware of his surroundings. No longer did Na'im look at Waheedah with the eyes of a man who has spotted an oasis after countless days in the desert. Instead, his golden gaze had come to rest on Felicia, confusion deep within its depths.

Their eyes locked. Gold and brown. Felicia's breasts heaved incessantly as she willed him to recognize her.

Waheedah was totally infuriated by what she saw and stepped between them. "Just what do you think you are doing? Do you think that because you have allowed Na'im to use you at his convenience he belongs to you? That he actually wants you? You are a fool."

"I don't think so. It's you that he doesn't want or he would have claimed you before now. So you decide to force him to choose you, nearly drug him out of his mind so that he doesn't know that he's agreeing to marry you. But that doesn't matter to you, does it? You'd get him any way you can."

Loud shouts rose from the crowd announcing the return of the runner. Out of breath from his efforts, he passed the Book of the Ancients, wrapped in animal skin, to Hambir.

Time stood still as the councilman searched the book for the necessary passage. At last he found it and recited for all in Arabic and English.

"The Book of the Ancients says, 'A foreigner is allowed to challenge *Awya*, but they must have a spiritual leader of Egyptian ancestry to open their way to the ancient rites'," Hambir recited to the crowd. Closing the book he declared, "Felicia Sanders has fulfilled the requirement of the ancient ones. Her challenge of Waheedah Farouk is accepted."

The crowd roared with anticipation. The majority of the villagers had never seen a challenger of *Awya*. This one was being challenged not by an Egyptian, but a foreigner.

Felicia could feel the adrenalin pumping in her veins as she listened to Hambir's declaration. Leaning over to Aisha, she told her she had an additional request.

"There are a group of Nubian musicians among the villagers that I would like to play for me. Would you tell that to Hambir?"

Without hesitation, Aisha imparted the request to Hambir and the others. "The challenger, Felicia, requests her own musicians from among the villagers of Karib. They are of Nubian descent. Their music she finds more to her taste."

"This is an outrage!" Waheedah blurted out. "If she cannot..."

Hambir silenced her by raising his hand. "The request is accepted."

Aisha smiled. "It is now up to you, my child."

The platform was literally divided in half by the bodies of four of the men who led Na'im's procession. In a straight line, they stood with their hands on their hips and their feet spread apart.

Felicia was instructed to take her position on the left side, while Waheedah stood waiting on the right.

Felicia looked out into the eager faces of the crowd. She had danced many times as a youngster before an audience, but it had been many years since she'd done so. None of the people behind her had ever thought of her as a dancer, only a scientist. Yet Felicia knew in her heart her first love had always been to dance. She would not have been a scientist if she'd had her own way. Fate had stepped in that summer before she could take advantage of a scholarship with the Alvin Ailey Dance Theatre. Her mother became very ill, and Felicia had to stay in Memphis to take care of her.

It was a slow recovery and Felicia began to pursue her second interest: science. She took classes at Memphis State University. As time passed, she became convinced, with the help of others, that she would make a good research scientist. Finances also played a heavy part in her decision.

Life could be strange. Now the career of a research scientist had led her back to where she always wanted to be--on stage as a dancer.

Felicia struck a pose reminiscent of the Egyptian dancers of old, elbows and wrists bent, flat palms extended upward. Dark brown flesh protruded through the shreds of gold as her knees flexed in readiness. Then the drums began. It was the kind of beat that struck a cord in Felicia's heritage and spewed up natural rhythm within her.

Never moving her feet, she allowed her upper body to respond in a way that the crowd knew was only the beginning. The rhythm commenced within her head and worked its way down, as Felicia's toned frame became the embodiment of the bongo beat. The beads of her top amplified her movements, while the strips of gold about her lower body became floating sparks of energy around her.

Trim legs were raised high, forming angles and spear-like lines, as she brought forth her dance training, jumping and spinning with the agility of a cat, yet harnessing the lightness of a bird in flight. Felicia quivered with the ending vibration of prolonged bongo beats and cymbals.

She was so dynamic, the crowds initial response was shocked silence, until Phillip hurled his compliment up toward the platform, clapping his hands high above his head, "Do it to 'em, Filly!"

The challenge had begun. Back and forth, Waheedah and Felicia danced, different in style but evenly matched in skill. Felicia, a fireball of gold and brown, her dance a mixture of modern jazz and African dance; Waheedah, a sea of blue, a belly dancer at her best.

Competition was at an all-time high. Felicia matched every exotic step executed by Waheedah with a blast of kicks, twists and twirls.

Na'im responded well to the additional time allotted him by Felicia's challenge. He had completely recovered from the altered state the "drink of the one who waits" had brought upon him. Now his chiseled features were the epitome of attentiveness as he watched the two women perform.

As time passed, his jaw began to clench with impatience. Glancing at the merciless sun, Na'im knew the two women could not keep at it much longer. Already their bodies were drenched with perspiration.

Suddenly the crowd's attention was no longer on the stage. Felicia stopped abruptly as some of the villagers ran, shouting and pointing toward the workers' homes.

There was no way for her to see what they were pointing at from where she stood. But she didn't need to see, for already a huge ball of black smoke was billowing upward into the sky.

"Smoke," she shouted, turning toward Na'im, "and it's coming from the direction of the schoolhouse and the lab."

Felicia was off the platform in seconds, pushing her way through the crowd. Na'im was not far behind. His huge bulk enabled him to travel fast through the hordes of people.

Na'im instructed several men to transport water from the west wing of the house and from the well nearest to the lab. There was no running water inside the workers' homes.

It took Felicia a couple of minutes to reach the lab site, her exhaustion forgotten in the excitement. Phillip and the others had already arrived, and they stood watching as the back end of the small building went up in flames.

Large mud bowls were being brought from the well by several workers, but no one knew where to throw the minute amounts of water.

William pointed to the fodder that had been on top of the building. "It must have caught fire first. It's burned a hole completely through the roof. Our living quarters are just about gone."

"What about the completed formula?" George asked in exasperation.

"It's still in the file cabinet," Felicia quickly answered.

"There's a chance that we can get it out of there," Phillip interjected, "the fire seems to still be contained in the living quarters."

"You're right, Phillip, and I'm the only one who knows exactly where it is inside that cabinet," Felicia said with finality.

Phillip remained unconvinced. "Now wait a minute, Filly. Maybe George and I can get in there and bring the whole file cabinet out."

"By now the file cabinet is too hot to carry. And there's too much smoke in there for any of you to see what you're doing. I know where it is, and we're wasting time standing here discussing it."

Felicia ran to the smoke-filled lab door before anyone

could stop her. She started to cough and gag immediately from the thick smoke that burned her eyes and shot up her nose. Closing her eyes and covering her nose and mouth, she grabbed for the lab coats that always hung near the door. She used one of them to shield her face as she progressed into the room.

Her bare foot rammed into an object on the floor, causing her to nearly fall. Coughing spasmodically, Felicia pressed her face into the bunched up garment. Her mind told her to hurry, but she also knew that many of the containers in the lab held highly flammable materials. If only one of them broke, exposing the contents to the extreme temperatures in the room, the entire lab would be blown to smithereens. So she progressed cautiously, but as rapidly as she could.

Na'im reached the scene moments after Felicia had gone into the lab. Wild-eyed with concern, he grabbed George by the shoulders and demanded to know where Felicia was.

"She ran into the lab before we could stop her, Na'im. Phillip and I tried to..."

"She's in there?" Accusing eyes turned to Phillip. "Why didn't you go in after her? Give me your shirts!" Na'im demanded.

Without hesitation, they did as he asked, while Na'im removed his shirt as well. He hollered to a man carrying a large earthen jar filled with water. Snatching the two shirts from George and Phillip, Na'im met the man and submerged both shirts into the water. Hurriedly, he covered his body as best he could with Phillip's shirt. Running toward the lab, he removed the water from the second one and placed it up to his face.

"Felicia!" he called, as he entered the smoke-infested room. He could hear her coughing as he entered.

Felicia was surprised to hear Na'im calling her from inside the building. Pulling her face slightly away from the lab coat, she mumbled, "I'm over here."

Na'im went in the direction of Felicia's voice. The room was not a large one, so he was able to follow the sound of the metal drawer scraping as Felicia attempted to pull it open.

The file cabinet drawer was so hot, Felicia couldn't stand to touch it. Using the dangling end of the coat, she managed to pull it open slightly. By then, Na'im was at her side. Deep coughs began to wrack Felicia's body as it rejected the unwanted smoke.

"Get back outside!" Na'im ordered her.

"But the files," she responded between coughs and sputters.

"I'll bring them. Now go!"

Felicia shuffled her way back to the lab door. Choking and overcome by heat, she stumbled across the threshold. William and George dragged her away from the building, while one of the women wiped her face with a cloth soaked in water from the well.

The workers had made a line where a continuous flow of jars filled with water traveled, but they did little to extinguish the fire.

The fodder was being removed from the roof of the schoolhouse, and water was being poured on the side nearest to the lab. They did not want it to go up in flames too.

By this time, the fire had spread to the interior of the lab. Na'im yanked the file drawer open the remainder of the way. Thrusting his hand inside, he snatched up the few files he found and placed them under the shirt he wore. Swiftly, he turned toward the door, knocking over several glass beakers in his wake.

As Na'im approached the doorway, the building exploded. His body was hurled out of the building by the impact. The gold material from the pants of the ceremonial *galabia* ignited like paper, engulfing his legs in flames. A cry like a wild animal in extreme pain broke from Na'im's lips.

Felicia watched as the building exploded in fire and Na'im's body was thrown through the air. Screaming insanely, with flailing arms she pushed away from Phillip and the others as she rushed toward Na'im.

Chapter Thirty-Seven

Several workers had already reached Na'im. Removing their own *galabias*, they covered Na'im's blazing legs and smothered the flames.

"Na'im! My God! Na'im!," Felicia wailed over and over. Crying uncontrollably, she knelt down beside him and pulled his head onto her lap.

His face was covered in black soot from the smoke, and his long brown eyelashes were singed. He did not respond to Felicia's lamentations. The pain from his burning legs was so acute, it had rendered him unconscious.

Aisha, Fatimah and Kareem emerged from the crowd that had gathered.

Distraught over Na'im's condition, Fatimah asked, "How did this happen?"

"It is my fault. He came in after me. Into the lab, when I was trying to save the formula. This never would have happened if it hadn't been for me." Felicia's shoulders shook as she sobbed uncontrollably.

"It is too late for that, my child," Aisha told her. "We must remove these clothes from his legs. They will blister and we do not want the cloth to stick to his skin. It will be difficult to remove if we wait any longer."

Gingerly, Aisha peeled the pants of the *galabia* away from Na'im's legs. Felicia was not prepared for what she saw. She did not know much about burns, but there was no doubt that Na'im's burns were very severe.

For a moment, deep concern crossed Aisha's usually calm features. "We must get him back to the house. We cannot let these burns get infected."

Felicia looked up at George.

George responded immediately. "I will bring the truck around. And we'll need some blankets to put in the back so he can lay back there. Kareem, go and tell the sheik and Yasmin what has happened so they will have someone waiting to take him into the house."

The explosion had ended the workers' efforts to save the lab. It was completely engulfed in flames and still burning profusely. All attention was now given to the schoolhouse, which was repeatedly doused with water.

George arrived with the truck and Fatimah covered its bed with blankets from the worker's homes. Carefully, Phillip, William and George placed Na'im upon the blankets and in the arms of a waiting Felicia.

Minutes later, they arrived at the front of the mansion. Na'im's parents were waiting anxiously, along with Waheedah. Four male servants were there to carry Na'im into the house on a sheet that was used as a stretcher. They were instructed by the sheik to place him in the first bedroom in the west wing. It was the closest to the entrance.

Overwhelmed with guilt, Felicia simply watched as the group followed Na'im's progress into the house. She felt depleted of energy, her mind tortured with the pain of Na'im's situation. She wished with all her heart that she could undo what had just been done, if only it was in her power.

"Now look what you have done," Waheedah's accusing voice interrupted Felicia's thoughts. "This would never have happened, if not for you. You, your lab and your formula. A woman should bring a man pleasure, not pain and destruction as you have. I am sure once Na'im regains consciousness and has time to think, he will realize he does not need a woman like you in his life. I believe he cares for you, but his duty to his people is most important. Your chemicals and solutions help to destroy and will do more harm than good. Our people are better off without your kind." Then she left behind the others.

Felicia had no response to Waheedah's accusations. Maybe she believed they were true. She did not care. She only wanted Na'im to be well again. The thought of his beautiful golden body marred with scars so deep, or that he may never walk again, overwhelmed her. She'd take all the guilt and blame in the world if it would help him.

A ceaseless flow of tears dropped onto the folders Felicia held in her lap, the formula now only a reminder of Na'im's terrifying situation.

Chapter Thirty-Eight

Sheik Rahman sat beside his son's bed. He and his wife had held a vigil there for several hours. He had ordered everyone out of the room except Sahim (Sah-heem), the village doctor.

His mind told him that Aisha would be the one who could help Na'im, but his emotions spoke against it. She had been brought here by the woman, Felicia, and it was because of her that his son lay unconscious with his legs brutally burned.

He had spoken harshly to Fatimah and George after the accident, refusing to give his permission for George to marry her. He, too, was being punished for his heritage.

Yasmin had remained quiet while Sahim applied a liniment to Na'im's third degree burns. She did not agree with her husband, but his grief was so powerful she decided to wait and see if Sahim's medicine would help. Yasmin knew her husband's negative attitude toward Aisha had been fueled by Waheedah. She'd made it clear that none of this would have happened if the foreigners had never come, and a man in power like the sheik did not need such evil in his own home.

Waheedah's voiced concern over Na'im's welfare was weakened in Yasmin's eyes when she showed no affection toward her son, only concern for herself.

"Please excuse me now while I bathe and change my clothes into something more comfortable," she had said. "All that dancing has made me sticky, and the air is stifling in here. I will return later, after Na'im is cleaned up. I cannot stand this sort of thing."

For Yasmin, Waheedah had proven she did not love her son.

Fever had begun to set in as Na'im squirmed with discomfort, rubbing his badly burned legs against the sheets of the bed. Before long he began talking out of his head, and the name he called over and over was Felicia's.

Na'im's parents listened as a semi-conscious Na'im tried to explain and justify things in his life to the images in his feverish mind. He talked of his father's illness, his obligation to his people and his love for Felicia.

Then he went into the past, and it was a tearful Na'im who recounted the first love in his life, Tahillah, Kareem's mother. Out of respect for his father and his people, he had never told anyone how he felt about her. Even she never really knew. But Tahillah's mother had known, and she had expected Na'im and Tahillah to build a life together, a better life for her daughter. That is why he felt responsible for Kareem. Because he was the future leader of Karib, he felt his first obligation was to his people and not to his heart.

Yasmin held her son's hand as he spoke of his current inner battle to claim the woman he loved, or do what his dying father felt was best for his people.

Tears flowing down her cheeks, Yasmin could no longer resist telling her husband how she felt.

"We cannot allow our son to undergo such mental torment. He loves this woman Felicia, and I believe she is good for him. On her own, she brought our villages relief from Hassan's grief and madness, and today she proved she is willing to honor our customs and ways if she has to. We want a strong woman as our son's wife, and she has shown that and more. I love you, my husband, even now after everything I have learned, but we cannot let our son bear the burden of your mistake. We know Kareem is your son, and he can help prolong your life. It is through Kareem that the burden can be lifted from Na'im's heart."

Sheik Rahman stared into his wife's tormented eyes and he knew what she had said was right. He nodded his head in submission.

"Let us send for Aisha. I believe she will know how to help Na'im."

"It is unfair for my uncle to decide all foreigners are bad. He was the one who sent Na'im to the United States to learn more about the western civilization. He said we would learn much from your technology and it could help us to progress. Now he has completely changed his mind, and does not want to have anything to do with anyone who is not 'his own'."

"You must calm yourself, Fatimah. Your uncle is distressed about your cousin. He is not thinking rationally now, and when he spoke to you he spoke out of concern for you." A slim smile crossed Aisha's lips. "It does not mean he is right. Give him a little more time."

George rose from beside Fatimah, who sat on the couch. Impatiently, he paced back and forth across Na'im and Felicia's sitting room.

"I just don't understand it," George pondered. "It appears the fire started directly over our living quarters, because that's where the fodder ignited."

"It is a common thing here in Egypt, George," Fatimah responded, "for the fodder to be a source of fire. It has happened to many homes in many villages. This is not a strange thing."

"I can understand that. But I could have sworn the fodder was directly over the lab portion of the building."

"What difference does it make now," Felicia commented. "The damage has been done. Na'im is suffering because I was rash and played the heroine. I'll never forgive myself for this. Never."

"You magnify your own pain, Felicia, by having such thoughts. It is more important now to send Na'im feelings of love and healing to help his life force fight off the infection that will surely set in without the proper help," Aisha advised her.

"Well, I've been here long enough. Talking about this isn't going to change anything. I'm going outside to find Phillip and William and see if I can be of any help."

"I will come with you, George." Fatimah followed him as he approached the door.

"No. In light of what your uncle has said, I think you'd better stay here."

Disappointment crossed Fatimah's young face.

"Don't worry. I haven't give up on the situation. I just need a little time to myself to think about this." George pressed a light kiss to Fatimah's lips and then he was gone.

Silently the women waited together. Aisha had given them both tea to help calm them.

Suddenly, they heard rapid footsteps outside the door. The knocking that followed was abrupt, demanding immediate attention.

Felicia rushed to the door, feeling the person brought news about Na'im. It was one of the servants. She greeted all the women, but her message was addressed to Aisha. The sheik had sent for her. Na'im was getting worse.

Aisha wasted no time in following the young woman to the room where Na'im lay. Felicia and Fatimah were close behind.

Fresh blood stains covered the sheets underneath Na'im's legs, where he had tossed and turned until the blisters had burst and the skin had rubbed away. No sooner had they entered the room than a delirious Na'im called out Felicia's name. She needed no further urging to hurry to his side. Yasmin gave her her son's hand.

Na'im's hand felt scorching hot within Felicia's. She reached out to touch the face that she loved so well. It, too, felt extremely hot and dry under her palm.

Sheik Rahman was sick with worry. He looked at the elderly woman that he'd sent for. Her face was completely inscrutable as she examined Na'im. Yet, the feeling of peace that she emanated was a comfort to him.

"Can you help my son, Aisha?"

There was no more pride or hate left in him; only the love a father has for his son.

"I can. But I must use the power of the word to do so. His burns are so severe, I must talk the fire out of his legs. Because we have waited, the flame of infection from these burns has made him delirious. Once that is done, we can begin to treat the blisters."

"What can I do?" Yasmin asked with a mother's concern.

"Once I have exorcised the heat from his body, I will need linseed oil. Go to my room. It is in the large pouch that I carry. Bring it to me."

"What do you plan to do?" Sheik Rahman asked with

uncertainty. "I have never heard of talking the fire out of someone who is badly burned."

"There are many things that exist that you may not be aware of, Sheik Rahman, but that does not mean they are not so. The spirit of the fire must be persuaded to leave Na'im's body. For the longer it dwells there, the longer it will take the burns to heal and the damage could be crippling."

Fatimah moved closer to her uncle, taking his arm to comfort him and finding comfort in the gesture for herself as well.

An air of skepticism mixed with hope hung in the room as Aisha instructed Felicia to move away and stand back with the others.

Making sure she did not injure the burns any further, Aisha positioned Na'im's legs so they did not touch at any point.

"When I am ready, I will motion for you to turn him over on his stomach so that I can continue the healing."

All three answered with a positive reply.

Aisha bent over Na'im's feet, placing her face and mouth as closely to the burns as she could without touching them. She began to speak, but Felicia could not understand what she was saying. Her voice was soft but strong, and she spoke at a very rapid pace. As she progressed, the sound of the letter 't' could be heard over and over again. Aisha emitted a light spray of saliva as she spoke.

Felicia could tell Aisha was expending much energy in her deed, even though her physical movements were slow and deliberate as she worked her way up from Na'im's foot to above his knee on one leg, and back down the same path on the other. With a flick of her wrist, Aisha signaled for Na'im's body to be turned, but she never stopped the continuous string of words.

Felicia thought it would be difficult to turn Na'im, and feared they would cause even worse injury to his massive burns while trying to turn his body as he squirmed and raved with fever. But to her astonishment, Na'im had calmed down immensely only moments after Aisha had begun the healing. Turning him was just a matter of managing his weight, while Aisha stood back to give them room. Once done, she duplicated the movements she'd performed before on the back of Na'im's badly burned legs.

As Aisha approached the end of the rite, her thin body was soaked in perspiration; droplets of sweat fell from the gray tendrils that formed around her face.

She was not alone, for Na'im's face was covered with a moist sheen that quickly turned to opulent rivulets of sweat.

In moments, the entire upper half of his body was wet, making Phillip's tee shirt that he wore cling to his chest.

Aisha looked at Na'im's moisture-covered body and said, "It is done. His fever has broken."

The rest was fairly simple. Aisha cleansed Na'im's legs with water and aloe, and then she applied the linseed oil. The smell of the liniment was enough to scare away the infection, Felicia thought, but after seeing Aisha "talk the fire out" of Na'im, there was no way she would complain or comment on the medicine she used to heal his burns.

Na'im regained consciousness while Aisha applied the amber-colored liquid that thickened and hardened moments after it was applied. Weak from the ordeal his body had just endured and still in pain, he managed to display a sense a humor. "With all of you here, I know I am not dead, but I sure smell like it."

They all laughed. But it was a laugh of relief and joy. One that could have easily turned to tears.

"Can a man get something cool to drink around here?" Na'im asked through parched lips.

"Yes, my son. It was brought only moments ago and placed beside your bed. We knew you would be thirsty when you awoke."

Na'im tried to sit up with considerable effort. Grimaces crossed his face as his blistered legs rubbed against the sheets.

"Do you need help?" Felicia could not stand by and watch him struggle. She had to be close to him, no matter what he thought of her; even if the things Waheedah said were true.

Misty gold eyes rose to look at her as she stood ringing her hands. He could see a mixture of emotions in her eyes. Fear. Uncertainty. But most of all, love.

This was the woman who dared to cross over into his world--a world of ancient customs and rituals--to proclaim her love for him before everyone. For her, love knew no bounds.

In a husky voice, filled with emotion, Na'im replied, "Yes, I believe the drink would be even more satisfying, Felicia, if I received it from you."

His words washed over her like a cool rain shower on a hot Memphis day. Proudly she crossed to his bedside, for she knew those words in front of his parents, Aisha and Fatimah carried so much meaning. And so did they.

While Na'im drank from the cup held by Felicia, clean bedding was brought in by one of the servants. It took some maneuvering, but soon fresh linen had replaced the soiled ones. Na'im lay back exhausted once the task was accomplished, and it wasn't long before he had fallen into deep sleep. This had been expected, for the cool fruit drink was an elixir prescribed by Aisha so that he would rest.

Chapter Thirty-Nine

Something prodded Felicia to wake up, even though her body was fatigued and cried for more sleep. Her back felt as if she'd been involved in heavy manual labor, as she lifted her head and neck off the bed upon which Na'im lay.

As soon as she opened her eyes, they were met by Na'im's gold ones. Evidently she had fallen asleep in the chair next to his bed, and at some point during the night, she'd stretched over the arm of the chair and placed her head on her hands and continued to sleep. She wondered how long he had been awake, and how long he had been watching her.

"Good morning, *aros al bher.*"

Felicia had heard Na'im call her his little mermaid many times before, but this time there was a special tone in it. A much more endearing sound. Almost a note of sadness.

His eyes held hers as he waited for her reply. During those few seconds before she spoke, she could see him taking in every part of her face as if he were branding her features into his memory, and she wondered why. Last night he had made it clear to everyone that she was very special to him. So why would he need to remember what she looked like?

"Good morning, Na'im."

His observation of her did not waiver, and something inside of her, a jittery nervous feeling, told her something was wrong. Felicia's voice was barely higher than a whisper when she spoke the next time. The thought that Na'im had decided to choose Waheedah after all made her feel physically weak and a little breathless.

"How do you feel?" Felicia's black lashes swooped down in an effort to hide what she was really feeling and thinking. "You gave us all quite a scare yesterday. The burns had brought on a fever, and you were delirious until Aisha performed the healing."

"And did I talk out of my head, telling my deepest and darkest secrets to everyone?" he taunted her.

Stutters filled Felicia's reply. He had caught her off guard with his playful attitude.

"I...I don't really know. Your father ordered all of us out of your room, except for your mother and Waheedah."

She looked directly at Na'im when she called Waheedah's name. She didn't really know what she expected to see, but his reaction told her nothing.

"When the sheik summoned Aisha, I came with her and the only thing I heard you say was my name."

"That didn't surprise you, did it?"

"It wouldn't have a few weeks ago. But so many things have happened recently. We had really grown apart."

"That's true," Na'im said with unparalleled seriousness, "and that is one of the reasons I have come to a decision."

Felicia braced herself for whatever Na'im was about to say.

"I am the future leader of Karib and therefore my first allegiance must be to my people and then to myself. They will look to me for guidance and I must have the strength to do what is right..."

Na'im's monologue was interrupted by a great commotion in the hallway. Na'im and Felicia were surprised when George, Ilyas and several other workers appeared in the doorway.

Startled by the abruptness of their appearance, Na'im asked if something else had gone wrong. George was the first to speak up.

"No, Na'im, nothing else has gone wrong. But you can thank Ilyas for starting that fire at the lab yesterday."

"Ilyas!" Na'im said in total disbelief.

"Yes. These workers saw him fiddling around the lab during the ceremony. They'd had some last minute business to tend to of their own, so they were late in getting there. They were pretty far away, but this guy says he saw someone on the roof. And they saw Ilyas walking back toward the crowd from the direction of the lab."

Na'im looked at the group of workers and asked if what George said was true. One by one they answered yes. Then he turned to Ilyas.

"Ilyas, is it true what they are saying?" he questioned his longtime friend and worker, who'd been loyal all these years.

Defiantly, Ilyas answered yes. While looking from George to Felicia with pure hatred, he gave a fiery explanation for his actions, one that neither George nor Felicia could understand. But they did understand their names when they were called and the names of Fatimah and Waheedah.

Na'im's face turned ashen under his golden brown skin as he listened, urging Felicia to ask for an interpretation.

"What did he say?"

"He says it was Waheedah's idea to torch the lab. But he would not do such a thing just because a woman suggested it. He did it because you and your kind, foreigners, were bringing changes to Karib that were not good. He burned the lab so your work would be over and you would have to return home."

"But didn't he know he could have burned down all the workers' homes had the fire spread. Was taking revenge against George and me important enough to him to risk that?"

Sheik Rahman entered the room as Felicia spoke.

"What has happened?" he asked, observing Ilyas' angry face and Na'im's pale one.

"Ilyas started the fire at the lab under Waheedah's suggestion," Na'im stated, supplying the answer that his father sought.

Astonished, Sheik Rahman turned to Ilyas.

"These kinds of actions cannot be tolerated. Ilyas, you are now banned from Karib. Do not show your face again or action will be taken against you. I want you men to make sure he follows my orders."

Proudly Ilyas turned toward the door, showing no remorse as he left.

"Well, I hope this changes your mind about my marrying Fatimah," George asked with great anticipation.

"I must admit it does. During the last twenty-four hours I have changed my mind about many things," he turned to face his son and Felicia.

"I have something I must discuss with you, my son."

"Well, this sounds like a family affair. I think I'll go and tell Fatimah the good news." George could not wipe the grin from his face as he backed out of the room into the hallway.

"Well, I guess I should take that as my cue to leave as well," Felicia said, standing up and crossing toward the door.

"No, Felicia, don't leave. Come back and sit down. I think this concerns you as well."

Shocked by the sheik's response, a wide-eyed Felicia sat back down.

"For years I have tried to guide the people of Karib in the direction I thought best for them. As I got older and my health began to fail me, my main concern has been what will happen when I can no longer be their leader. Therefore, all my thoughts and energies have been toward preparing you, Na'im, for that role. I knew you had a strong feeling of obligation toward Karib and I used that to my advantage, even when you were a very young man. Your love for your people has always been first in your heart. I knew that when you were in love with Tahillah and wanted to marry her, but I would not let you, pointing out your different stations in life as the reason. I depended on your innocence that had not yet tasted the fruits of manhood.

"But that was not the whole truth, Na'im. I did not want you to marry Tahillah because of my involvement with her. I did not want you to be hurt by my weakness, in taking advantage of such a young woman and fathering a child I did not suspect to be mine–Kareem. It is because of this, Na'im, and no doubt what Ilyas has just confessed, that I know my decision is right. I advise you to follow your heart. Your mother has always said 'The One' speaks to you for your highest good through your emotions, and this time I must agree with her. So do what you have to do, my son, to be happy."

Felicia could tell that a weight had been lifted from the sheik's shoulders by telling Na'im the truth. By doing so, he had accepted that each individual has the right to make his own decisions, whether they are right or wrong.

It was an awkward moment for the three of them. Sheik Rahman stood regally, a deep sense of remorse surrounding him, and Na'im was visibly shaken by what his father had said.

At last Na'im was able to voice his feelings. "There is nothing we can do about the past, my father, but we must do what we can to create a satisfying future. Does Kareem know that you are his father?"

"No, but I will tell him today. His mother tried to tell him in his dreams. That is why he fell ill. He felt her love so strongly that he wanted to join her. All of this has been very strange. Even from the other side, she held no ill feelings toward me. She told Kareem he must live to help me. I believe we will find that Kareem has the blood type I need for my transfusions."

"Then all of this has been for good, my father, and you should not judge yourself too har-"

An overly sweet, seductive voice broke in before Na'im could finish speaking. Waheedah approached the doorway, extravagantly dressed. She had her eyes closed as she pressed one hand to her forehead and the other against her abdomen.

"Please excuse me, Sheik Rahman, if I look a mess this morning. Yesterday's *Awya* completely tired me out. I had every intention of coming back to check on poor Na'im, but..." Waheedah broke her performance in mid sentence when she saw Felicia sitting beside Na'im's bed.

"Why is this woman sitting beside my fiance's bed after all the trouble she and her friends have caused us?"

It was Na'im who answered her. "Felicia happens to be my fiancee, and it is you who is no longer welcome in

Karib. Ilyas has told us of your involvement with the fire."

Na'im's outspoken tone surprised both Felicia and Waheedah. Felicia, in mild shock, studied his magnificent profile after he unblinkingly announced they were to be married.

Waheedah's discomfort was much more obvious. She was comical, to say the least. Holding her neck at its base and stretching it somewhat like a goose, she swallowed audibly while trying to regain her composure.

"Well, my family and I will not remain where we are not wanted." Pouncing on the sheik, she continued. "Sheik Rahman, I hope you know the extent of damage this will have on Karib."

"You have had a hand in any damage that has been done, Waheedah Faruuk," the sheik replied.

With the proper tone in her voice, she managed a haughty, "Well," and flounced away.

"I will leave you now as well, my son. It is time that I told Kareem the truth." With a swish of his elaborate *galabia*, he was gone.

Chapter Forty

Na'im turned to face Felicia, who still looked stunned over what she'd just seen and heard.

"*Habibi*, why did it shock you so when I said that you are my fiancee? Was that not your intent when you challenged Waheedah at *Awya*?"

Embarrassed by his directness, Felicia began to ramble. "In a way...I just knew I couldn't stand by and let that fatal attraction in Egyptian clothing just snatch you right from under my nose."

Na'im lifted a large hand and placed it gently under Felicia's chin. "So *azizi*, are you saying you do not want to marry me, you only wanted to keep Waheedah from having me?"

Felicia could feel her insides turn to jelly as Na'im touched her, and she knew as she looked into his handsome face she could never belong to anyone else.

Love filled Felicia's very being and she replied, "I'd marry you today, Na'im Raoul Rahman."

"Well, you will have to wait, *aros al bher*, at least until I am up and around," he said, planting an affectionate kiss on her willing lips.

"I have waited all my life for the right man to come along, so a few more days won't matter a bit."

Gold eyes gazed into brown ones.

"You are some woman, *aros al bher*," Na'im proclaimed as he held her face and kissed her once again.

Dark eyes locked with gold ones as he straddled her, both revealing the love they shared. They knew it was not their first time...but in a way it was. This time he would take her basking in the light of full acceptance of their love for one another.

His descent was slow and purposeful as he murmured over and over again, "I love you hubibi, I love you," causing her body to raise in invitation.

"I love you too. I believe I have always loved you, but I know I always will."

Her body was just as warm and embracing as her words. Spontaneously, her womanhood parted like the petals of an opening blossom to engulf him. Her mind raced with thoughts of love for him while her body displayed the pleasure he gave her, which she could not help but return.

In the heat of his passion, he proclaimed his love almost ritualistically. "Our love will burn like the fiery sands. It will never wane. The sincerity and trust upon which it is built will be its noonday sun, replenishing it from day to day."

As they reached their peaks together, his chiseled lips covered her full ones, sealing the affirmation.

Felicia looked down at the pleasant expression covering Na'im's sleeping face. It was obvious he was having a wonderful dream. She hoped he dreamed of them and their life together.

For once in her life she was content with what life had given her in the way of love. Yes, it had taken a trip halfway around the world for her to find the love she wanted and needed.

Life was no longer black and white for Felicia Sanders. She was a believer. And maybe it was the belief itself that had made the difference.

ABOUT THE AUTHOR

Born in Gary, Indiana, Eboni Snoe grew up in a small family, consisting of her parents and one sister.

A love for reading, dance, speaking and performing permeated her life. She attended Fisk University, after which her life took many turns personally, geographically and philosophically.

Eboni Snoe's life took the journalistic path at the beginning of the eighties, when she secured her first part-time street reporter's job at one of the oldest Black radio stations in the nation, WDIA, in Memphis, Tennessee. From there, her career advanced, including full-time street reporter, part-time TV anchor and finally news director.

During this time of her life, reading became the medium that would take her away from daily stress and strain, specifically, the reading of women's fiction.

Today, she is a full-time wife, mother and writer, living in Roswell, Georgia.

Ms. Snoe is a member of Romance Writers of America. ***A Sheik's Spell*** is her first novel.

ROOMS

OF THE

HEART

Glamour Romance

For six long years, Tempest Dailey had maintained her secret. Then, without warning, her carefully constructed world began to crumble down around her.

This is the compelling and passionate story of a highly successful black interior designer who is torn between love and obligation.

He held her fiercely against him, absorbing her very being through his pores; afraid that if he should dare to let go, this miracle that he had found would slip away like so many particles of sand through his fingers. How could he be so blessed as to have a second chance with the woman of his dreams? He wanted to shout out to the world his joy and his frustration; that what he held in his arms was still just out of his reach.

DONNA HILL

Yamilla

Historical Romance

The moonlight on her bare dark skin reflected what looked like diamond dust. Never had Cal seen such an exquisite, perfectly formed figure. Her short hair fitted almost cap-like around her head. She was tall, slender, with long, lean bones. Her ebony skin seemed flawless in the moonlight. Unaware of Cal's presence, the young woman moved slowly; walked towards the water's edge dreamlike, as if to an inner beat of majestic sounds.....

Set in America during and after the Civil War this fictional romance vividly portrays the strivings, frustrations and triumphs of three sensuous black women.

Mildred E. Riley

Contemporary Romance

From the moment she laid eyes on him, Sylvia found Justin as appealing and intriguing as his art. Never before had she met anyone who had such a profound impression on her in so short a period of time. Tall, dark and mysterious, he represented all she had ever desired in a man.

Justin was an enigma. A difficult, arrogant man, he was capable of deep kindness and thoughtfulness. However, he sent conflicting signals regarding his love for her and the talent he so jealously guarded.

She wondered why his work always managed to come between them. Perhaps someday she would find out.

BARBARA

STEPHENS

INDISCRETIONS

Contemporary Romance

Khendra Phillips is at the height of her legal career when the handsome, smooth talking attorney, Sean Michaels, bursts onto the scene and threatens to capture not only her love with his irresistible, relentless charm, but her glorious reign in the legal profession as well. Can she combat both the demons that plague her heart as well as the ensuing bitterness toward the man who shattered her dreams?

Another beguilling love story from the author of "ROOMS OF THE HEART"

DONNA HILL

DARK EMBRACE

Alexandria St. Clair had it all...a promising career, wealth and love. Steadfastly building her own photography business, her list of clientele included some of the most prestigious names in the city.

John St. Clair, her doting father and a multi- million dollar magnate, had one obsession: ensuring his daughter's happiness and well-being.

Christopher Mason--whose love for Alexandria is unsurpassed--has vowed to win the beautiful woman who lifted him from the stranglehold of despair when his dreams were shattered.

Then tragedy struck , hurtling them down a path which led to vengeance, manipulation, deceit and guilt, and threatened to unravel the fiber of their lives.

CRYSTAL
WILSON - HARRIS

My Love's Keeper

Nicole Moore felt the ravages of frustration whenever she was near Zachary Regan. She loved him, but he didn't want her love. What did he want? She wanted to belong to him totally.

Zachary Regan found this beautiful, intelligent woman more desirable than any woman he had ever known. But could her love for him break through the barrier of fear that held him captive; release him to love her unselfishly and with the promise that he could share his life with her--a life free of nightmares of his loving and losing?

''**My Love's Keeper**'' is a sensitive and passionate story of love and commitment.

Rochelle Alers

ODYSSEY BOOKS, INC.
P.O. BOX 13210
SILVER SPRING,MD
20911

PLEASE SEND ME THE FOLLOWING BOOKS

	QTY	TOTAL
YAMILLA $4.75 U.S./$5.75 CAN	____	____
ROOMS OF THE HEART $4.25 U.S./$5.25 CAN	____	____
MIDNIGHT WALTZ $4.50 U.S./$5.50 CAN	____	____
INDISCRETIONS $4.75 U.S./$5.75 CAN	____	____
DARK EMBRACE $4.75 U.S./$5.75 CAN	____	____
MY LOVE'S KEEPER $4.50 U.S./$5.50	____	____
PLEASE INCLUDE $1.50 FOR POSTAGE AND HANDLING FOR EACH PURCHASE. MARYLAND RESIDENTS ADD 5% SALES TAX	**TAX**	____
	TOTAL	____

NAME____________________________

ADDRESS_________________________

STATE/ ZIP_______________________